Tom Gratson

Merry Christmas

Life is what you
make of it

Robert Schultz

MASTERS OF
NEW YORK

Robert Schultz

authorHOUSE®

AuthorHouse™
1663 Liberty Drive
Bloomington, IN 47403
www.authorhouse.com
Phone: 1-800-839-8640

Published by AuthorHouse 5/22/2013

ISBN: 978-1-4520-8847-1 (sc)
ISBN: 978-1-4520-8848-8 (hc)
ISBN: 978-1-4520-8846-4 (e)

Library of Congress Control Number: 2010915651

Printed in the United States of America

This book is printed on acid-free paper.

Certain stock imagery © Thinkstock.

Dedication

To the ones I love: my wife, Kim;
my children, Cheyenne and Savannah;
my parents, David and Joyce; and
my brothers, Dave and Paul.

Introduction

I'VE WRITTEN THIS BOOK to inspire all the people that feel trapped or enslaved by our current society. It is my intent to help free our minds by introducing the simple idea that the power of man's free will is stronger than that of any sanctified arguments of pre-destiny.

My journey in writing this book started with my deployment to Iraq while I was in the United States army. First, I must explain the situation. I was a single parent in the infantry, raising twin daughters on my own from the time they were five years old until they reached the age of eight. Prior to our deployment, I had to make arrangements to have my daughters, who had become my left and right arms, flown from Honolulu back to Detroit and to their lying, deceitful, and wretched excuse of a mother.

On our first day after entering into the combat zone, all seemed well. It was February 10th, 2004. Warm and sunny, at first Kirkuk was not much different from Hawaii if, you could believe it, with a whole lot of sand. We thought it was going to be a breeze. Then day two came. Eleven soldiers standing near me suddenly exploded in all directions, wounding nine, and two very seriously; those two soldiers were medi-vacked back to Germany. We were all in shock, and the thought that we were in a real war was suddenly obvious.

One day, after living on adrenaline for months and not knowing if I was to make it home alive or not, one of my older sergeants said to me, "Relax, Schultz, there is no way you are going to die. You have two loving children at home waiting for you. God won't let you die out here in this hellhole." What did he mean? And what in the hell did he know? I'd seen many of our soldiers get it: men who were married, single, loved, or perhaps hated. I thought there was no difference between who was going to get it and who was not.

With seven more months ahead of me on the battlefield, the question came to mind: who was going to die this week, this month, or even in the coming year? There was no distinct pattern, though I tried looking for one. I wanted to know if I was to ever see my children again. Did I lack faith? Are our destinies predetermined? Do we enjoy free will?

After returning to the paradise of Hawaii, I resolved to take every history, philosophy, religious, and government college class I could. Still with no answers, I turned my search for truth to the Internet. I've read every conspiracy theory, nut job cult stories, and the general philosophies from the Greeks to the Far East. I've studied the backgrounds of far-off religions, from the beliefs of the Cathars to Zoroastrians.

Still not satisfied, after finishing my personal journey in the quest for knowledge and understanding, I wrote this book. Though it is not a retrospective of any religious, philosophical, or political argument, I wrote it to lift the hearts of men. I have narrowed my thoughts in this book to a purely American perspective and placed the setting in New York City. After all, it is my perspective. Writing this book has allowed me to exorcise some of the demons within me. I have tried my best to keep it a happy read and easily understandable.

All the facts pertaining to the colony of Rensselaerswyck and the Van Rensselaer family are true, to the best of my knowledge, as are the facts surrounding the Rockefeller family as well.

Acknowledgements

I HAVE NO ONE THAT I know personally to acknowledge except a few authors, storytellers, and raconteurs that I hold dear to me. I'll start with the following:

David Icke, the only man I know who has connected all the dots and has made sense of our world.

Alex Jones, a good man fighting the good fight every day and exposing the New World Order for what it is.

Benjamin Fulford—without his story, there would have been no novel to write.

Dr. Henry Makow, a person who has revealed the darker nature of man and how it affects our world.

H. I. Hester, a great teacher who has made the New Testament so understandable to us laymen.

Mitch Albom and Dan Brown for bringing joy and happiness into a dark world. You keep writing, and I'll keep reading.

Prologue

Streets of New York, September 10, 2010

THE PROPERTY VALUES IN Midtown Manhattan have escalated to astronomical levels since the island's colonization in the early seventeenth century. This does not bode well for David, the patriarch and controller of the great Rockefeller family fortune. The crown jewel of their empire, Rockefeller Center, consists of nineteen buildings that rest on twenty-two acres of land. The land that the buildings rest on has been owned historically by Columbia University and dates back to time of the college's inception in 1784. This afternoon, David intends on meeting with the co-owners of the property, the Red and Green Societies from Asia, to try to negotiate a deal to repurchase the property, which can only be accomplished with the approval of the regent of Columbia University. The regents of the New York State educational system have appointed Mr. Alex Van Rensselaer as regent of the Morningside Heights district, which includes Columbia University. The Rockefeller brothers, David and Laurance, are standing just outside of their Upper East Side New York City residence, awaiting the arrival of a private limousine and their new driver, Joey.

"I took the liberty of having our agents retrieve some information on our friend Mr. Van Rensselaer," David says.

"Van Rensselaer, that name sounds familiar. Did you say his name was Alex?"

"Yes, you courted one of his sisters back in the day. Your memory is definitely not what it used to be, Laurance."

"You don't intend on meeting Mr. Van Rensselaer alone, do you? What unscrupulous plan did you come up with this time?"

"My plan is not your concern. I just need to convince our driver that it is my full intention to meet Alex this afternoon," David says.

"One of your old Indian tricks, I assume."

"Well, if it all falls apart, at least our driver will testify to my intent of meeting him," David says to his brother Laurance.

"Of course, David, your standard operating procedure of investigating business rivals before meetings. I'm sure you will be quite convincing, and besides, the whole thing may keep me entertained on our trip downtown," Laurance says.

"One can never underestimate one's opponent when it comes to business or finance," David says, reassuring his brother as the two gather together with a small private security taskforce on the sidewalk in front of the turn-of-the-century brownstone.

"Oh, yes, that will no doubt put your mind at ease prior to the negotiations," says Laurence. "Let me guess—he is some academic or law professor perhaps, hmmm?"

"You'll be surprised what our team has found out, I can assure you," muses David. "We'll review it in the car on our way to the ceremony," David says.

"Well, it is already ten after ten. The new driver you hand-selected is late. You should fire him on the spot," Laurance says.

"It is his first day on the job, and I need him. Remember, patience is a virtue."

Chapter one

New York City's Upper East Side

Joey Patroni is racing the limo, a stretched silver Chrysler 300 model that he was hired to chauffer to an unfamiliar address, northeast of Central Park. Joey and his limo are now twelve minutes late to East Sixty-fifth Street and Lexington.

"Oh, shit, was that a left at the Armory or a right? Lexington must be one street over. Screw it, let's go right," Joey shouts to himself, as he's unfamiliar with this part of town. "There it is. I'll pull up next to these stiffs and park. They look harmless enough."

Joey powers down the right side window, and before he can say anything, one of the old gentlemen shouts at him. "Are you the chap from Manville Limousine Service?" David asks.

"Why, yes, I am, am running late. Say, do you ..." Joey says franticly as he is cut off.

"You are twelve minutes late, to be exact. It is ten-twelve," bemoans David. "Now let's get to it."

"Oh, yes, right away," Joey says very professionally as he climbs out of the car and onto the curb. "Allow me to get the door for you, sirs. Beautiful weather we're having, isn't it?"

"No time for small chat. My brother and I are due at Building Six, World Trade Center, in less than an hour. I trust you can get us there without incident or accident," says David.

"Oh, yes, not a problem, sirs. You mean Ground Zero," Joey says as he shuts the car's rear door.

Joey climbs back, turns over the engine, puts the limo in drive, and proceeds by turning right on East Sixty-fourth street.

"I think it would be best if we took Park Avenue south," Joey says.

"That will be fine," David answers.

"I have to apologize in advance," Joey says. "This particular limo's partition is broken. I can't get it to go up or down. The limo I was supposed to pick you up in went to the airport earlier, and ..."

"How long have you been driving for the Manvilles?" David asks.

"Well, about five months now. I got back from Iraq in January and was released from military custody, I mean duty, in February." Joey laughs, as his joke was found to be unfunny by the brothers.

"I've never met any of the Manvilles, though. They friends of yours?" Joey asks in his thick New York accent.

Laurance interrupts. "Yes, the Manvilles are of the Connecticut Manvilles—Southbury, Connecticut, in particular, I believe."

"I was lucky enough to find this job. I mean, in this economy and all," Joey says.

"I believe the economy is doing just fine," David states.

"What, do you live in an igloo or something?" Joe says. "It might be okay for you Wall Street types, but not us Main Street types," Joey says as he eyes the back seat so as to gain a clue as to his occupants. Knowing the men to be of great wealth was obvious.

"I'm sorry. I did not catch your name?" asks Laurance.

"Oh, oh, my name is Joey—Joey Patroni from the Brooklyn Patronis. My ancestors moved here back in the ..." Joey says, trying to state his importance.

"I'm sure it is the most interesting story, but my brother and I have some issues to discuss before our afternoon meeting," says David.

"Oh, I'm sorry. I just thought it would be a long drive through the city, and ... ah, I guess it's not important. I'll try and be quiet, but if you knew my family, you'd know that it's hard for us Patronis to shut up," Joey says as he releases some nervousness.

"Thank you for serving our country, young man. We do require our drivers to have some security training. You seem a bit old to be in the military so recently," says David.

"Oh, yes, I just turned thirty-eight, but I've had all kinds of military training. Down at Fort Benning, Georgia, I went through weapons training, jungle training, interrogation training, and get-down-and-do-some-push–ups training. I had a lot of that. Probably because I talk too much—my drill sergeant told me to shut my cock holster once. The guy was hilarious," Joey says laughingly. "Sorry, I didn't mean to swear. It's just my upbringing. As far as my age, yeah, I got a late start in the army. I mean, I got laid off back in '01, and then some knuckleheads flew those planes into towers on 9-11. So I got pissed off and joined the army on 9-12. I went through the army basic training at the age of thirty-three. I'm the last line of the Patronis. I had two girls, and all my cousins had girls as well. So when I go, I am the last male in the family of Patronis here in America."

"Quite a chatterbox we have," Laurance says.

"Yes, indeed. A driver blessed with so many talents. And you are always complaining at the lack of entertainment, Laurence," states David as the limo makes its way through one of New York's most exclusive neighborhoods.

Chapter two

7:32 am Greenwich Time, London, England

Alex Van Rensselaer's and Wally Niles' day starts early as they arrive at Heathrow Airport, London, in the early morning fog. Alex and Wally gather their bags from the trunk of a London cab just as Alex's Gulfstream G650 is arriving at a private terminal just after sunrise.

"No time to waste, Wally. We must get a move on," Alex says as he directs his personal secretary into the airport and they start their way through the crowded terminal. Alex wearing is a double-breasted suit of the highest accord and, being by a full head the taller of the two, stands straight, proper, and regal, with the ability to see over most of the patrons. "We need to head north. This way, Wally," Alex says, directing their actions.

"Alex, please show some patience. Our plane has just arrived. It will be some time before they're done fueling," Wally, the consummate professional, learned, lawyerly, and some what clumsy at times, says to Alex as he tries to keep up.

"Do you think they will allow us to board?" Alex asks.

"No, I don't think so. Allow me to run and get us a cup of coffee," Wally answers.

"Yes, you go ahead—that's a good idea. A small cream, no sugar, please," Alex says as he strides his way along.

After Wally completes the purchase, he turns and hurriedly walks toward Alex, spilling hot coffee onto his hands as he fumbles with their luggage. Alex, who has made himself comfortable in a chair close to the terminal door in which his aircraft is parked, unfolds and begins to read the morning newspaper.

"Here you go, Alex. Cream, no sugar," Wally says as he reaches out carefully, delivering the hot coffee. Wally quickly organizes their luggage and takes special care of his laptop bag. Wally sits down near Alex, crosses his legs, and begins to fiddle with his watch.

"Well, you had a heck of a day yesterday," Wally announces.

"What are you getting at?" Alex asks, half ignoring Wally as he makes time to read over the morning newspaper.

"Well, it's not every day one gets to speak to the Queen of England," Wally says as nonchalantly as he can, perhaps even prying for information.

"Well, she did invite me back, come this spring. She wishes to know more about the geldings that will be born from our stables in Kentucky. And I've been invited to a ceremony christening one of Her Majesty's ships this April," Alex says as he goes over the daily headlines.

"The horses, Alex? That is not why we fly all the way to London, is it?" Wally asks again.

"No, of course not. In my official capacity, I was only allowed one question of Her Majesty," Alex answers. "My brief encounter with the queen lasted less than half an hour."

Wally, acting nervously and trying not to be too blatant,

pauses before quickly blurting out, "My god, man, what in the world did you ask her?"

"It was a simple question. I asked her something to the effect of how she intended to stop the growth of inequity," Alex says.

"You asked her how to stop the growth of inequity?" Wally repeats. "What in the world do you mean? You get to speak to the queen once in a life time, and that is what you asked her?" Wally asks, quite dumbfounded.

"Yes. You see, on June 2, 1953, during the Queen's coronation, she swore an oath to God that she would stop the growth of inequity," Alex answers. "So I felt it was a pertinent question to ask of her, and how she has done addressing the issue."

"So this year, you were honored enough to be given this opportunity?" Wally asks sheepishly.

"It's more like being thrown to the dogs, Wally."

"Was she kind enough to answer? I mean, how did she respond?"

"She answered with grace and humility," Alex answers with the high authority of a statesman in his voice.

"You know that is not what I meant, sir," Wally says.

"If you must know, she answered by telling me that the gap between the rich and the poor can be measured by more than just money. She went on about the equality of education, health care, and life expectancies," Alex answers as he folds back up his newspaper.

"We all know that the gap between the rich and the poor is greater now than ever before," Wally says. "Do you think she knew the question was coming?" Wally asks. "I mean she really didn't answer the question, then."

"Of course she knew it was coming. She didn't fully answer

the question to my satisfaction, but after all, she is the queen and a true politician, as you know. Every five years or so, all the members of the lodge that I belong to write their questions months ahead of time. And after a vote, five questions are presented to the queen, and after some consultation from her staff, she gets to pick which one she would prefer to answer," Alex explains.

"That is a great honor, sir. I mean, your question being accepted by the queen and all. And that is what brought us over here?" Wally says.

"Well, yes, it is. I thought the question was pertinent, anyway," Alex says. "I was formally invited to meet the queen weeks ago. One does not turn down an opportunity to meet with the queen. You, being a Brit, should know that. In fact, a refusal may be construed as an insult."

"Are you a member of the Temple Lodge here in London, sir?" Wally asks.

"No. Why do you ask, Wally?" Alex asks as he folds one leg over the other and looks about the corridor as if he were uninterested.

"Well, I've been a member of the Temple Lodge for just over ten years now. I'm only considered a twelfth-degree mason, though. I'm still sort of the new guy, I guess," Wally says.

"Oh, you are in the brotherhood as well. Then you know I can only tell you that I belong to the New York Lodge Number One of St. James. How have they treated you on this side of the pond?" Alex asks.

"Just fine, I guess. The Temple Lodge's claim to fame is that they possess an ancient book. They call it the Book of Ages. It's our big secret, I guess," Wally says.

"That is fascinating, Wally. What in the world is the Book of Ages?" Alex asks.

"I don't know; I've never seen it. I hear they keep it in Italy or Holland somewhere, I think. I'm not privileged enough to know for sure, I guess," Wally answers.

Just then, a beautiful young lady comes through the doors of the gate marked 6H and asks, "Are you the Van Rensselaer party?"

"Yes, we are," Wally answers.

"The captain informs me that your plane is fueled and ready. You may begin boarding now."

Wally and Alex stand up and begin to gather their luggage.

"Let me help you with that," Alex offers as both the men eye the young beauty.

"Thank you, my dear." Alex nods at the young woman as she turns toward the airplane with a smile.

"Right this way," she says as she escorts them down a ramp and onto the waiting private plane. "Have a nice flight."

Chapter 3

Joey glances back into the rearview mirror as David turns to his briefcase and opens it up. "Now let's get started. As I was saying earlier, Laurence, our people have provided us with a sort of dossier on our old friend Mr. Alex Van Rensselaer," David says while reaching for his reading glasses inside of his jacket.

David turns the folder open, adjusts his glasses, and says, "The majority of our dossier is attributed to W. W. Spooner of *The National Historic Magazine* and also to a book in the Harvard library written by one of the Van Rensselaers themselves. Let's see, inside this first folder we have a paper labeled 'Section 1: Family History.'

"It seems to be in chronological order, with some excerpts from some newspaper clippings. The paper starts in 1602 with one Kiliaen Van Rensselaer. He was the 'First Patroon of Rensselaerswyck,' in capital letters," David reads.

"Today is your lucky day. I just happen to be a history major over near Columbia University. I've read plenty about the *patroons*. They were the original Dutch settlers here in New York," Joey says as he tries to remember anything else about them.

"That is a great school here in New York," says Laurance. "Have you been a Lion long?"

"I said I go to school near Columbia, not at Columbia. I'm a student at the City College of New York over on Convent Avenue. *Patroon* is a Dutch word. They were the original settlers here in what was New Amsterdam," Joey says, almost repeating himself.

"I took quite a few history classes myself, back in the day. I graduated from Princeton, of course," Laurance says.

"What year was that?" Joey asks.

"I graduated in1932, my boy, 1932," Laurance answers. "My brother here was just a young pup, as I recall."

"Wow, that was during the Depression," Joey says.

"You're quite the talker this morning," David says to Laurance, staring over his reading spectacles. "It says Kiliaen's uncle was the one of the founding members of the Amsterdam Stock Exchange in 1602."

"That was the beginning of capitalism as we know it. The VOC was the original trading organization set up for the Dutch East India Company," Laurance replies.

"The VOC also started the Dutch West India Company to explore and colonize the new world," Joey adds as the car slowly moves through traffic.

"Yes, we know, Joey." David continues, "It says Kiliaen was the only child of Captain Henry Van Rensselaer, who was a sailor and major trader of his day. Kiliaen was a leading pearl and diamond merchant at the time. Kiliaen was on the board of directors of the States-General."

"Yeah, that is like the Dutch government, because there was no Dutch king at the time, even though Prince William of Orange lived there in Holland at the time," Joey says.

"Yes, we know, Joey. If you paid attention to your driving duties, it would be much appreciated," David says.

"I'm just trying to help. I just took a European history class last semester," Joey says.

"'Kiliaen was the chief investor in the commissioning by the States-General of the exploring vessel *Half-Moon*,'" David reads.

"Hey, that is the ship Henry Hudson sailed to America and discovered Manhattan and the Hudson River."

"Yes, we know, Joey," Laurance chimes in. "Would you please drive on? It's a green light."

"I got something you don't know. Did you know John Coleman? One of his crew was shot in the neck with an arrow by one of the local Indians. He died that same day. It was on the sixth of September, 1609, about this time of year," Joey adds. "I remembered that because it happened on my birthday."

"Yes, and on September 11, 1609, he discovered and mapped Manhattan for the first time," David adds.

"I've got one for you," Laurance states. "Did you know that fool sailed not back to Holland but to Dartmouth, England? I'm sure that Mr. Van Rensselaer and the States-General were quite upset."

"Of course, Hudson was an Englishman. Maybe he thought he would get away with it—I mean, turning over all that information to the English. At best it was espionage and at worst treason," David says.

"Upset? I'd say so. Did you know on his next trip, the Dutch crewmen mutinied and set Captain Henry and the English crewmen a drift in a frickin' rowboat? They were never seen or herd from again," Joey says, slowing the vehicle and stopping at a red light. "I guess they had it coming."

David says, "I have here an article dated 1907 and attributed to *The National Historic Magazine* by W. W. Spooner. It reads:

"'Kiliaen was a well-educated man and succeeding to the leadership of the family, and was of great influence. Being one of the wealthiest citizens in Holland, and of noble birth, he kept close friendship with the House Orange, the non-reigning monarchial family of Amsterdam.

"'In earlier times, large iron baskets were placed on castles and the gates thereof, where fires were kindled in them for the purpose of illumination in the celebration of great events. Hence the Van Rensselaer crests. On the night of Henry Hudson's return to Holland, the illumination of the Van Rensselaers' fires so far outshone all others that the Prince of Orange requested the head of the house to substitute for his ancient motto that of *Omnibus Effulgeo*—"I outshine all."

"'The Dutch merchants created the Dutch West India Company with much insecurity, thinking the British would try and undermine the twelve-year truce. Their just and ambitious attempts at colonizing of the new world failed at all levels. It was a time when profits were on the minds of men. The fight of the powerful global conglomerates in this gigantic contest was shortly to ensue. Kiliaen Van Rensselaer was one of the organizers and original directors of the Dutch West India Company. While trading prospered during the truce, none except one in the west looked promising. Beverwyck, a small trading post, on the Hudson, always provided shells, beads, and furs continuously from its inception in 1614 until the places were settled.'"

"Beverwyck—that is the old name for Albany, New York, isn't it?" Joey asks.

"Yes, our great city and our state capital," Laurance says.

David continues after taking a short breath. "'The Dutch West India Company was chartered in July 1621, with a capital investment of seven million florins, being granted exclusive authority and trade privileges in the Dutch possessions of the two Americas and the coast of Africa from the Tropic of Cancer to the Cape of Good Hope.

The quests of this enterprise were first, to "establish an efficient and aggressive Atlantic maritime power in the struggle with Spain" and second, to colonize, develop, and rule the Dutch American dependencies, one of which was the splendid country known as New Netherland. Great expectations of commercial and financial advantages are being based upon the extensive privileges and imperial powers conceded in the charter. The wealthy merchants of Holland subscribed for the stock in the newly formed company with exuberance. The affairs of the company were administered by a directorate known as the "Assembly of the XIX." Two executive boards of nine members were selected to manage the concerns of the company and that of New Netherland, and Kiliaen Van Rensselaer was a member of both of these controlling bodies.

"'In the Dutch West India Company, Van Rensselaer was one of its mainstays, allowing several of his vessels at the company's disposal and twice advancing money to save its credit. His name is conspicuously identified with all its measures of policy, including the original settlement of Manhattan Island in 1624,'" David reads.

"Image a land full of beaver! Why in the world were the beavers even worth trading for?" laughs Joey. "You know, I took a boat ride up north on the Hudson River once. It's where all those rich families live—you know, the Van Cortlandts, Vanderbilts, and Rockefellers. They're not just mansions, but entire estates. It's like the whole Eastern establishment."

"We are the establi ..." Laurance starts to say.

"Shhh," David interrupts. "Most of the beaver pelts were used to make hats and were very valuable. No, no, let's entertain him for a while. Let's see if he can figure it on his own, and besides, I want to know if he has any common sense and not just muscles for brains.

"Yeah, we got up there near the Roosevelts' Hyde Park and turned around. I guess it was getting late, and we were getting drunk," Joey says as he thinks back about his experience. "Hey, we are coming up on Grand Central. I'm going to take a right on East Forty-sixth Street and a left onto Vanderbilt Avenue. It will help us loop back around to Park Avenue. It's a private shortcut of mine."

Chapter 4

ALEX'S PERFECT MANNERISMS ARE impressive, as he has the grace of a man from the Victorian age. His character seems at odds a bit; one of a world-renowned politician mixed with the character of a modern-day playboy, very European, but yet distinctly American. He and his private plane, the newest Gulfstream, the G650, are a fit to a tee. After all, he did have the interior costume fitted to his personal likings. These included a wet bar, which would insure he would never miss a drink while in the air, and a kitchenette as well. As Wally and Alex take their accustomed sitting positions, with Wally facing the aft of the plane and Mr. Van Rensselaer facing forward, the captain's voice comes over the speaker system.

"Where would you like to go today, Mr. Van Rensselaer?" the captain asks.

Alex pushes an intercom button on his armchair and responds. "We're headed to home base, Jimmy. We need to get to John F. Kennedy Airport, New York, please," Alex says.

"No problem, sir. It will be just a few minutes before we gain clearance," the voice responds.

"Is that you, Jimmy?" Alex asks, as the voice sounds a bit harsher than normal.

"No, sir. My name is Raymond. I'm a friend of Jimmy's; we share a flat together in New York. He was taken ill last night after our dinner. I think it was the fish. He'll be better in a few days. He asked me to make this flight for him."

Alex pushes his intercom button and says, "Very well, then. Are you familiar with this type of aircraft?"

"Yes, I've flown many of the Gulfstream models over the past few years. I've logged thousands of hours in flight time in crafts just like this. We should have smooth sailing," Raymond says as Alex's mind is put at ease.

"How did you acquire this plane, the Gulfstream G650?" Wally asks. "It's not even on the market yet. The prototype has not even finished its air trials yet."

"This is the prototype, Wally. And the G650 and we will be conducting the air trials here in just a few minutes. I do have an interest in seeing this plane on the market within a year or so," Alex answers.

"Is it safe to fly?" Wally asks nervously.

"Well, we'll soon find out, won't we? Fasten your seatbelt, please," Alex says as he does the same.

"You were once a pilot yourself, weren't you?" Wally asks.

"Yes. I had to give it up. My love of drinking outweighs my love for flying. I had become far too reckless at times. It's been quite a few years now since I have gotten behind the controls. Hiring my pilot Jimmy has been a godsend."

"We have a full agenda ahead of us when we get to New York, Alex," Wally says as the men settle into what will be an eight-hour flight. Wally opens up his carry-on bag and pulls out his laptop computer.

"I have it all right here, Mr. Van Rensselaer. Give me a moment to boot it up," Wally says professionally, as if he were starting another busy day at the office.

The Gulfstream G650 slowly taxis toward the tight 180-degree turn near the start of the runway.

"That will have to wait, Wally. You know how I love the takeoffs and landings. This is my favorite part of flying," Alex says, pressing his face to the window like a child.

The private plane turns and lines up for takeoff. In an instant, the dual engines roar to life, sending the plane speeding down the runway. Within twenty seconds, the plane is airborne.

"That gets me every time. I feel like a kid on a rollercoaster," Alex joyfully explains as Wally turns pale.

Chapter 5

"So this guy, Van Rensselaer, you plan on meeting—he claims he's royalty or something," Joey says.

"I believe Mr. Van Rensselaer does descend from a long line of royal ancestry, I'm afraid," Laurance says.

"Well, does the Van Rensselaer family still live here in New York?" Joey asks as he maneuvers the car through some more traffic.

"If you had kept traveling north on your boat trip, you would have discovered the Manor of Rensselaerswyck far north on the Hudson," Laurance says. "The property was practically its own colony."

David says, "You are absolutely right, Laurence. Now please allow me to finish the article."

"Wait a minute. See, that is what I'm talking about. So this guy, he has money, he has ships, and he owns property, but still there are no people. It's the people that make a place. And my cousin Toni, she's got a nice boat. Sorry it's not a yacht like you all are used to," Joey says.

"Joey, you are not part of this conversation. Just drive the car, please. I'll read it out loud for your entertainment, just no interruption, please. Section 2 of the dossier," David reads.

"'Long before the Eastern establishment of New York City, there was a family much more wealthy and more powerful, that of the Van Rensselaers. They defined the establishment. North along the Hudson, beyond the estates of the Whitneys, Delanos, and Astors, there is an estate so large that it dwarfed that of all other American patronages and in fact was larger than many European principalities.

"'Of the early Dutch colonial families, the Van Rensselaers were the first to acquire a great landed estate in America under the *patroon* system. The Van Rensselaers were among the first, before the English conquest of New Netherland, to have their properties legally made into a "manorial estate" by the British crown, predating those of the Livingstons and Van Cortlandts in what would become the state of New York. They were, in the first place, nobles in the old country, which cannot be said of any other manorial families of New York, although several of these claim noble descent.

"'Their territorial possessions were from the first of grand proportions—some twenty-four by forty-eight miles. Thus, in becoming *patroons* and later manorial lords in America, the Van Rensselaers enjoyed an extension in kind of aristocratic dignities which had already been theirs for generations. Measured by the standard of American antiquity, they take precedence over every other New York family of present consequence, their *patroon*ship having been created in 1631, only eight years after the first permanent settlement of the Dutch on Manhattan Island.

"'Their special privileges were the highest accorded to any family in America, either under the Dutch regime or under the English. The 750,000-acre domain, as originally acquired by the founder of the house with the sanction of the Holland government, constituted a distinct colony, not subject in any manner to the political control or jurisdiction of the general administration of New Netherland; and indeed, their independence was so sharply defined that the governor of the province and director of the Dutch West India Company, Peter Stuyvesant, in a dispute with the Rensselaerswyck director regarding territorial rights, could find no other recourse than an act of war,'" David reads.

"Did you say seven hundred and fifty thousand acres? That is bigger than the state of Rhode Island. How come I never heard of this guy? What in the heck are you meeting him about?" Joey exclaims.

David begins to read again as he looks over his reading glasses toward Joey with a judgmental grin that shouts for him to be silent. "'The "powers and exemptions" that the Rensselaerswyck estate enjoyed included the power to police, appoint, and control all necessary officials and administer justice; the right to appoint church officials; and the right to coin money. Indeed, the aristocratic master class had arrived on the shores of the new world.'"

"They could print their own money? I can't stand bankers. They are going to ruin this country," Joey says.

"It was bankers who started this country, Joey," David says.

"You are wrong on that one, mister. It was the hard work of ordinary people that made this country great and not some merchant selling shares of stock to the highest bidder," Joey says.

David continues on. "'The *patroon* was also allowed to select a special deputy to the general assembly of the province. As a matter of course, the head of the family or his representative took this position. Again, the position of the Van Rensselaer family as one of the foremost in the aristocratic order in America was secured as long as the estate should endure by application of the law of primogeniture, requiring the perpetual transmission of the entire landed estate in the eldest male line.

"'The exceptional position conferred upon the Van Rensselaer family, and for generations sustained, by virtue of its great propriety estate, is naturally the most conspicuous fact in the history of New York and the United States. From its inception and for the next two hundred years, the manor of Rensselaerswyck has been maintained as the greatest hereditary property in the state of New York and the United States.

"'Throughout this period of two centuries, its character as a strictly private estate remained unchanged until the American Revolution. The principle of primogeniture was abolished, but the ancient features of the estate and single ownership of the soil and the terms of a feudal tenantship were preserved to the last,'" David reads.

"It sounds like a Southern slave plantation, except it was here in the North," Joey says as the men travel south on Park Avenue near East Thirty-fifth Street.

Chapter 6

THE GULFSTREAM GENTLY REACHES the overhead cloud canopy at twenty thousand feet and levels off. The captain's voice confidently breaks the temporary silence. "Our arrival time in New York is estimated at 1:30 PM eastern standard time. Our total flight time will be about eight hours from ground to ground."

Wally's laptop comes to life with a few keystrokes. "Here it is, September 10, 2010," Wally says as he reads from his digital day calendar.

"Hotel check out, ride to Heathrow, flight from London to New York—we need to arrive at JFK no later than 2:00 PM eastern standard time to be safe," Wally says as he looks at his watch and tries to calculate their exact landing time.

"Make sure you call the airport an hour before we land in New York. We need to make sure the helicopter is ready on time. I'm meeting with some very important business clients this afternoon," Alex says as he closes his eyes and tries to relax.

"Yes, of course. I have it listed here as 'Rocky at 4:30 PM," Wally says. "But prior to that, we have stops at the Holland Society, and don't forget our meeting at the Ritz-Carlton, sir," Wally reminds Alex.

"Oh yes, indeed. What time do we need to be there?"

"The Holland Society is at 2:30 PM, and the Ritz-Carlton is at 3:30 PM."

"That is a pretty tight schedule, Wally. I'm only one man. Do I need to be at both events?"

"Well, yes, both are quite important. You had me put two stars next to each of them. It is your highest mark, sir. And you've asked me to put together a report on the Rockefellers as well. I have it here."

"Yes, we'll get to that in a second. Why are we going to the Holland Society?" Alex asks.

"Well, the Holland Society is giving your mother an award for her generosity. She has given the American Cancer Society a huge charitable gift. Her lady friends and you are to present her with a birthday cake as well," Wally says.

"My goodness, is it that time of year again?" Alex asks sarcastically. "It is her eighty-sixth birthday, right, Wally?" Alex asks unconfidently.

"No, sir, eighty-seventh this time around," Wally answers as he browses his notes.

Alex pushes his call button to inform the pilot. "Raymond, warp drive, please. Let's break some records. I forgot it is my mother's birthday today. I don't wish to disappoint her," Alex says.

"Yes, sir. I'll take the shortcut. It might be possible to get there in six and a half hours, depending on our wind speeds. Your plane, sir, she is a beauty," Raymond announces. One would not have noticed the change in speed except for the long smooth fire that blazed out the exhaust of the twin engines.

"My goodness, how fast can this plane fly?" Wally asks.

"This particular model can go nearly eight hundred miles per hour," Alex answers.

"The Ritz-Carlton meeting I'm not so sure about, Alex. I have it noted as just the Green and the Red," Wally says with a questioning look in his eyes.

"It's a private conference with some old friends of mine. Your attendance will not be needed. Just make sure I make it there on time, please," Alex says.

"Yes, sir, we'll try," Wally says, not trying to press the issue. "But if it is a business meeting of any kind, sir, I have to advise you, as your lawyer, that it would be best if I attended as well."

"Tell me, where did you earn your law degree?" Alex asks.

"Well, I earned my law degree at Cambridge, but I learned far much more with my internship at the Tavistock group."

"What do you mean?"

"Well, I was in charge of psychological evaluations of some of our British troops before they deployed, and I conducted interviews upon the troops' return," Wally says. "I would record the mental changes in the troops' personalities. It was all quite fascinating."

Chapter 7

Joey asks, "If your meeting is in Midtown, why are we headed downtown?" with an unashamed voice.

"The first event on our agenda is a brief ceremony at Ground Zero. And later, if you must know, we have a business meeting to negotiate some property that we used to own that does not concern you," David says.

"Property? Well, what kind of property is it?" Joey asks excitedly. "You mean here in New York City?"

"Yes, Joey, some land in Midtown Manhattan that used to be owned by Columbia University," Laurance says.

"I've been over there a lot. There is no vacant land over there. You mean a building of some sort. I know—you sold someone an old, broken-down money pit, and they want their money back, right? I hope you brought your wallets," Joey says.

"What do you mean?" asks David.

"There is nothing but skyscrapers in Midtown. This guy you're meeting, he is American royalty of some sort. His family owns the land and has been here since prehistoric times. In my neighborhood, we'd have to call him by another name. He's like the boss of bosses. Good luck—it won't be cheap," Joey says in his best imitation of the Godfather's movie voice.

"He is nothing of the likes of the Mafia. But I think the boy is on to something, Laurence," David states as he looks to confer with his brother.

"First of all, I'm not a boy. I'm thirty-eight years old, and I've been in combat, serving my country," Joey says as his voice gets anxious.

"Well, I'm ninety-one, and everyone under eighty is still wet behind the ears to me," David says as he turns back to his brief.

"Ha, that is funny. I'm proud of you, your first joke in what, ten years? And I would swear you don't look a day over a hundred and ten," Joey says jokingly and lightening the conversation. "Now, that was funny, you have to admit."

"So, how did this *patroon*ship get any people—I mean pilgrims or settlers—to move over here?" Joey asks as he returns comfortably to his driving duties. "I mean, he must have promised them some kind of freedoms or something."

Chapter 8

W<small>ALLY MAKES A FEW</small> keystrokes on his laptop and finds the folder labeled "The Rockefeller Report."

"I have always wanted to learn how to operate a computer. One of these days, could you sit down with me and show me how it works? I've just never seemed to get around to doing it," Alex says as he leans his head back for comfort.

"It's not so hard once you get used to it. The computer kind of runs itself. I'll be glad to show you sometime, sir," Wally says as he scrolls the mouse up and finds the beginning of the report. "Shall we begin the report, sir?"

"Yes, indeed. If I fall asleep, just give me a nudge," Alex says with a smile as he tilts his chair back, removes his shoes, and slips into a more comfortable position.

"You're not saying my reports are boring, are you, sir? I do try and keep them jazzy, sir. That is a grand idea," Wally says as he slips his shoes off as well. "Here we go. William Avery Rockefeller Senior was born in Granger, New York, in 1810."

"You're kidding. My family used to own that property way back when. It's in the interior of the state of New York, west of the Appalachian mountains, if I recall properly," Alex says as he fights the urge to sleep.

"Of course, sir, your family owned most of the property there in the state of New York at one time, even the property where William grew up as well, in Moravia, New York," Wally says as he increases the volume of his voice to help Alex stay awake. "Are the Rockefellers relatives of yours, sir?" Wally asks to keep Alex involved with the conversation.

"No, the Rockefellers are of German descent. My family came from Holland," Alex explains. "What were William's mother and father's names?" Alex asks.

"Her name was Lucy Avery, and his father's name was Godfrey," Wally answers as he reads from his own report.

"Oh, yes, I've heard she was a descended from Mary Boleyn, Anne Boleyn's sister," Alex says, leaning upright before lying back down. "Some say she could justly claim descent from Edmond Ironside, the English king, crowned back in 1016, I think it was."

"Bravo, sir, you do remember your history. William Avery's father, Godfrey Rockefeller, was born in Albany, New York, in 1784," Wally says, returning his eyes to the computer screen.

"'William Avery Senior was known as "Big Bill." He labeled himself as a botanic physician and sold fanciful elixirs. He was an entrepreneur of sorts, selling salts, produce, and timber. William was frequently gone for lengths of time, but when he was at home, he taught his boys to always get the better part of any deal. Big Bill once said, "I cheat my boys every chance I get. I want to make 'em sharp." William Avery socially married up in 1837 to Eliza Davison. Her father was a rich man for his times. William Avery was responsible for moving the family to the Cleveland area in 1853. In 1856, William changed his name to William Livingston and lived briefly in Canada before moving to North Dakota and then on to Freeport, Illinois. Joseph Pulitzer offered a reward of eight thousand dollars for any information about the hiding "Doc Rockefeller," on account of his bigamy,'" Wally reads.

"Yes, I've heard he married another woman while he was still married to his first wife. Quite controversial for the day. The Tiger Woods of his day, I guess. I'm sure the press had a field day with it," Alex says.

"Some gilded age gossip, I suppose," Wally says.

"When did William Avery pass?"

"Let's see here. May 11, 1906—that would have made him ninety-five years old," Wally answers.

"Well into the times of his son's enormous fame. It seems that all the Rockefellers live quite long. It must be in the genes," Alex says as he adjusts his high-backed chair.

"He, of course, was the father of eight children, including the three boys John Davison, William Junior, and Franklin Rockefeller," Wally reads.

"Franklin? I've never heard of him," Alex says.

"Let me Google him," Wally says.

"Google? What on earth is that?" Alex asks.

"Let me show you," Wally says as both men lean toward one another. "On the Internet, it works as a search engine. You just type in words or names that you're interested in, and voila. The world is at my fingertips."

"That is amazing. Can I play with that when we're done?" Alex asks.

"I'll make sure we get you a laptop as soon as we get to New York," Wally says, leaning back and pulling his laptop away as if it were his most precious commodity.

"'Franklin was the younger brother of John Senior and William Junior. He fought in the Civil War, while his brothers hired substitute soldiers to fight in their places.' I suppose many rich northerners of the day paid to avoid combat. It says here that he had a falling out with his brothers and moved from Cleveland to Columbus, Ohio. 'He invested heavily into the Buckeye Steel Castings Company of Columbus, Ohio. He became president of the company in 1905 and served until 1908, when the president of the company became Samuel Prescott Bush. Frank stayed on as vice president of the company after Prescott Bush took over as president.' It says he refused to speak to his brothers up until his death," Wally reads.

"Is that the same Prescott Bush that I think it is?"

"Yes, sir. He was the father of US senator Prescott Bush and grandfather of former US President George H. W. Bush, and not to mention ..."

"Please do not mention the idiot great-grandson of his to me. Do you think Frank was pissed off about the American Civil War?" Alex asks.

"Yes, I almost forgot, your least favorite president, sir. I don't know for sure, but both of Frank's brothers did attended his funeral on the fifteenth of April, 1917. He was seventy-one years of age," Wally reads from his report. "May I ask you a question, sir?"

"Sure, go ahead."

"It seems we have gone through this before a few years back. Your meeting is with David alone, so why go through all of the family's background?"

"Well, you know, Wally, that the apple doesn't fall too far from the tree."

"Yes, of course, sir."

Chapter 9

DAVID ROCKEFELLER TURNS A few pages and announces, "Yes, yes this next section should answer some of our questions. It's titled 'Section 3: History of Rensselaerswyck.' Should I bore you by reading it, Laurance?"

"Yes, indeed. At this point, the more we can learn, the better prepared we'll be," says Laurance.

"I hope this is good. I mean, who in their right mind would want to move to a wild and uncultivated land filled with savage Indians?" Joey states.

"Savage Indians? Au contraire, Joey—the Lenape Indians of the area were quite friendly. I've read they traded beaver pelts, along with growing maize and kidney beans," Laurance says. "I believe the northern part of the Hudson also had many Mohawk and Mohegan Indians as well."

"Well, I'm sure they were nice and peaceful before us white guys showed up and started stealing their lands. Go ahead—I'll be quiet," Joey says as he stares at a red light at Thirty-third Street.

David reads on. "'It was Kiliaen Van Rensselaer who introduced the plan of "Freedoms and Exemptions," along with several of his colleagues. The authors devised a plan to encourage the masses and the wealthy to make the investment in the New World. Kiliaen realized that special measures would be needed to stimulate growth in the colonies. So he and his colleagues at the Dutch West India Company introduced the plan to the States-General. Under this plan, it was provided that any member of the company who desired to do so could select lands in the province of New Netherland and erect them into a *patroon*ship under their exclusive personal proprietorship and governmental authority, the conditions being the necessary satisfaction of the natives. The cost of transportation would be the responsibility of the *patroon*. Ownership of said properties, as bona fide settlers, must include that of "fifty souls, upwards of fifteen years old, one-fourth to be sent during the first year and the remainder before the expiration of the fourth year." Upon each *patroon* was conferred the right "to forever possess and enjoy all the lands lying within said boundaries. The *patroon* shall fully own all fruits, minerals, rivers, fish, and fowl, at the exclusion of all others, to be held as a perpetual inheritance."

"'The act of "Freedoms and Exemptions" was ratified by the States-General of Holland in June 1629. Kiliaen Van Rensselaer, who pushed for the adoption of the plan, quickly took energetic steps toward availing himself of its privileges. He employed as his agent Sebastiaen Jansen Crol, an officer of the company in command at Fort Orange, who, in a series of purchases from the Indians beginning in 1630 and continuing until 1637, acquired for him all the land on the west side of the Hudson River from twelve miles south of Albany to Smack's Island, "at the mouth of the Mohawk River, stretching two days' journey into the interior," and also a tract of about the same dimensions on the east side, both north and south of Fort Orange and twelve miles into the wilderness." The possessions of Kiliaen Van Rensselaer encompassed parts of four different counties,'" David reads on.

"'Rensselaerwyck was a fully acquired estate by fulfillment of the condition of the settlement and was duly confirmed to Kiliaen on the eighth of January, 1631, at a session of the Assembly of the XIX. The States-General proclaiming "that he in good faith was *patroon* of all said lands that lay claimed, having in view the colonization of his lands and their development for the benefit of his descendants, there is not the slightest of doubt." The deed would therefore be "Holden in Zealand." With his grand wisdom, it was Van Rensselaer's policy to settle his colonies in close proximity to one another; in which he secured the advantage of intercourse, of union for defensive purposes, and of progress of sharing of ideas within the community. The point chosen on the property was that of Fort Orange. Kiliaen seeing the obvious advantages being near the fort and the trading post of Beverwyck, he started to exercise control of the colony from afar. Kiliaen started dividing up parcels to settle and also erected the first church. For his tenants, he provided seed, livestock, and farm equipment. Van Rensselaer built his own fort, supplying his own soldiers, cannons, and firearms. A flag with the Van Rensselaer crest flew over the fort. Justice was administered in his own name. The colonists, upon becoming his subjects, swore an oath directly to him and his lands.'" David finishes his reading.

"Fifty souls—that sounds like a pact with the devil. The 'subjects' they refer to are real people. They shouldn't have sworn an oath to anybody but their lord, Jesus Christ. Don't you guys read the Bible?" Joey says, stating his opinion. "I'm sure no good Catholics joined up. It sounds like indentured servants or even slavery to me."

"You are right to a point, Joey. Most of the new settlers in America came seeking religious freedoms: Quakers, Puritans, and Huguenots," Laurance explains. "And some people were indeed servants, slaves, and perhaps even prisoners. It was all quite legal back then."

"Legal, maybe, but slavery is the same, no matter how you dress it up," Joey says as drives the limo across Thirty-second Street.

Chapter 10

Raymond the pilot comes over the radio and announces, "We're taking the most northern route possible, sir. It may get a little cold inside."

Alex ignores the pilot and asks Wally, with eyes barely open, "What about John D. Senior's brother, William Avery Junior? I don't know that much about him either."

"William Avery Junior—he was the co-founder of an oil company with his older brother, named Rockefeller and Andrews, which later would become the Standard Oil Company. He was considered far more personable and receptive a man than his older brother, John D. Senior," Wally says.

"So John D. Senior was older than William Junior. I've got it. I'm sure he was adept in business matters. Did he have any formal education?"

"No, he went to public school and was mentored by a man named Rufus Osgood Mason. 'In 1886, it was William Junior who bought property along the Hudson River from General Lloyd Aspinwall, where he built Rockwood Hall. The mansion is located within the estate of Pocantico,'" Wally reads.

"Isn't that the place they call Kykuit?" Alex asks.

"Yes, it is. Have you been there, sir?" Wally asks.

"Oh, yes, once or twice," Alex answers as he leans back once more. "You know, *kykuit* is a Dutch word. It means 'lookout.'"

"'In the 1890s, William Junior joined Henry Rogers in forming Amalgamated Copper Mining Company,'" Wally reads.

"That's the company that pulled the scam on the Anaconda Copper Company. They made off with thirty-six million dollars—pretty slippery, I'd say," Alex says.

"He also had interest in railways and public utilities, and he built up the National City Bank of New York, now part of Citigroup. It says here that upon his death, his estate had to pay $18,600,000 in inheritance and estate taxes," Wally says.

"My goodness, he must have been worth a fortune," Alex says.

"'He died in 1922 in Tarrytown, New York, and was interred in the Sleepy Hollow Cemetery,'" Wally reads.

"Is there a real Sleepy Hollow Cemetery? When I was a child, my mother would have me read *The Legend of Sleepy Hollow*. It was a short novel written by Washington Irving," Alex says.

"Yes, I know, sir, and yes, there is," Wally says. "'William Avery Junior married Almira Goodsell. They had six children, four of which lived to adulthood. His son William Goodsell Rockefeller married Sarah Elizabeth Stillman. She was the daughter of James Stillman, the president of First National Bank. William Goodsell's brother Percy graduated from Yale and was a member of Skull and Bones. He married Sarah's sister Almira.'"

"That is one of those secret societies at Yale. There are a few of them up there. I've never been to New Haven before.

We should make a note to go there someday, Wally," Alex says.

"Sure, it's not too far. I think you go north on the Taconic Highway and then East on I-84. I'll check on it," Wally says as he types a note into his day planner.

"'William Goodsell's second son Godfrey Stillman served as a second lieutenant during World War One. He also was a member of Skull and Bones in the graduating class of 1921 and served as a second lieutenant colonel during World War Two. Godfrey served on many corporate boards and was the director of Freeport-McMoRan from December 1931 until his death in 1983,'" Wally reads.

"'William Goodsell's third son, James Stillman Rockefeller, won a gold medal in rowing at the 1924 Summer Olympics in Paris.' That's funny—it reads that he joined the Scroll and Key while at Yale and not the Skull and Bones like his brother and uncle did. 'James worked at Brown Brothers Harriman and served as president from 1952 to 1959 and chairman from 1959 to 1967. Brown Brothers Harriman later became part of Citigroup. Prior to the time of James' death, he was America's oldest living Olympic champion and the earliest living subject of *Time* magazine. James was on the cover July 7, 1924, and lived to be 102 years old,'" Wally reads.

"'John Sterling, the forth son of William Goodsell, attended Yale and was another member of the Scroll and Key. John donated Kent's Island in the Bay of Fundy to Bowdoin College under the condition that it remained a bird sanctuary and a place the students of all institutions could study,'" Wally reads.

"What about Percy? Do we have any information on him?" Alex asks.

"'Percy Avery Rockefeller was a member of the 1900 class of Skull and Bones. He was the founder and vice president of Owenoke Corporation and a board director of no less than twenty-two other corporations, including Remington Arms, Western Union, New York Edison, and Bethlehem Steel. Percy was the father of five daughters and no boys.' My dossier states that his daughter Winifred killed herself along with her two daughters. 'She had suffocated herself and her daughters by leaving two cars running in a garage,'" Wally reads.

"Oh, my, that is terrible," Alex says as he more closely pays attention.

"'William Avery Junior's youngest daughter, Geraldine Rockefeller, married Marcellus Hartley Dodge Senior, president of the Remington Arms Company. At the time, she had brought into the marriage an estimated net worth of 101 million dollars, while Marcellus was worth just over 60 million dollars himself,'" Wally reads.

"My goodness, what year was that?"

"It was in 1907, sir. 'Their only son unfortunately was killed in a car crash in France in 1930,'" Wally reads.

"Oh, yes, I remember their story. She and her husband lived separately but on adjacent properties in New Jersey. They say that the path that connected the two houses extended for miles. I think the names were Giralda Farms and Hartley Farms. They are two huge properties. I think his property is listed on the National Register of Historic Places," Alex says.

Wally gets up from his chair and says, "I'll heat some water up on the burner, sir. Perhaps we have some tea or coffee in here somewhere." Wally begins to search the plane's small galley.

Chapter 11

"Section 4 of our dossier on the Van Rensselaers reads, 'Arms of Rensselaerswyck,'" David says.

"Hold up—I'm making a left on Fourteenth Street. There is going to be less traffic this way," Joey announces.

"'Kiliaen loaded the sailing vessel *The Arms of Rensselaerswyck* with more than just goods; he included two distinct gentlemen. The highly distinguished Arendt Van Corlaer became the first director general of the estate. And Dr. Adriaen Vander Donck, being the first lawyer in New Netherland, was sent over to be sheriff and treasurer of the Rensselaerswyck colony,'" David reads. "There is an added note here; it reads, 'The Van Rensselaer family commissioned the ship *The Flying Dutchman*.'"

"That's funny, another joke. You're killing me. That was not a real ship," laughs Joey. "That was from one of those pirate movies."

"I'm afraid it's true. *The Flying Dutchman* was a real ship," Laurance says. "It was commissioned by the VOC sometime in the 1640s. It was more of a trading vessel than a warship."

"So the Van Rensselaers were shipbuilders too. I'm making a right onto Third Avenue," Joey says.

David reads on. "'Upon the arrival of the first director of Rensselaerswyck in 1641, forests were cut down, homes were built, a fort erected, and crops planted, all at the toiling of the colonists. The colonists worked in every endeavor except the profitable fur trade; this alone was held as a monopoly saved for the Dutch West India Company. Another eminent character dispatched to America by Van Rensselaer was Domine Megapolensis, who took charge of the spiritual welfare of the people of the colony and was the most learned and accomplished of the early Dutch divines on this continent,'" David reads from the dossier.

"Well, sure, why not? If you're going to be a slave worker for someone else, you should be a happy, churchgoing slave. It seems the early churches in America worked the same way as our television and sports teams work today. They're just here to pacify us. They keep our minds off real issues like running an honest government," Joey says.

"That is a pretty negative point of view you have, Joey," Laurance says.

"Remember Leopard? He once said that 'Things must change so they can remain the same.' Things haven't changed for the common people since before the time of the Roman Empire. We all just slaves on a big farm called America," Joey says without hesitation.

Chapter 12

Wᴀʟʟʏ ᴀɴᴅ Aʟᴇx ʙᴏᴛʜ straighten up in their chairs as the plane hits a pocket of air, causing some slight turbulence.

"You know, I remember in the year 2004, when John Kerry ran against George Bush for the presidency of the United States, there was some flack about both of them belonging to the Skull and Bones up there at Yale. A great many of the Van Rensselaers went to Yale, but I don't recall any members of our family joining any of the Yale secret societies. I think my mother would have informed me of that. And besides, knowing more about them could prove helpful to us in the end," Alex says. "Could you look up what year those secret societies came into being? You have me curious."

"Didn't you find that election odd, sir?" Wally asks.

"What, the fact that they controlled both candidates of the election? No, I don't—it's an old trick. Let me tell you something, Wally: we here in America have a one-party system. It does not matter who is elected; there has been a higher authority running both the parties for many years now. The real control of politics lies in the hands of men with money and power. Presidents aren't elected—they are selected," Alex says as he leans forward in his chair.

"Who selects them?"

"The rich and powerful select them, that's who. You should know that by now, Wally. With a little more research, perhaps we can find out for sure," Alex answers.

"I've found here what they call the big three at Yale. I'm not sure what the differences are between the Skull and Bones, the Scroll and Key, and the Wolf's Head Society. I think I can just punch it in on Google and do a quick search," Wally says as he taps a few keys on his keypad. "Is there a reason you are interested in secret societies, sir?" Wally asks.

"Yes, the Red and the Green societies that I am meeting later today are two such societies," Alex starts to explain.

"Are they from America, sir?" Wally asks as he waits for his computer to finish its search.

"No, they are Asian societies. One from Japan, and the other from China, but both of them claim to stem from the old Ming Dynasty," Alex says.

"I just so happen to belong to the Temple Lodge, London, myself. The members there are very secretive," Wally says.

"Is that a fact, Wally?" Alex asks. "Let's check out these Yales first."

"How do you think they originate, sir?"

"I think most come from men of means that get together and are either unhappy about their own government or are ex-militia men that contrive together for more power."

"I think men of ideas sometimes come together for a particular cause. You know, to gain a better lot in life, perhaps. Well, either way, you've got me curious as well. Let me try the Skull and Bones Society first," Wally says. "It says the society's alumni organization, the Russell Trust Association, owns the real estate property and oversees the organization. It is named for General William Huntington

Russell, who co-founded Skull and Bones with classmate Alphonso Taft in 1832, and is the oldest of the secret societies at Yale."

"Alphonso was the father of our twenty-seventh president of the United States, William Howard Taft. Did you know Alphonso served as Attorney General and Secretary of War under President Ulysses S. Grant?" Alex asks.

"No, I didn't. It does show that the societies were a powerful outfit from the start," Wally says. "Listen to this: 'Alphonso's great-grandson, Robert A. Taft, supported the founding of the Wolf's Head Society, and Howard Taft IV worked in the Republican administration under George W. Bush. Another recent Taft was Robert A. II. He served as the governor of Ohio from 1999 until 2007,'" Wally reads.

"Amazing. Go on," Alex says, now resting back in his chair.

"'The Russell Trust was founded by Russell and Daniel Coit Gilman. Gilman later became president of the university. The members are known as bonesmen. The emblem of Skull and Bones is a skull with crossed bones over the number 322.'"

"Reminds one of the old pirate flag, I suppose," Alex adds.

"'In 1991, all living bonesmen mailed in a vote that permitted the society to go co-ed. William F. Buckley attempted to block the move by changing the locks on the doors to the Tomb. The vote was 368-320 in favor of allowing females in.'"

"That means there are just fewer than seven hundred members at any given time. Very interesting, Wally," Alex says.

"'There are rumors that the members take on nicknames. Averell Harriman was named Thor, Henry Luce was named Baal, and George H. W. Bush was named Magog,'" Wally reads.

"I'm not interested in rumors, Wally."

"Yes, sir. 'The society has been accused of possessing the stolen skulls of Martin Van Buren, Geronimo, and Pancho Villa,'" Wally reads.

"Again, I am not interested in unproven accusations either," Alex says.

"I suppose you don't want to hear anything about witchcraft or satanic rituals either, then," Wally says with a grin.

"No, I don't. None of that is our concern," Alex says.

"Sorry, sir. There is a long and illustrious list of members, but Percy is the only Rockefeller listed to be a member. It is obviously a mistake," Wally says.

"Tell me about the Scroll and Key," Alex says.

"'The Scroll and Key is the second-oldest secret society at Yale and was founded by John Porter, with aid from several members of the class of 1842, in 1843. After disputes over elections to the Skull and Bones, Porter got together with William Kingsley and others to form the Scroll and Key Society.' There is a picture here of their tomb, very Moorish, and very beautiful," Wally says, leaning over to show Alex.

"Ah, yes, very nice. Do you have anything on their members?"

"Yes, there is a list here. My goodness, they are all affiliated with the war department, the CIA ... there are mayors, governors, and ambassadors on the list of members as well. Sargent Shriver is on the list," Wally says.

"Yes, he married into the Kennedy family—John's sister Eunice, I believe," Alex says.

"Yes. The Rockefellers, of course, are on the list, along with Cornelius Vanderbilt III, Gilbert Colgate of toothpaste fame, and Stone Philips—you know, that guy on *Dateline NBC,*" Wally reads.

"Yes, of course. Is anybody else from New York on the list?" Alex asks.

"I'm not sure. The last entry is William Delano. Let me try him, and we'll see what comes up," Wally says as he punches keys on the laptop.

"I know of some of his work. He was an architect," Alex says.

"'William Delano was born in New York City, a member of the prominent Delano family. William attended Yale and graduated from Columbia's school of architecture. William formed a partnership with Chester Holmes Aldrich in the firm of Delano and Aldrich in 1903. They designed and built in the Beaux-Arts tradition for elite clients in New York City. Almost immediately won commissions from the Rockefeller family building townhouses, country houses, churches, schools, banks, and social clubs for the Astors, the Vanderbilts, and the Whitneys in the Georgian and Federal styles, combining brick and limestone, which became their trademark,'" Wally reads.

"Did you know that I hold the Delano and Aldrich archives?" Alex asks. "I keep them in the drawings and archives department in the Avery Architectural and Fine Arts Library at Columbia University."

"No, I didn't know that, sir. It must be some collection."

"It's a fantastic collection. The design of Kykuit, the mansion on the Rockefeller family estate, is in there, along with the Knickerbocker Club, the Willard Straight House—that's where the National Audubon Society is located—the Colony Club over on Park Avenue, and the Harold Pratt House on Sixty-eighth and Park," Alex says with some pride.

"The Pratt House—isn't that the Rockefellers' headquarters for the Council on Foreign Relations?" Wally asks.

"Yes, it is. The design is similar to the Union Club over on Sixty-ninth and Park Avenue, another Delano masterpiece. I think their best work was Oheka, though. It is a French-style chateau on Long Island. It was built for the financier Otto Kahn. I believe it is the second largest residence in the United States. It has 127 rooms, 109,000 square feet of living space, a golf course, and an airstrip. It's more of a castle than a home, beautiful," Alex says.

"Wow. Do you know what is considered to be the biggest estate here in America?" Wally asks.

"Of course I do. George Vanderbilt's Biltmore Castle is considered the biggest, but I think Oheka served as the inspiration for the Gatsby estate in F. Scott Fitzgerald's *The Great Gatsby*. The state of New York is filled with many wonderful homes," Alex says.

"Yes, sir. The Wolf's Head Society, sir?" Wally asks.

"Yes, entertain me, Wally."

"'The Wolf's Head Society consisted of fifteen members of the Yale class of 1884. It is an undergraduate secret society located in New Haven, Connecticut. It is owned by the Phelps Trust Association. The founding members thought that they had been overlooked by the other societies. It is composed of fifteen to sixteen members that are tapped from Yale College students annually,'" Wally reads. "'Stephen V. Harkness's three sons helped found and sustain The Third Society, later known as Wolf's Head Society, at Yale in 1883,'" Wally reads. "I remember that John D. Rockefeller had a silent partner named Stephen V. Harkness."

"Yes, Wally, you're right on with that one. Why did they name it Wolf's head?" Alex asks.

"I'm not sure. It says here that the wolf head symbolizes eternal life, rather than death. 'Its pin is a stylized wolf head on an inverted ankh, an Egyptian hieroglyphic known as the Egyptian Cross or the key to life,'" Wally reads.

"Sounds like some ancient magic mumbo jumbo to me, Wally. Is there anyone of significance as a member there?" Alex asks.

"Yes, does James Smith Bush count? He was the father of our Samuel Prescott Bush. Or maybe Douglas MacArthur II—he was the son of navy admiral Arthur MacArthur III and was named after his uncle, General Douglas MacArthur. How about Erastus Corning II?" Wally asks. "He is from your neck of the woods. He was mayor of Albany, New York, for more than forty years. His great-grandfather, Erastus Corning, founded the New York Central and was also the mayor of Albany, winning the election of 1834."

Alex leaned forward and with excitement says, "Of course I knew Erastus! He was a friend of my father's. Our families go back for generations. I'll tell you a story. Erastus the first owned and operated the Albany Nail Factory. It eventually became the Rensselaer Iron Works, but Erastus managed it so well that my great-great-grandfather offered him the presidency of our Albany State Bank. Our families have been in the railroad business together for years. Erastus was also put on the board of regents of the University of the State of New York as vice chancellor. He held that position for over thirty years. Erastus II passed back in 1983, not before he had built the Empire State Plaza in Albany along with Laurance Rockefeller, one of the five Rockefeller brothers. Did you know it was my father who proposed to Queen Wilhelmina of the Netherlands to make Erastus an officer of the Order of Orange-Nassau in gratitude for his aid following World War II?" Alex asks.

"No. He must have accomplished quite a bit. Sir, do you know the queen of Holland as well?" Wally asks.

"Of course I know Queen Beatrix. She is my mother's third cousin twice removed or something like that," Alex answers. "I've never kept track of those things. My mother makes it her job to remind me of certain genealogies of our friends and family alike, you know."

"Whatever happened to the ironworks that your family owned?" Wally asks.

"Rensselaer Iron Works became the Troy Iron & Steel Company. In its time, it was the largest iron and steel manufacturer in the United States, but the company eventually went out of business," Alex answers, somewhat sorry.

"Do you still own a piece of the New York Central Railroad?" Wally asks.

"Oh, dear, no. My mother may have, but I do not. Our family had at one time or another owned the Utica and Schenectady, the Mohawk and Hudson, and the Mohawk Valley Railroads. My great-great-grandfather Stephen Van Rensselaer IV sold out to the Vanderbilts right after the Civil War. I think it was the last time any Van Rensselaers owned any railroad stock, except over in New Jersey—at least, I haven't," Alex says.

"As head of the family now, sir, don't you think you should know more of your family's business?"

"I know of a nephew who works as the director of marketing over at AT&T."

"Prove you really know. What is his name?" Wally asks.

"I … I think his name is ah … Kiliaen. Yes, that's it, Kiliaen."

"That sounds like a wild guess to me, sir," Wally says as he returns his attention back to his laptop. "Listen to this one. This is great. 'Wolf's Head Society member William Clay Ford, owner of the Detroit Lions, in 1973 actually drafted another Wolf's Head member, Dick Jauron. Dick actually made the Pro Bowl in 1974 for the Detroit Lions,'" Wally reads.

"Isn't he the head coach of Buffalo Bills now?" Alex asks, returning to his slumber position.

"Well, yes, he was last year, but I think he is with the Philadelphia Eagles now," Wally answers.

"Either way, it is a bit off topic. Let's get back to the Rockefeller report," Alex says.

Chapter 13

THE ROCKEFELLER LIMO IS traveling south on Third Avenue until it slows for a red light at East Tenth Street.

David turns a page in the dossier. "There is quite a bit more to go over. Section 5 looks like an obituary of sorts. 'One would have recognized the passing of such a grand dignitary with no doubt, as a parade of horses, carriages, arms, and flags in Kiliaen's funeral procession would pass along the streets from Amsterdam to his final resting place in Nykerk, Holland. Neither Kiliaen nor his first son Johannas Van Rensselaer, the second *patroon* of the estate, would ever go and visit the grand domains of Rensselaerswyck. The colony, being in its adolescent state, had much anxiety over the passing of Rensselaerswyck's first *patroon;* as he died at such a young age, it could be thought of as a bad omen. No such omen could stop the rise of the estate as the second *patroon,* Johannes Van Rensselaer, would indeed exemplify his namesake.

"'Johannes, with his unwillingness to move to the new world, did direct the colony from afar. Immediately upon his father's death, he decided to hire Brandt Arendt Van Slichtenhorst to replace Van Corlaer. Van Slichtenhorst may have traveled to America with Claes Van Resonvelt, the ancestor of the Roosevelt family, and Cornelius Vanderbilt's great-great-grandfather, Jan Aertson, who was a Dutch farmer from De Bilt in Utrecht, Netherlands, who immigrated to New York as an indentured servant in 1650. Under Van Slichtenhorst's direction, the estate rose to flourishing heights, its prosperity even exceeding that of the city of New Amsterdam.'" David pauses.

"Are you saying Albany was once bigger than New York City?" Joey asks.

"Yes, apparently it is true, Joey. Our staff double- and triple-checks all the reports before they reach us," Laurance says.

"It's ironic in the fact that the Vanderbilts first came here as indentured servants and ended up becoming one of the riches families in America. The American dream that was is now dead," Joey says. "The land of opportunity doesn't exist. It's a sad myth, perpetuated to keep the slave classes working."

"America is still growing and is boundless with opportunities," David says. "You just need to know where to look."

"'These two men had laid the foundation of Albany. In those times, it was known as Beverwyck. At this time, Indian wars were rampant throughout all the other colonies, while Rensselaerswyck never felt or had any difficulties with the Indians. The good fortunes of escaping such ravages were due to the prudent and just policy of Van Corlaer and Van Slichtenhorst, both of whom were revered as friends of the Five Nations. In fact, the colony befriended the Indians more than any other, which added to their security and strength in their prolonged struggle for supremacy with the French to the north,'" David reads.

"'With the tragic death of Johannes, his younger brother Jan Baptist Van Rensselaer became the director of Rensselaerwyck. He came to the colony in 1651, along with his younger brother Ryckert. Jan Baptist became the director on the eighth of May, 1652. During his stay at the manor, he lived in a style befitting his position, having brought furniture, silverware, and other personal property of great wealth. While the first Dutch Reformed church was being constructed, it was Jan Baptist who placed the windowpane representing the Van Rensselaer arms in the Dutch Church of Beverwyck. He stayed only a few years, and on the arrival of his brother, Jeremias, he returned to Holland in 1658. Jan Baptist became one of the richest men in Amsterdam, where he died in 1678,'" David reads. "I'll go on with section 6," David says.

"'Pieter Stuyvesant served as the last Dutch director-general of the colony of New Netherland from 1647 until it was ceded provisionally to the English in 1664. He built the protective wall on Wall Street. He had a peg leg, and his nickname was "Old Silver Leg." In 1648, he started a conflict with Brant Van Slichtenhorst. He claimed he had power over Rensselaerswyck, despite special privileges granted to the Van Rensselaer family. In 1649, Stuyvesant marched on Fort Orange with a military escort. The conflict allowed Stuyvesant to erect a fort at Beverwyck in 1650,'" David reads.

"Hey, we just passed Stuyvesant Street and the Hamilton Fish House," Joey states. "Is that the same guy?"

"Yes, Joey, it is. Mr. Fish is a descendent of the Livingstons, as are our presidents, Bush One and Bush Two," Laurance says. "Mr. Fish was intimate with most of the Van Rensselaer family. He not only served as our sixteenth governor, but was a trustee to Columbia University for fifty-three years."

"I must agree, Laurance. Mr. Fish was a descendent of the Livingstons on his father's side, and, of course, his mother was Elizabeth Stuyvesant, a direct descendent of Peter Stuyvesant herself," David says.

"Though parts of the Livingston and the Van Rensselaer families intermarried, Hamilton Fish and the Bushes are not directly related to the Van Rensselaers," Laurance says.

"You know, the history of the United States all started right here in New York," Joey says as he accelerates at a green light on Third Avenue. "I mean, everything happens here. You gotta love this place."

"You know, in 1673, the Dutch recaptured New York City and then traded it for Suriname in 1674 back to the English," Laurance says.

"So the Dutch traded New York to the British for some island I never heard of. And I thought the Indians were dumb when they sold Manhattan for a thousand dollars." Joey laughs. "You guys might have a shot at that property deal after all."

"Suriname is not an island. It's part of the mainland in South America," Laurance corrects Joey.

"Same thing. What's the difference?" Joey says.

Chapter 14

"Mr. Van Rensselaer! Mr. Van Rensselaer, sir! *Alex!*" Wally shouts as Alex Van Rensselaer awakes after dozing off.

"I was not asleep. I was just resting my eyes," Alex says untruthfully.

"We are a good three hours into our flight. Would you like some coffee or tea, sir? You seem to be a bit tired," Wally says as he pours each of them a hot cup of water as their flight takes them over parts of Greenland.

"Yes, some tea would be nice, thank you," Alex answers.

"I have some hot water right here. Perhaps some caffeine is in order, sir, and it will keep you from dozing off. All we have are these lousy teabags, I'm afraid," Wally says as he gets up from his chair.

"Where are we in the report, Wally?" Alex asks.

Wally returns to his seat and opens his laptop.

"Your favorite part, sir, John D. Rockefeller Senior. As I recall, we've gone through this report once before. I've added this part from an early report that you had created in 1985. I was not in your service at that time, sir," Wally says as he looks it over.

"Yes, it was in the midst of the sale of property that the Rockefeller Center sits on. It was in 1985. You see, the trust at the Columbia University used to own the land. We sold the property to the Rockefeller Group at the extremely low price of four hundred million dollars, but my father had the Rockefellers agree to put a provision in the deal that the regents would have to approve any resale of the property due to its proximity to some other properties in the area. We used the same provision again when the Rockefellers sold the land to The Green and Red Soc ..." Alex stops and corrects himself. "I mean, the Mitsubishi Group in 1989," Alex says, knowing he overspoke.

"I was a new hire in 2000, but I recall that it was Jerry Speyer who purchased the property, along with the Lester Crown family of Chicago," Wally says.

"No, not all of it. Mr. Speyer's real estate company owns the land and the fourteen older buildings. He represents the Rockefellers' interest in the property. The five newer buildings are still owned by the Mitsubishi Group," Alex explains.

"These two groups, the Red and the Green—are they part of the Japanese Triads?" Wally asks.

"No, the Triads are gangsters. The Red and the Green are more like financers and politicians," Alex says.

"Is there much of a difference?" Wally asks sarcastically.

"It's funny—Mr. Speyer and I graduated from Columbia College in the same year, 1962, but I've never met him personally. I only conversed with him over the phone. He seems to be a nice fellow," Alex says as he gets up from his chair. Alex looks into the empty refrigerator for some food.

"Will Mr. Speyer be at today's meeting with David?" Wally asks.

"I don't think so. David said that we will be meeting alone," Alex says. "I'm getting a bit hungry; are you?"

"Yes, anything sounds good right about now. Would you like me to accompany you to the Ritz-Carleton meeting this afternoon?" Wally asks. "I would advise it—I mean, if it has anything to do with our business meeting with David Rockefeller later."

"Well, all right, but those guys are a bit touchy when it comes to strangers. If you could just lie low, I'm sure everything will be fine," Alex says.

"Of course. It's an Englishman's job to be discreet," Wally says.

Alex finishes his cup of tea and pours a second.

"Please proceed, Wally," Alex says, sitting back down in his chair. "That is a bit odd."

"What is it, sir?"

"Look out the window, Wally. Tell me, what do you see?"

"I just see the sunrise, sir."

"Yes, but wouldn't you think the sun would be a little more behind us if we were heading from London straight to New York?"

"Yes, it is at an odd angle, I'd say. Perhaps Raymond has diverted a little to avoid a storm."

"What, and not tell us? I'd swear he is heading toward the west coast. Is it possible to retrieve our flight path from that computer of yours?"

"Well, all pilots must submit a flight plan before take-off. I can try. You don't think he would purposely fly us off course, do you?"

"I'm not sure, but we are definitely not heading toward New York."

"Let's see. I'm on the FAA website. Our flight number, as I recall, is NC12098. He has us flying to Seattle. My goodness, sir, you are right."

"We have got to do something," Alex says, trying to think of something as fast as he can.

Chapter 15

Davɪᴅ ʀᴇᴀᴅs ᴏɴ ɪɴ section 7 of the dossier. "'The third *patroon,* Jeremias Van Rensselaer, was the third son of the first Kiliaen. He was born in Holland in 1632, received a superior education, and, in 1658, came over to take the place of his brother Jan Baptist. He was the first in the family to establish himself permanently in America, being devoted to the governing of the colony, which he exercised with great prudence, energy, and distinction. He became a man of great influence among the Indians; they apparently guarded the estate as carefully as they did their own. The French in Canada regarded him as one of the ablest of men and a great representative of the entire colony. He had the good judgment to get along with Stuyvesant, who had troubled the administrations of his brother and Van Slichtenhorst. During the time in which the Dutch were the authority of New Netherland, Stuyvesant was the governor. In early 1664, when the *landtsdagh,* or diet, was summoned by Stuyvesant to deliberate on the critical condition of the province, which included all manorial estates of the Dutch, it was Jeremias who served as the presiding officer of that body. They talked about the viability of the colonists to defend themselves from the British. Thus being the first general assembly held within the state of New York.

"'The Dutch colonists decided to surrender to the British rather than fight and have all their valuable assets destroyed. After the surrender to the British in September of 1685, Jeremias took an oath to the new government, and all the rights and immunities enjoyed by his family in its colony of Rensselaerswyck were recognized, although the future of the estate was still not settled. Jeremias failed in his attempt to get a re-grant of the estate in his family's name. His lawyer had advised him to seek the patent needed as an individual, being qualified to hold real estate by virtue of his British citizenship and so obtained the re-grant of Rensselaerswyck in his personal name. Jeremias started and wrote the newspaper *New Netherland Mercury*. He married Maria Van Cortlandt, she being the sister of Stephanus Van Cortlandt, the founder of the Van Cortlandt Manor,'" David reads.

"I think Stephen Van Cortlandt was the mayor of New York for a while," Joey interrupts.

"Yes, he was, Joey." David pauses before he continues. "Although Jeremias died at Rensselaerwyck October 12, 1674, the British patent was held as a provisional grant until 1685. This British patent came from Governor Andros to the heirs of Kiliaen Van Rensselaer in 1685."

"Governor Andros—he is the guy that saved Christmas. Did you know the puritans outlawed Christmas back in the 1650s? This Governor Edmund Andros guy had to pass a law to save Christmas. Can you believe that? In Boston, the people still did not celebrate Christmas until the mid-1800s. It's true," Joey states.

David continues. "Jeremias opened the Albany Savings Bank in 1686 and, with others, would eventually create the New York pound, the colonial scrip that would be used up until the American Revolution,'" David reads.

"Wow, so the *patroons* were allowed to print money of their own? I wonder how much they made. I would have made millions," Joey says.

"They could, and they did," Laurance states.

"He sounds like he works for the Federal Reserve. Did you know those guys are allowed to print money whenever they feel like it, right out of thin air?" Joey says. "It just doesn't feel right. I mean, I'm not one to return to the gold standard, but I think money should be based on some sort of metal. I think that is in the Constitution somewhere. Maybe the treasury should create money based on a metals index of some sort. You know, like an average of gold, silver, copper, and platinum," Joey says.

"Now, that is not a bad idea," Laurance says.

"Don't encourage him, Laurance," David states.

"Listen to me. I almost sound like I know what I'm talking about," Joey says. "You like that idea? I've got a million of them. You would think the congress would do something about the Fed. I mean, curb their power or something. I don't think the president can do anything either. Say, you guys look familiar," Joey says.

"Please hurry, Joey. We don't wish to be late," David says as he tries to change the subject.

"You know, my mother has a crazy idea that our government is really run by a secret government. She says that the Rockefellers ..." Joey pauses with excitement. "Hey that's who you guys are—you're the Rockefeller brothers, right? I knew I recognized you. Holy shit, imagine me driving around the Rockefellers. That property you mentioned earlier, you meant Rockefeller Center, didn't you? You're telling me, with all those buildings, you guys don't actually own the land? This Van Rensselaer guy is going to ass-rape you during negotiations. You better grow some balls before your meeting. I mean balls the size of church bells," Joey says.

"I had faith he would figure it out," Laurance says to his brother.

"It is important we get there on time," David restates with a lack of amusement.

"We're still twenty minutes away, plenty of time. Why are we going to Ground Zero anyway?" Joey asks.

"We are laying a wreath in commemoration of the losses the NYFD sustained on September 11, 2001," Laurance announces.

"Yes, that was a tragedy, but today is only the tenth. Shouldn't you being doing this tomorrow? Joey asks.

"We've done this every year, and every year it gets worse," Laurance says.

"What gets worse?" ask Joey.

"We are doing this today because there will be too many protestors there tomorrow," Laurance says.

"Yes, the protestors, there is a wacky bunch. I mean, they say the buildings were blown up from the inside and fell at freefall speeds. I'll only say one thing about that. Those buildings here in New York City kicked those airplanes' asses. I mean really. You know, my whole family was stonemasons. We've worked on a lot of the building sites here in New York for years. My grandfather started back in the 1920s. I belong to the Masonic Hall here in New York City," Joey says.

"Is that right? How else did you think you got this job?" David asks sarcastically.

"Well, yes, a friend of a friend, you know how it works," Joey says. "When my grandfather was a stonemason, he helped build all these skyscrapers you see every day. Most of my uncles are carpenters, electricians, plumbers, or stonemasons—you know, union guys. We built most of the churches and bridges too," Joey says. "There is no way those buildings just fell down."

"I'm happy you two are enjoying this chat, but we need to get through this dossier," David says as he looks at his watch.

"Yes, do go on, David," Laurance says.

Chapter 16

"I'VE GOT A PLAN, Wally. You walk up front with the pot of hot water and offer the pilot some coffee. While you have him distracted, I'll pretend to have a gun in my pocket, and ..." Raymond the pilot has moved his way to the back of the plane.

"I've put the plane on auto-pilot for a moment, sir. Is there a latrine I may use?"

"Yes, of course. It's right there," Alex says, pointing the way.

"Thank you. I won't be a moment," Raymond says.

"Now what are we going to do?" Wally says, frantically whispering.

"When he comes out of the bathroom, block his way, and I'll grab him from behind," Alex says.

"And then what?"

"Shhh, here he comes."

After the bathroom door opens, the men smile at each other graciously. The plane hits a gust of turbulence as Wally is still holding the hot pot of water. He decides to douse Raymond with it. As Raymond screams in bloody horror,

Alex whacks him in the back of the head with his cane, knocking him out.

"Wow, nice shot, sir."

"Good thinking, Wally," Alex says.

"It was more of an accident than anything, sir."

"The controls, I've got to figure out how to fly this thing," Alex says as the two rush toward the cockpit. "Drag him back into the bathroom and wedge the door shut before he wakes up," Alex says as he takes a seat in the pilot's chair.

After a few moments of banging and bruising, Wally has succeeded in moving the man who called himself Raymond into the bathroom. Wally keeps the door shut by tying the straps of their luggage together and stringing one end to the handle of the door and the other end to the steel framework of the nearest chair.

Wally moves to the front cabin and sits back and makes himself as comfortable as he can in the high-backed leather chair as Alex frantically tries to turn off the auto-pilot. "I think I've found it," Alex says as he pushes a button with a blinking red light on it. "Now, let's see. These here are the thrusters, and that is the altimeter ... that there controls our landing gear—we're going to need that, of course—and this is the steering column, no doubt," Alex says as he gets acquainted with the instrument panel.

"Are you sure you can fly this plane, Alex?" Wally asks, slightly terrified.

"Is our friend secure?"

"I think so. I did the best I could."

"I'm not worried about the flying as much as I am about the landing," Alex says, not very reassured. "Now let's slow this thing down a bit," Alex says, pulling back on the thrusters.

"We need to get a heading," Alex says as he banks the plane to the left. "Can you see any landmarks down below us?"

"I think we are somewhere over Canada, sir, but this plane has a state-of-the-art navigation system. Let me try and figure this out," Wally says as he pushes a few buttons of the onboard navi-computer. "There we are, sir. We are just north of Nova Scotia. You need to turn a degree or two to the south."

"How is that, Wally?" Alex says calmly, turning slightly more left.

"We should be right on, Alex. We need to send the FAA a request for an airborne reroute."

"Do whatever it takes, Wally."

"Yes, sir," Wally says as he tries to make contact with the FAA in Canada.

"We'll need to return to your report soon."

After a busy few minutes on the computer, Wally says, "We have approval to fly into JFK, sir. Do you think the queen may have done this, or perhaps the Asians?"

"No, I'm sure Mr. Rockefeller had something to do with switching our pilot. Somewhat clever, I suppose."

"Do you think he intended on killing us?"

"No, that is not his style, I don't think. Perhaps he was wishing we would miss the meeting with him today."

"Maybe he wanted us to miss the meeting at the Holland Society or the meeting with the Green and the Red."

"He's afraid of something, that is for sure. Do you have your computer handy?"

"Yes, it's right here, and it is still running."

"Please proceed," Alex says as he pushes the thrusters back to full throttle.

"'Mr. John D. Rockefeller Senior, the founder of the Standard Oil Company of Cleveland, Ohio. As a boy, he earned extra money selling turkeys, potatoes, and candy. When John D. was sixteen, he got his first job as an assistant bookkeeper working for a small produce firm. He was particularly adept at calculating transportation cost.' This is odd for a boy his age. It says that young John D. donated six percent of his pay to charity, and by age twenty, he was donating ten percent of his earnings to the church. 'In 1859, John D., along with a partner, Maurice Clark, started their own produce business with four thousand dollars in capital and never had a losing year during the rest of his life,'" Wally reads from his report.

"That seems hard to believe, going through the Civil War years and living through the Great Depression," Alex comments.

"'Rockefeller, along with Samuel Andrews, Maurice Clark, and Clark's two brothers, built an oil refinery in 1863 while the commercial oil business was in its infancy,'" Wally reads.

"I've read that whale oil had become too expensive for the common folk of the time, so the masses desperately needed something cheaper to illuminate their homes and heat their ovens," Alex says.

"One would think candles and firewood would do the trick," Wally replies.

"That just begs us not to buy into everything we read," Alex says.

"I agree, Alex. 'In 1864, John D. married Laura Spelman. They, of course, had four daughters and one son. He credited her by stating, "Her judgment was always better than mine. Without her keen advice, I would be a poor man." In addition to John D. hiring soldiers to substitute for him during the Civil War, he also gave money to the Union cause. Near the end of the war, John D. bought out the Clark brothers at auction for $72,500. He said himself, "It was the day that determined my career." In 1866, John's brother built another refinery in Cleveland, and John was brought into the partnership. In 1867, Henry M. Flagler became a partner, and the firm of Rockefeller, Andrews, and Flagler was established. By 1868, the two refineries, along with a marketing subsidiary in New York made up the largest oil refinery in the world,'" Wally reads.

"It's amazing—with their longevity, David Rockefeller's grandparents go back prior to the Civil War. I'll bet there are not too many people who can say that," Alex says.

"Yes, that is an incredibly long stretch for just three generations," Wally says.

"'The Standard Oil Company was founded in 1870 by the thirty-one-year-old merchant; the company emerged as the giant among the oil refiners. Rockefeller exploited every possible means, fair and foul, to gain advantage over competitors. When competitive wars in the refining industry started, it was Standard Oil that emerged victorious because Rockefeller was the toughest, most imaginative, and the most efficient refiner in the business. Standard Oil obtained ten-percent rebates from the railroads and cut prices locally to force small independents to sell out or face ruin. Standard supplied kerosene, meat, sugar, and other products at artificially low prices in an effort to crush the stores that carried other brands of kerosene. The company employed spies to track down customers and offer them bargain prices,'" Wally reads.

"Sounds a lot like today's world of business. It's known that John D. would bribe members of the legislature. The only difference today is they call it a campaign contribution," Alex says.

"'By 1879, he controlled ninety percent of the oil refining capacity of the United States, along with a network of pipelines and large reserves of petroleum still in the ground. Rockefeller knew little about the technology of petroleum, but was a meticulous organizer and a ruthless competitor. John D. would prefer to persuade other refiners to join him so they could all enjoy profits rather than crushing them. Standard Oil developed over three hundred oil-based products such as tar, paint, Vaseline, and chewing gum. After achieving his monopoly, Rockefeller created a new type of business organization, the trust,'" Wally reads.

"It's a widely known fact that John Jacob Astor created the first private trust in America, not Rockefeller," Alex says.

"I'm sorry, sir, but the Standard Oil Trust was the first legal commercial entity of its kind. I'll explain. At that time, many state legislatures had made it difficult to incorporate in one state and operate in another. So Rockefeller hired a lawyer named Samuel Todd in 1879, who incorporated the forty-one companies that were operating in different states and assigned nine trustees to run them as one business. In fact, it was a corporation of corporations, but it had no legal charter. Todd, in fact, invented the stockholder. The individual investors would receive trust certificates, on which dividends were paid. For many years, few people outside the organization knew that it existed. The public and press were suspicious of this newly devised entity, but other businesses, seeing the efficiency of a centralized management team, emulated it," Wally says.

"I'm sure that fact further inflamed public sentiment against all the trusts of the time," Alex says.

"'In the 1880s, Standard Oil created certificates of issuances against oil stored in its pipelines. Those certificates started to be traded by speculators, thus creating the world's first oil futures market. It was genius because now Rockefeller benefited by creating an auction block for his product and guaranteeing the highest prices and most the profits. In 1882, the National Petroleum Exchange opened in Manhattan to facilitate these trades. Knowing that New York was the trading center of America and perhaps the world, Rockefeller moved the Standard Oil Company's headquarters to 26 Broadway and became a central figure in the city's business community. He moved his family to Fifty-fourth Street, near the mansions of other magnates such as William Vanderbilt, in 1884,'" Wally says.

"I've heard he used to take the elevated train to his downtown office daily. I'm sure he had to deal with threats from vagabonds and pleas for charity. It's a strange world we live in," Alex says.

"'The management of the trust was turned over to John D. Archbold as John D. bought Pocantico Hills, an estate north of New York City, entering semi-retirement, taking up bicycling and golf,'" Wally reads.

"It's a wonder why the Hudson River has always attracted the rich and industrious right from the beginning, after its discovery," Alex says.

"'In 1901, US Steel, controlled by J. Pierpont Morgan, having bought out Andrew Carnegie, offered to buy Standard's iron interests. John D. and his son were given stock in the company and were board members on the company's board of directors. In full retirement at age sixty-three, John D. Rockefeller Senior earned over fifty-eight million dollars in investments in 1902,'" Wally reads.

"That is a lot of money, but I thought Standard Oil was found to be in violation of the Sherman Antitrust Act?" Alex asks.

"Yes, they were, sir. The Sherman Antitrust Act of 1890 was originally conceived to control unions, but in 1911, the Supreme Court of the United States found Standard Oil Company of New Jersey in violation of the act," Wally says.

"Yes, the court ruled that the trust was using illegal monopoly practices and ordered it to be broken up into thirty-four new companies," Alex says.

"'Standard Oil became Conoco, Chevron, Mobil, Esso, Amoco, Exxon, and many others. Rockefeller held over twenty-five percent of the shares at the time of the breakup. In return, he received twenty-five percent of all the new companies that were created. As the company's stock rose in price, Rockefeller's personal wealth would make him the world's first billionaire,'" Wally reads. "Will reading about David's grandparents really help you in your business deal?" Wally asks.

"Well, you remember your grandparents, don't you, Wally? All of David's traits must originate somewhere. So why not research from the beginning?" Alex asks.

"Yes, quite well, actually, but I don't think I have any of their mental traits. I mean, we grew up in different generations and all, although anything is possible, I suppose," Wally answers.

"I can see John D. Senior got his business tactics from his father and his philanthropic side from his mother. Would you agree, Wally?" Alex asks.

"Yes, of course. I have a great deal of information dealing with his philanthropy. 'John D. Senior was a lifelong Baptist. John D.'s wife, Laura, along with her parents, was abolitionist and joined his congregation of Northern Baptist. It is Laura who is the namesake of Spelman College. The Rockefellers continued to donate ten percent of their income to charity at that time,'" Wally reads.

"Did you know that John D. Senior adhered to total abstinence from alcohol and tobacco throughout his entire life? That surely is not his father's doing," Alex says.

"Maybe that's the reason the old man William Avery left all the time—his wife was henpicking him. The man simply needed a drink," Wally laughs.

"You know, he was a lifelong Republican as well. Now the head of the Republican Party is charging tabs at voyeurism clubs," Alex says. "How times have changed."

"'John D. Senior was advised primarily by Frederick T. Gates from 1889 until 1924 in business and philanthropy,'" Wally reads.

"That is some thirty-five years. Sort of a Rasputin, was he? That fact alone should inform us about the man. Can you research Gates from twenty-five thousand feet over the Atlantic Ocean?" Alex asks.

"I'm already searching for him, sir," Wally says. "'Frederick Taylor Gates was the son of a Baptist minister. He was born in 1853. He graduated from the Rochester Theological Seminary in 1880.' Let's see, that would have made him fourteen years younger than John D. I would have thought the opposite. 'In January of 1889, Gates met Rockefeller Senior, suggesting designs in hope of funding for the creation of the Baptist University of Chicago. He subsequently served for many years as a trustee on its board. John D. Senior ended up donating eighty million dollars to the college. He then became Rockefeller's key philanthropic and business adviser, where he oversaw investments in many companies and real estate holdings, but never in John D.'s personal stock in the Standard Oil Trust.' What do you make of that?" Wally asks.

"It tells me he didn't fully trust the man. Pretty smart, I would say. Let that be a lesson to us. The only thing someone should ever fully trust is one's own conscience. Good job, Wally; we've learned something important about the man," Alex says.

"'Gates worked in the newly established family office in the headquarters at 26 Broadway. In his capacity, he steered Rockefeller money into syndicates arranged primarily by the investment house Kuhn, Loeb, and Company and some lesser amounts to J. P. Morgan. At the time, Rockefeller held a securities portfolio of unprecedented size for a private individual, but it was Gates that served on the boards of many of the companies in which Rockefeller had a majority share. Rockefeller himself regarded him as the greatest businessman he had encountered in his life,'" Wally reads.

"That sounds like a slap to the face of men like Henry Ford, Andrew Carnegie, and William Vanderbilt," Alex says.

"'Gates served as president of the Rockefeller-created General Education Board, in which Rockefeller gave 180 million dollars to establish,'" Wally reads.

"That was set up to help educate medical students and poor blacks in the South, which helped to teach them general farming practices," Alex says.

"He sounds like a brilliant man. For example, 'After changes in the tax codes, as well as the advent of the Federal Reserve Act of 1913, it was Gates who designed the Rockefeller Foundation. Gates also started shifting donations away from churches and moved more and more toward modernizing medical facilities and reforming education. They helped sponsor research to identify and cure diseases like hookworm. Rockefeller himself believed in folk medicines, but upon Gates' advice, the billionaire set up foundations and agreed to let experts run them,'" Wally reads.

"Folk medicine, that shows John D. was a bit old-fashioned even for his time. I can see that same trait in David sometimes," Alex says.

"That is a bit of an oxymoron, don't you think, to say that a ninety-two-year-old is a bit old-fashioned? Anyway, 'In 1924, John Junior was on the board of advisors and refused Gates when Gates asked for 265 million dollars to support the China Medical Board,'" Wally reads.

"Well, John D. Rockefeller Senior did give away about 550 million dollars in his lifetime. I remember stories that he would hand out dimes to adults and nickels to children on his way to work," Alex says.

"I've found a poem written by John D. He wrote it at the age of eighty-six," Wally says.

"Well, let me hear it, Wally," Alex says, crossing his legs and having full attention.

> "'I was early taught to work as well as play.
> My life has been one long, happy holiday,
> full of work and full of play.
> I dropped the worry on the way,
> and God was good to me every day,'"

Wally reads with a smile.

Chapter 17

Dᴀᴠɪᴅ ʟᴏᴏᴋs ᴅᴏᴡɴ ᴀɴᴅ finds section 8 of the dossier. "This section is labeled 'Nicholas Van Rensselaer.'"

David reads on: "'The fourth *patroon,* the Reverend Nicolaus Van Rensselaer. Nicolaus was born in Amsterdam, Holland, about 1638, was well educated, and obtained a degree in theology. While in Europe, he met the exiled King Charles II and had the politeness to predict his speedy restoration to the throne. A few years later, Charles being restored, Nicolaus was recognized by the king and was presented with a gold snuff-box, which is still preserved as a family heirloom to this day. In 1674, he came to America with his brother Ryckert, with a letter from the Duke of York, who recommended that he be put in charge of the Dutch churches in the colonies. In fact, Nicolaus tried to become the head of the Dutch Reformed Church. He was put in jail, because of complaints from Jacob Leisler and Jacob Milburne, for some time for this act. Nicholas had married Alyda Schuyler, the daughter of Philip Schuyler. Nicholas died in 1678. Alyda remarried a year later in 1679 to Robert Livingston. Ryckert Van Rensselaer moved back to Holland,'" David reads.

"There is a guy with some balls. I mean, he tried to declare himself the pope of the Dutch Reformed Church, and he got his ass thrown in jail. I like him already," Joey says.

"Please, Joey," David says as he insists on him being quiet while he reads.

"'The Estate of Rensselaerwyck was undecided by the late Jeremias' last will and being descended to the third generation from Kiliaen. The crown in England was unwilling to grant the manorial title until a male descendent was born unto the male line. Kiliaen, the son of Johannas, became the first lord of the manor under British law. Kiliaen quickly granted a one-mile-by-sixteen-mile-long tract of land to the city of Albany, which was given to the government of the province of New York as commons to the king. The administrator of the Dutch West India Company, Stuyvesant, had intended this property for the company, it being the most valuable property in upstate New York. He fought to stop this grant through arbitration with Governor Dongan. The governor sided with the Rensselaers, stating, "The town of Albany lies within the Rensselaers' colony … They settled the place.""'" David reads.

"I wonder what it would be like to live back then. I mean, with the Indians and with no electricity and no running water," Laurance says, wondering out loud.

"Please, Laurance; you are as bad as Joey," David says.

"I can tell you how it was; it sucked. Us guys that were in Iraq, we didn't have any electricity, running water, or toilet paper for four months. I used to wipe my ass with the empty water bottles," Joes says.

David clears his throat and begins anew. "'The early death of Kiliaen, son of Johannas, and leaving no male heir, in 1678 moved the ownership of the estate to the Kiliaen, his cousin, the son of Jeremias. This Kiliaen became the second lord of the manor. Kiliaen, on behalf of his cousins, brothers, and sisters, still owned much property back in Holland. He, representing the American half of the family and negotiating with another cousin named Kiliaen, son of Jan Baptist, representing the heirs in the old country, settled on the lands in America going to the American heirs and the Holland lands going to the Holland heirs as according to English customs,'" David reads as he turns a page in the dossier.

"You're killing me with this stuff. Don't you have anything interesting in there?" Joey cries.

"Ah, yes, indeed. Here is a typed note; I'll read it to you," David says. "Section 9: 'Captain William Kidd was hired in 1694 by the Van Rensselaer agent, and now family member, Colonel Robert Livingston. A plan was orchestrated by Kidd, Livingston, and the governor of New York, Bellomont, to attack a list of pirates that they had created and any enemy French ships. Kidd was presented with a letter of marque from Van Rensselaer, signed by King William III of England,'" David reads.

"We must not forget that King William III of England was of Dutch descent," Laurance adds.

David continues, "'The ship, the *Adventure Galley,* was built and weighed 184 tons. It had 34 cannons, oars, and 150 men. The cost for the venture was paid for by the Van Rensselaers and their friends, which included a duke, an earl, and a baron, none of whom shall be named. As the new ship weighed anchor and sailed down the Thames River in London, Captain Kidd failed to salute a navy yacht at Greenwich, as it was customary. The yacht then fired a shot to try and make him show some respect, but Kidd's crew turned and slapped their naked backsides in disdain,'" David reads.

"So Captain Kidd mooned the British Navy. That is awesome. I love it. My balls feel bigger already," Joey says.

"'After a long career in the pirating business, Captain Kidd was hanged on May 23, 1701. He was to hang in an iron cage over the River Thames, London, for twenty years as a warning to future would-be pirates,'" David reads. "Was that interesting enough for you, Joey?"

"I believe the term used is *gibbeted,*" Laurance says.

"Yes, that was great. What about that Robert Livingston guy? Isn't he the guy that signed the Declaration of Independence?" asks Joey.

"No, no, Robert Livingston the Elder was the grandfather of Robert R. Livingston and a great-uncle to Philip Livingston. Robert R. was actually on the committee of five that wrote the original draft. He was recalled to Albany by Van Rensselaer prior to July 4, 1776, and did not sign the Declaration, but his cousin Philip Livingston did sign," Laurance adds.

"How in the world do you remember all that?" David asks. "I thought Thomas Jefferson wrote the Declaration of Independence," David says.

"Well, I read a lot," Laurance answers. "I've also learned that during the Glorious Revolution in Britain, it was Van Rensselaer ships that brought William of Orange from Holland to London. The crew also brought and distributed real oranges on the streets of London. The Van Rensselaer faction was also present when parliament authored that 'William of Orange was made king by grace of parliament, not God,'" Laurance says.

"You have done some homework, Laurance," David commends his brother.

"Yes, it is called the library, my dear boy," Laurance says, not hesitating to ridicule his brother.

"New York became something of the capital of privateering in those days," Laurance adds.

"So four hundred years, later nothing has changed. What were the pirates then are the bankers now," Joey says.

"Watch the road, please," David says as Joey slows the limo down and stops at Third Avenue and East Houston Street.

"So what happened to the king?" Joey asks.

"What king?" Laurance asks.

"What happened to the old king, King James the II, the Catholic king?" Joey says.

"It is not important. I believe he moved to France or something," answers Laurance.

"Yes, what is important is that Queen Anne succeeded William of Orange on March 8, 1702," David says.

"Wasn't she the last of the Stuarts to sit on the throne?" Joey asks.

"Yes, quite right, Joey," Laurance says.

"Well, what about her?" Joey asks.

"Well, we're getting to it. We would be farther along if you two would be quiet long enough for me to read through it," David says as he removes his glasses and gives them a quick cleaning. "Just give me a minute here, and we'll start again."

Chapter 18

THE GULFSTREAM G650 SOARS through the air, passing its flight trails with a world of ease and speed. "I'd get you something to eat if we had anything," Alex says.

"Do we have any water onboard, sir?" Wally asks.

"Yes, we do have plenty of bottles of water, thank goodness. Look in the refrigerator in the back," Alex says as he concentrates on flying the plane. "I think I'll have a drink. Do you care for one?" Alex asks Wally.

"No, thanks, sir. It's a bit early for me," Wally replies.

"Would you be a dear and mix me one? I have a bottle of whiskey in the cabinet back there somewhere."

Wally finds the bottle of booze and mixes Alex a drink, making sure it isn't too strong.

"Let's get on with it, then," Alex says, easing himself back into his chair after he accepts the cocktail from Wally.

"'John D. Rockefeller Junior grew up amongst his four older sisters, Elizabeth, Alice, Alta, and Edith, and was invariably referred to as Junior,'" Wally reads.

"Yes, born to wealth during the Gilded Age, he was the

father to Abby and the five famous Rockefeller Brothers," Alex adds.

"'Living in the family mansion at 4 West Fifty-fourth Street, he attended Park Avenue Baptist Church on Sixty-fourth Street with the entire family. He attended the Cutler School and then The Browning School, which was established for him and other children of associates of the family. It was an all-boys' school that was located in a brownstone owned by the Rockefellers on West Fifty-fifth Street,'" Wally reads and stops to gulp down some water. "'Junior initially intended to go to Yale, but was persuaded to enter the Baptist-oriented Brown University instead. He was nicknamed 'Johnny Rock' by his roommates,'" Wally reads.

"That sounds like a cool name of a rock band, like Kidd Rock. Performing live Saturday night, it's Johnny Rock!" Alex says as he enjoys his first drink of the day.

"I don't think so, sir. Our report states that Junior joined the glee and mandolin clubs, taught a Bible class, and was elected junior class president," Wally reads.

"He sounds like a bit of a bore. Was he a teetotaler like his father?" Alex asks.

"Yes, he was, very much so," Wally answers.

"'After graduation, he joined his father's office on 26 Broadway. In August 1900, Junior was invited by the powerful Senator Nelson Aldrich of Rhode Island to a party aboard President William McKinley's yacht, the *Dolphin*, on a cruise to Cuba. The outing was of political nature, but Junior's future wife, Abby Aldrich, was included in the large party. The two had been courting for over four years at the time,'" Wally reads.

"As I recall, their wedding was seen at the time as the consummate marriage of capitalism and politics. It was held at the Aldrich summer mansion at Warwick Neck, Rhode Island, and was attended by the great executives of the age. Did you know that after his first wife's death, he later remarried at the age of seventy-seven to a woman named Martha Allen?" Alex says.

"I'll take your word for it, sir. Perhaps he was lonely," Wally says. "You are starting to sound a lot like your mother, sir."

"Yes, at times, the gossip that plagues man is usually the oracles of a fool. But besides that, the strange thing was, Martha Allen was the widow of his old college classmate, Arthur Allen," Alex says.

"I see nothing wrong with marrying his friend's wife, sir," Wally responds.

"Well, you just caught me thinking out loud."

Alex passes his empty glass to Wally as he wishes for another drink. "A refill, please."

"Are you sure you want another drink, sir? You do have to land the plane."

"Just one more drink, Wally, to calm my nerves."

Wally quickly returns with the whiskey and water.

"Please go on, Wally."

"In April 1914, the Ludlow Massacre occurred at the coal mining company of Colorado Fuel and Iron. Senior owned a majority of stock in the company, and Junior sat on the board. Although Junior was an absentee director, he was called to testify in January 1915 before the US Commission on Industrial Relations. Junior was being advised by William Lyon Mackenzie King and, in a precedent-setting move, hired the pioneering public relations expert Ivy Lee. King was later to say that this testimony was the turning point in Junior's life. Restoring the reputation of the family name would become one of Junior's lifelong traits. You're laughing, sir. May I ask why?" Wally asks.

"Yes, of course, don't you see the irony? He actually felt

guilt over the Ludlow Massacre. Most people view the rich oligarchs as uncaring or unscrupulous devils. I've read that after the incident, he went out there to Colorado and had conversations with the union organizer Mother Jones, as she was called. You see, having a conscience while doing business is rare nowadays, but it just proves that we're all humans. It goes back to good, old-fashioned family values. You know, having both a mother and a father and perhaps attending church, I believe, gives a child a more rounded and secure upbringing. It's kind of sad our world of today has lost so much of that old spirit," Alex says.

"Bravo, sir. I have to admit I'm a little surprised hearing that coming from you. Of course, you did come from a strong family whose parents did stay together."

"Well, of course, my parents stayed married for over sixty years, until my father died. On the other hand, they had their ups and downs. Perhaps people's lot in life has a lot to do with it. I heard over eighty percent of divorces are due to some kind of financial issues. Wally, please make a note of this. At the end of the year, when we're doing our taxes, remind me to donate some money to one of the family advocacy groups," Alex says, returning to his seat.

"No kidding, sir?" Wally asks as he types away.

"I'm dead serious. Just make sure it's not one of those feminist groups or anything that favors fathers' rights. You know, something neutral to the family and the children."

"I have it noted, sir. Now, on to a happier note, sir. Junior, during the Great Depression, had developed and was the sole financier of the vast fourteen-building real estate complex in the geographical center of Manhattan, Rockefeller Center. As a result, he became one of the largest real estate holders in New York City," Wally reads.

"Allow me to interrupt just for a second, Wally. It was Junior who originally leased the space from Columbia University in 1928. We, or I should say it was my grandfather, William

Bayard Van Cortlandt Van Rensselaer, wrote the lease that allowed John D. Rockefeller Junior to build on the land. The original lease was for twenty-four years with three twenty-one-year renewals, for a total of eighty-seven years," Alex says. "The vast real estate holdings that you refer to were not the amount of land, but the amount of office space that was created."

"Okay, let's see—that would take us out to 2015. Why, then, did you renegotiate in 1985?" Wally asks.

"My father renegotiated the deal just prior to his death. He actually sold the land against my mother's better judgment. The details are held in my father's private safe. I need to speak with my mother to gain access to it," Alex says.

"You're kidding, right?" Wally asks.

"Sadly, I am not. She is on our schedule. She'll understand my concerns," Alex says, sipping down the second drink. "Ice, we need some ice," Alex says.

"I think you've had enough, sir. Can we try and land while you are still sober?" Wally says as he takes the empty glass from Alex.

"I guess I can try. I haven't flown in some four or five years now," Alex says.

"Thank you, sir," Wally says as he returns to the report. "'John D. Junior influenced many leading blue chip corporations into moving their headquarters into the complex, including GE, RCA, NBC, RKO, the Associated Press, Time Inc., Chase National Bank, and Standard Oil of New Jersey. The family office, of which Junior was in charge, is called formally 'Rockefeller Family and Associates.' Junior moved the company from 26 Broadway to the fifty-sixth floor of what is now the landmark GE Building upon its completion in 1933. Informally named Room 5600, Junior operated the family business from floors fifty-six though fifty-eight. In 1921, his father gave him about ten percent of the shares of Equitable Trust Company, making him the bank's largest shareholder. In 1930, Equitable merged with Chase National Bank and became the largest bank in the world at that time.'"

"Chase National Bank was known as the Rockefeller Bank until it merged with JP Morgan in the late 1960s. My friend David was the president of Chase National bank for some twenty years," Alex says.

"'In 1932, Junior, well-known for his abstinence from alcohol, wrote a letter to Nicholas Butler, an editor at the *New York Times,* arguing against the continuation of the Eighteenth Amendment on the grounds of the increase in disrespect for the law. The letter was printed on the front page of the *New York Times* and became the singular event that would push the nation to repeal Prohibition,'" Wally reads. "That is interesting. I almost forgot about that little American experiment."

"It is amazing how their name alone commands so much respect in New York and Washington. The man just voiced his opinion, and it changed the constitution," Alex says.

"I agree. I don't believe there is anyone in our time that commands that much respect, sir," Wally says.

"I'm interested in knowing if Junior carried on any of his family traits, Wally," Alex says.

"Yes, he would have been regarded as one of the greatest philanthropists in the world," Wally says.

"It's such a long flight. We have the time to dig into this a little deeper," Alex suggests.

"Of course. I have it all right here. For example, 'In 1900, he persuaded his father to support cancer research. With the money, Junior built a medical laboratory on the campus of Cornell Medical Center. Decades later, it became the world-renowned Memorial Sloan-Kettering Cancer Center. He established the Bureau of Social Hygiene in 1913. It was a major initiative that investigated such social issues as prostitution and venereal diseases. It supported both studies in police administration and research in support of birth control clinics. Junior owned properties at 4, 10, 12, 14, and 16 West Fifty-Fourth Street. All the land was gifted to his wife's Museum of Modern Art,'" Wally reads.

"I've been there on several occasions. Most of the artwork is now located in the basement of the Time-Life Building in Rockefeller Center. It was Junior who founded the Museum of Primitive Art as well. It is now part of the Metropolitan Museum of Art in New York City," Alex says.

"'John D. Junior founded the Laura Spelman Rockefeller Memorial in 1918, which was folded into the Rockefeller Foundation in 1929. During the 1920s, junior also donated a substantial amount towards the restoration of major buildings in France that were damaged during World War One: Rheims Cathedral, the Chateau de Fontainebleau, and the Chateau de Versailles. For this, he was awarded France's highest decoration, the *Grand Croix* of the *Legion d'Honneur.* In 1921, Junior financially supported programs of the League of Nations and funded the ongoing expenses of the Council on Foreign Relations. In November of 1926, Junior came to the College of William and Mary for a dedication of an auditorium built in memory of the organizers of Phi Beta Kappa. Junior being a member, and the fraternity having been founded in Williamsburg in 1776, he helped pay for the auditorium. The next year after, he approved the plans already developed by the Reverend Dr. Goodwin that launched a massive historical restoration of Colonial Williamsburg. He also liberally funded the early excavations at Luxor in Egypt and the American School of Classical Studies for excavations and reconstruction in Athens; the American Academy in Rome; Lingnan University in China; St. Luke's Hospital in Tokyo; the library of the Imperial University in Tokyo; and the Shakespeare Memorial Endowment in England,'" Wally reads with a smile.

"What is it, Wally?"

"Nothing, sir. As a child, I visited the Shakespeare Memorial. I have quite fond memories of the place."

"Junior was a world traveler indeed. He provided the funding for the construction of the Palestine Archaeological Museum in East Jerusalem and the Rockefeller Museum, which houses the two-thousand-year-old Dead Sea Scrolls," Alex says.

"Didn't the Rockefellers finance the United Nations as well?" Wally asks.

"Yes, originally the United Nations was to be set up at the family estate of Pocantico, but Junior vetoed the idea. Sometime in 1946, right after World War Two, through negotiations by his son Nelson, he bought and then donated the land along the East River in Manhattan where the United Nations sits today. The library in Geneva was a gift from Junior to the earlier League of Nations, which today still remains a resource for the United Nations," Alex says.

"I'll move on to the churches Junior has donated to. 'Over the years, he has given substantial sums to Protestant and Baptist institutions, including the Interchurch World Movement, the Federal Council of Churches, the Union Theological Seminary, and the Cathedral of St. John the Divine, New York's Riverside Church, and the World Council of Churches,'" Wally reads.

"After all, that I'm surprised Junior had anything left to give. I have heard that Andrew Carnegie tried and failed to give all his money away before he died. He was still left with some thirty million dollars when he passed," Alex says.

"There is more, Alex. 'Junior had a special interest in conservation; he purchased and donated land for many American national parks, including Grand Teton, in which he hid his involvement behind the Snake River Land Company. In the case of the Acadia National Park, he financed and engineered an extensive carriage road network throughout the park. Both the John D. Rockefeller Junior Memorial Parkway that connects Yellowstone National Park to the Grand Teton National Park and the Rockefeller Memorial in the Great Smoky Mountain National Park were named after him. He was also active in making significant contributions to Save-the-Redwoods League, which enabled the purchase of what would become the Rockefeller Forest in Humboldt Redwoods State Park of California. Back on the East Coast in 1951, Junior established Sleepy Hollow Restorations, which brought together two historical sites he had acquired, Philipsburg Manor in North Tarrytown, now called Sleepy Hollow, and Sunnyside, Washington Irving's home. Junior bought the Van Cortlandt Manor in Croton-on-Hudson in 1953 and in 1959 donated it to Sleepy Hollow Restorations. His total investment was more than twelve million dollars in the three properties. In 1986, Sleepy Hollow Restoration became Historic Hudson Valley, which operates the guided tours of the Rockefeller family estate of Kykuit in Pocantico Hills,'" Wally reads.

"Over in Rockefeller Center, there is an inscription attributed to Junior. On a tablet, it reads Junior's noted life principle of 'I believe that every right implies a responsibility; every opportunity, an obligation; every possession, a duty.' What does that say to you, Wally?" Alex asks.

"Well, I'm no psychiatrist, but it may reflect his belief in a higher authority. It is kind of as if he was speaking from his conscience," Wally answers.

"Exactly, as if he were himself above it all. You know, my grandfather respected him so much that in 1935, he gave Junior the Hundred Year Association of New York's Gold Medal Award. It was in recognition of outstanding contributions to the City of New York," Alex says.

"'His wife, Abby Rockefeller, died of a heart attack at the family apartment at 740 Park Avenue in April, 1948,'" Wally reads.

"Seven-forty Park Avenue is considered the world's richest apartment building, Wally," Alex mentions.

"That is the place where Jacqueline Kennedy Onassis grew up. I heard her grandfather, James T. Lee, was the builder," Wally says.

"According to author Michael Gross, Lee's daughter Janet Lee Bouvier and son-in-law Jack Bouvier took the final open lease, perhaps even for free," Alex says.

"Is that near your place, sir?" Wally asks.

"No, not really. In general, though mixed, there are more people of German descent up that way from around Fiftieth Street and moving north, while at Forty-ninth and moving south, you find more people of the Dutch and British ancestries," Alex says.

"They had six children together: Abby Rockefeller Mauze, John D. III, Nelson Aldrich, Laurance Spelman, Winthrop, and David, of course," Wally reads.

"Junior died of pneumonia on May 11, 1960, at the age of eighty-six. He was interred in the family cemetery in Tarrytown, with forty family members present. I don't think I could even name forty members of my family, sir," Wally says as he takes a glance out one of the frosted windows.

Chapter 19

J~OEY HAS THE LIMO~ heading south on Third Avenue near Twelfth Street.

David starts to read from section 10 of the dossier. "'Agreeably to the customs of the time, a new patent to the manor of Rensselaerswyck was issued by Queen Anne, May 20, 1704, which confirmed it to Kiliaen and perpetually to his eldest male descent. A few days later, on June 1, he released to his younger brother Hendrick the lower manor, called Claverack Manor, of some sixty thousand acres that encompassed all of Colombia County. The lower manor consisted of all property on the east side of the Hudson. Hendrick also received part of the upper manor, that of Greenbush, and two islands located in the northern part of the Hudson River.

"'Kiliaen, first lord of the manor, also sold the Coeyman's Tract in a deal with the Massachusetts Bay Colony. Kiliaen maintained the upper tract and encompassed all lands on the west side of the Hudson. Kiliaen died in 1687 at Watervliet. He had married his first cousin Anna Van Rensselaer and had no children. The upper portion of Rensselaerswyck was passed to his cousin Kiliaen, the son of Jeremias,'" David reads.

"I'm confused—how many Kiliaens were there?" Joey asks.

"Three or four, and there might be more, the way it sounds," Laurance answers. "It's a green light, Joey."

"Yeah, right, Laurance," Joey says. "I thought it was illegal to marry your first cousin."

"There were different attitudes for different times, Joey," Laurance says.

David reads on in section 11 of the dossier: "'Kiliaen, second lord of the manor, was one of the most prominent citizens of his times, being continuously in public life from 1691 until his death in 1719. Kiliaen was the commissioner of Indian affairs. Rensselaerswyck having the right to send a special deputy to the legislative assembly of New York, Kiliaen sat on this body until he was elevated to the governor's council in 1704, where he would remain until his death. In this generation, there were two lords of the manor, one of the upper and one of the lower.'"

"So before New York became a state, it was a province, and before that, it was a colony, and before that, it was divided up into *patroon*ships?" Joey asks.

"I thought you were a history student, Joey. You should be able to explain that to us. Don't forget the Italian explorer Giovanni Verrazzano or the native Americans before that," David says.

"I'd have to go back and restudy my history, I guess," Joey says.

Chapter 20

A<small>FTER</small> W<small>ALLY</small> <small>RETURNS</small> <small>FROM</small> checking on their unwelcome passenger, he reads on in his Rockefeller report. "We are safe and secure still. I'll go on now. 'Junior's only daughter, Abigail "Abby" Rockefeller Mauze, was born September 11, 1903. She was known by the name of Babs. Unlike her famous brothers, she always remained out of the public spotlight. She held many positions in her life, including membership of the board of trustees of the Rockefeller Brothers Fund, which she and her brothers set up in 1940. She was an advisory member of the board of trustees of the Memorial Sloan-Kettering Cancer Center and honorary trustee of the Rockefeller Family Fund, founded in 1967. She was also benefactor of the Metropolitan Museum of Art, the YWCA, New York Hospital, the Museum of Modern Art, the New York Zoological Society, the Asia Society, the Population Council, and the American Red Cross.'"

"What in the world is the Population Council?" Alex asks.

"Well, its headquarters are in New York. The council has its roots in eugenics. The Rockefellers hired Frederick Osborn, who was the leader of the American Eugenics Society. They perform scientific research on the interrelationships between population and socioeconomic development in developing countries. I believe their goal was to develop contraceptives and to introduce family planning programs. The British medical journal *Lancet* said that the Population Council has changed the lives and expectations of hundreds of millions of people. On the other hand, some right-wing extremists in Britain and America have accused the council of inventing and spreading the AIDS and HIV viruses," Wally says.

"That sounds ridiculous. And what about the Asia Society?" Alex asks. "I've never heard of it either."

"The Asia Society is another non-profit organization setup by the Rockefellers, focusing on educating the world about Asia. Their aim is to build awareness about Asian politics, business, arts, and culture through education," Wally says.

"So the Rockefellers do business globally. Let me guess— the headquarters of the Asia Society is in New York City?" Alex asks.

"Yes, sir, that is correct. They have offices in San Francisco, Los Angeles, and Washington D.C., as well as Hong Kong, Seoul, and Shanghai."

"'In 1968, Babs created the Greenacre Foundation in order to maintain parks in New York State for the benefit of the public. She was married three times, and from her first husband had Abby Rockefeller Milton and Marilyn Rockefeller Milton. She died on May 27, 1976, at her apartment at One Beekman Place in New York City,'" Wally says.

"One Beekman Place, I heard that place was haunted," Alex says with a straight face.

"Are you serious, sir?"

"Of course I am. Look it up."

"Okay. One Beekman Place. Here it is. 'The street was named after the Beekman family, an influential family in the development of the city. The street runs from north to south for two blocks and is situated between First and

Second Street and Fifty-first and Forty-ninth Streets. The neighborhood was the site of the Beekman family mansion, Mount Pleasant, which was built by James Beekman in 1765. The British made their headquarters in the mansion for a time during the Revolutionary War, and Nathan Hale was tried as a spy in the mansion's greenhouse and hanged in a nearby orchard,'" Wally reads.

"See? I told you so," Alex says.

"I'm not finished yet. It says here that George Washington visited the house many times during his presidency."

Alex raises his arms in a ghostly fashion. "The ghost of Nathan Hale. 'I only regret that I have but one life to lose for my country.'" Alex laughs heartily.

"That is not funny, sir. He was considered America's first spy and a national hero," Wally says.

"That sounds a bit funny coming from a Brit," Alex says.

Chapter 21

Dᴀᴠɪᴅ ʀᴇᴀᴅs ᴏɴ ᴀs the vehicle heads south through Chinatown.

"'The upper manor was inherited by Jeremias Van Rensselaer; the third lord of the manor, born in 1705, represented the manor in the provincial assembly from 1726 to 1743 and was a member of the governor's council. Jeremias died unmarried and without heir in 1745,'" David reads.

"'Stephen Van Rensselaer the First, fourth lord of the manor, was born in 1707. He became the commissioner of Indian Affairs. Married Elizabeth Groesbeck and had seven children. Their third child, Elizabeth, married General Abraham Ten Broeck. It was Stephen who had the Ten Broeck mansion built for his sister, Elizabeth. Abraham was a member of the provincial assembly, representing the Van Rensselaer manor, and fought against the Stamp Act of 1765. He was a colonel in the New York militia, a member of the provincial congress of 1775, president of the state convention of 1776, a brigadier-general in the Revolution, later senator of Albany, judge of the court of common pleas, and president of the bank of Albany,'" David reads.

"'Stephen Van Rensselaer II was the fifth lord of the manor. During his minority, the affairs of the manor were administered by his brother in-law, Colonel Ten Broeck. Stephen II built the manor house at Greenbush in 1765. During his time, he witnessed the divisions of popular sentiment between patriots and loyalists to the British Crown. There was no member old enough in the upper manorial house to bear arms during the Revolution, all being too old or too young. In 1769, Abraham Ten Broeck became co-administrator of Rensselaerswyck, a position he held until 1784, when Stephen III came of age,'" David says, finishing the document and turning to the next section.

Chapter 22

Wally crosses his legs to get more comfortable and says, "We're moving on to John D. Rockefeller III, sir." The two hear screaming in the background. "I think our friend in the bathroom has finally wakened up. We need to make sure he was a Rockefeller plant. I could try and beat it out of him, sir."

"Be sure to put on another pot of boiling water first, just in case."

After Wally has finished in the kitchen, he makes his way back to the bathroom. He shouts through the door, "What is your name, and why are you on this flight?"

"My name is Raymond. I was hired to fly the plane to Seattle. That is all I know. Have you lost your mind? Let me out of here."

"Who hired you?"

"A man approached me in the hanger. He didn't say why. I'm just a pilot, that's all."

"You're lying. Now, who was he? I've got more water on the cooker if that is what you want," Wally threatens.

"I don't know what you're talking about."

"What happened to Jimmy, our regular pilot?" Wally asks and hears no reply.

Wally grabs the now steaming hot pot of water. He loosens the bindings holding the door shut. With a one, two, and a three, he swings the door open and douses the man with more hot water, quickly shutting the door and binding it tightly.

The substitute pilot screams in agony. "You can't land the plane. If you take it below ten thousand feet, there is a bomb rigged to go off."

"Why should I believe you? Why would you agree to fly a plane, knowing a bomb was on board?"

"They agreed to pay me in cash once we landed safely in Seattle. I never thought it would be activated."

"My god, man, you must have shit for brains. How can the bomb be activated from the air?"

"I don't know. I'm supposed to make a phone call a half hour before we land so they can deactivate it."

"So it is already activated. Where in the hell is it?" Wally shouts.

"It's in the cabin of the cockpit. The bomb is up in the storage bin above the pilot's head."

Wally makes his way back to the front cabin. "We have trouble, Alex. The idiot in the back has planted a bomb on board," Wally says as he opens the overhead bin. Wally finds the crude bomb hidden beneath a parachute. He sets the parachute on the floor of the cabin. He then pulls out three sticks of dynamite attached to a mercury switch.

"Let me see that," Alex says, looking over the crude device. "That should not be a problem. Untape the sticks and flush them down the toilet, and I'll exhaust the waste container over the Atlantic."

Wally looks in disbelief at Alex's calmness. "The sticks should fit in there one at a time," Alex says.

"I almost forgot. We have a passenger in the toilet, don't we?" Alex says as he slows the plane down and switches the control back to auto-pilot.

"And what if they blow up?" Wally asks, not sure he can handle the situation.

"Nonsense, trust me," Alex says as he moves toward the bathroom. After untying the door, he reaches in and grabs the pilot by the throat. "Now, you stay right here and be a good boy."

"But I swear I didn't do anything wrong. I was just following orders," The pilot says as Wally hurriedly cuts the tape that holds the sticks of dynamite with his teeth.

"The Nazis said the same thing at Nuremberg, and you know what happened to them, don't you?" Alex says, not loosening his grip.

"I think I have a better idea, sir," Wally says as he walks back and picks up the parachute.

"You're not thinking what I'm thinking, are you?" Alex asks.

"Put this on," Wally says to Raymond. "This is how he was going to escape," Wally says to Alex. "The son of a bitch was going to jump."

Alex helps to force Raymond to put on the parachute. Wally quickly tears the duct tape that holds the sticks of dynamite together and sticks it tightly to the back of the parachute. "If you could, please open the door, sir?"

"Gladly," Alex says as Wally gets ready to give Raymond the heave-ho.

With the plane at such a slow speed, it is easy for Alex to open the door and move back. Wally, with something of a running start, gives Raymond a hard shove toward the open door, and out he goes.

The bomb blows up at the same time Raymond's parachute begins to open, leaving nothing more than a pink cloud of human debris floating in the air behind them. The explosion jerks the plane upward and switches off the auto-pilot. As the plane soars skyward, Wally is slammed into one of the rear seats. Alex barely keeps his balance as he moves toward the cockpit and takes the controls. He slowly demonstrates his piloting skills as the plane levels out at nearly forty thousand feet. "We need to get back down near twenty thousand feet," Alex says as he pushes the controls down.

"Why is that, sir?" Wally shouts as he makes his way back to the front seat, just as a Boeing 747 crosses in front of their windshield and both men turn white as ghosts.

"It's because this airspace is reserved for the commercial airlines, Wally. I'll get us down in just a second or two."

After the plane levels out and the men are back in the correct airspace, Wally says, "I'll return back to our report, then, sir. 'John D. III felt that he was predestined to manage the family interests as the eldest son of his generation, a view with which his brothers, particularly Nelson, took issue. John D. III argued over politics with his father and struggled with Nelson over control of Rockefeller Center. John D. III felt that the Williamsburg restoration policies were anti-Semitic and racist. He took the lead role in organizing the Commission on Foundations, Council on Foundations, Foundation Center, and Independent Sector. He also made initial donation for the first academic research center to focus on nonprofits, which was set up at Yale University. In addition to his interest, Rockefeller made major commitments to supporting organizations committed to East Asian affairs, including the Institute of Pacific Relations, the Asia Society, the Population Council, and the Japan Society,'" Wally reads.

"I've read that he went to Princeton University, and after he graduated, he undertook a world tour," Alex says.

"Yes, mostly in Asia, sir. 'John D. III shortly afterwards became a member of the Foreign Policy Association and the Institute of Pacific Relations, and he sat on the Council on Foreign Relations,'" Wally reads.

"Isn't the Council on Foreign Relations the name of the secret government that runs the world, Wally?" Alex asks with a smile.

"No, sir, I believe the secret government that you are referring to is the Knights of the Round Table and is located in London," Wally says with British authority. "The Council of Foreign on Relations has had many American presidents on its membership rolls, including a friend of your father's, Dwight D. Eisenhower," Wally mentions.

"Yes, right after General Eisenhower returned from Europe, my father hired him as the president of Columbia University in 1948, but it was short-lived. President Truman made him the Supreme Commander of the NATO forces in Europe in 1950. He came back to the university in 1952 as president, but then he made the mistake of getting himself elected to the presidency of the United States," Alex says.

"Yes something of a non-factor in world events, I'd say," Wally says with his dry humor. "'John D. III also sat on the board of directors of Princeton University and set up the United Negro College Fund,'" Wally reads.

"I've heard rumors that John D. III traveled with John Foster Dulles to Japan to see General MacArthur after the Japanese surrender," Alex says.

"I wouldn't know, sir. What I do know is in the mid-1950s, JDR III assumed the leadership of a committee of civic leaders who were working to create Lincoln Center. 'He became the center's first president, and he served as chairman until 1970,'" Wally reads.

"Remember the Gold Medal Award my grandfather gave John D. Junior? Well, my father gave the same award to John D. III in 1959. The Hundred Year Association of New York, 'in recognition of outstanding contributions to the City of New York.' I suppose it's my turn to award it to one of the fourth generation Rockefellers one day," Alex says.

"'They named the Rockefeller College at Princeton in his honor in 1982. He had married Blanchette Ferry Hooker in 1932. Together they had one son, John D. Rockefeller IV, known as Jay Rockefeller, and three daughters, Sandra, Hope Aldrich, and Alida,'" Wally reads.

Chapter 23

Joey drives the men south toward New York's financial district.

"Section 12 of our dossier reads," David says, never looking up, "'The lower manorial estate of Claverack and Greenbush produced numerous male descendents. All twelve of the Van Rensselaers who participated in the American Revolutionary War came from this half of the family. The Hendrick line, having the superiority of numbers, played a larger role in the history of the United States than the older branch of the family. From Hendrick and the Greenbush lands, the historic mansion of the Van Rensselaers, "Fort Crailo," was built in 1642 by Hendrick. It was a massive structure styled as a military fort. Fort Crailo is the oldest continuously inhabited dwelling in the state of New York. It was here that Dr. Shackburg of the British Army wrote the lines of "Yankee Doodle."' Our report also states, 'This is where Benjamin Franklin stayed while he was in Albany discussing his Albany Plan,'" David reads.

"That was on the eve of the Seven Years' War," Laurance says. "The Albany Plan also inspired the Articles of Confederation and later our United States Constitution."

"'In 1715, the lower manor of Claverack gained a southern neighbor when King George I granted a royal charter to

Robert Livingston the Elder. His lands were just to the south of Claverack, where the Livingston Manor and Clermont Manor are located. The Livingston estate incorporated about 160,000 acres,'" David reads.

"So what you're saying is, the Van Rensselaers were neighbors of the Livingstons?" Joey asks.

"The Van Rensselaers and the Livingstons had already begun to intermarry, and most of their descendants came from that area. The Livingston estate lies just north of our Kykuit property," David says.

"'Fort Crailo is also where General James Abercrombie's troops were stationed in 1758. He was the British army general during the French and Indian war. General Abercrombie was commander-in-chief of North America of all British troops,'" David finishes reading.

Chapter 24

The air around the outside of the plane begins to clear, giving Alex and Wally a clearer view of the coast. "Tell me more about John D. III's children. They must keep close ties with David. After all, they work together at Rockefeller Center," Alex requests.

"Yes, sir, I'll look it up. 'John D. Rockefeller IV (Jay Rockefeller)' ... There seems to be some kind of split in the family due to Jay being a Democratic US senator from West Virginia. Prior to that, he was the governor of West Virginia from 1977 to 1985. 'He is the only current politician of the family and the only Democrat in what has been traditionally a Republican dynasty,'" Wally reads from the report.

"You mean he is the only elected politician in the family. They're all politicians of one sort or another. He won't be in office much longer. I heard he is retiring at the end of his current term," Alex says.

"'He is related to several prominent Republican officeholders. He is the great-grandson of Rhode Island Senator Nelson W. Aldrich, a nephew to banker David Rockefeller, Arkansas governor Winthrop, and former US vice president Nelson A. Rockefeller. He is the son-in-law of former senator Charles H. Percy of Illinois and cousin of Arkansas lieutenant governor Winthrop P. Rockefeller. He was born just twenty-six days after the death of his great-grandfather, John D. Rockefeller Senior. Jay studied Japanese for three years in Tokyo at the International Christian University before returning and graduating from Harvard with a B.A. in Far Eastern languages and history. After college, Jay worked for the Peace Corps in Washington, D.C., under John F. Kennedy and became friends with Robert Kennedy as he worked as an assistant to the Peace Corps director, Sargent Shriver. Jay, along with his son Charles, is a trustee of New York's Asia Society and a member of the Council on Foreign Relations. He actually voted against the 1993 North American Free Trade Agreement,'" Wally reads.

"That is odd. His uncle David was a heavy backer of that agreement. It makes you wonder what the family rift is about, if there is one," Alex says.

"'Jay resides in Charleston, West Virginia. He, along with most of the members of the family, has a ranch in the Grand Teton National Park in Jackson Hole, Wyoming. Bill Clinton, a friend of Jay's, and his family have spent summer vacations there,'" Wally reads.

"I thought he might make a run at the presidency back in 1992," Alex says.

"Well, in April of 1992, he was the Democratic Party's finance chairman and considered it, but after consulting family and friends, he pulled out," Wally says.

"I've heard Jay was a strong supporter of our nation's health care reform," Alex says.

"Yes, in 1993, Jay opened up his mansion in Rock Creek Park for the first strategy meetings dealing with health care, meeting with Bill and Hillary Clinton and the late Ted Kennedy," Wally says.

"Wasn't Jay Rockefeller the chair of the Intelligence Committee just prior to the start of the Iraq War?" Alex asks.

"Yes, and he was an outspoken critic of President Bush and the war. 'After releasing the final two pieces of Phase II Report on Iraq, Senator Jay Rockefeller said, "The president and his advisers undertook a relentless public campaign in the aftermath of the attacks to use the war against Al Qaeda as a justification for overthrowing Saddam Hussein,"'" Wally reads.

"That is fine and dandy, but in the end, how did he vote—in favor or against the war?" Alex asks.

"Well, sir, he voted in favor of the war in the end. 'He voted to go to war, and on October 10, 2002, he said, "There is unmistakable evidence that Saddam Hussein is working aggressively to develop nuclear weapons and will likely have nuclear weapons within the next five years ... Saddam Hussein represents a grave threat to the United States, and I have concluded we must use force to deal with him if all other means fail,"'" Wally reads.

"I wonder who handed that script to him—Dick Cheney, or maybe his uncle David?" Alex asks.

"'Jay has been a fighter to end television violence and had begun steering the Senate Intelligence Committee to grant retroactive immunity to the telecommunication companies who were accused of unlawfully monitoring communications of American citizens—this after he had earlier questioned the legality of warrantless wire-taps,'" Wally reads.

"So he is a flip-flopper. His conscience tells him one thing, and then after someone gets to him, he changes his mind. That doesn't quite fit into the Rockefeller profile, if you know what I mean," Alex says.

"'Jay has demonstrated that his public views do not always match his voting record. For example, he publicly deplores the use of torture, but when he was briefed on waterboarding and other secret CIA practices, and having the knowledge of the taped evidence of the interrogations, he opposed a special counsel or a commission inquiry into the destruction of the tapes, stating "It is the job of the intelligence committees to do that,"'" Wally reads.

"No wonder he isn't going to run for office again. It sounds like he has been forced to lie about many things. If he is being undermined by his lawyers, lobbyists, or his uncle David, I can see it being hard for such a rich man no longer wanting to do battle with his own conscience," Alex says.

"'Jay's sister, Hope Aldrich Rockefeller Spencer, pursued a career in journalism and has worked for Long Island's *Newsday,* Beijing's *China Daily,* New York's *The Village Voice,* and the *Washington Monthly.* She worked for the *Santa Fe Reporter* in the 1980s until she decided to buy the newspaper and became its publisher,'" Wally reads.

"That is one way to move up at the workplace. Just buy the frickin company," Alex says.

"'She married into the British royalty when she wed John Spencer, a descendent of Charles II, King of England and King of Scotland, in 1959. She continues to live in New Mexico and is considered the third-richest person in her state. Back in 1996, her net worth was estimated at 250 million dollars. John Spencer and Hope have three children together,'" Wally reads.

"You said Hope had two sisters?"

"Yes, Sandra Rockefeller and Alida Rockefeller Messinger. 'Alida is a trustee to the Rockefeller Family Fund and is a major donor to conservation and environmental organizations. At one time, she was married to US senator Mark Dayton of Minnesota. She is a regular contributor to the Center for Public Integrity,'" Wally reads.

"The Center for Public Integrity is a group of disgruntled news journalists," Alex says.

"What do you mean?"

"It was founded by Charles Lewis. He was a career

television reporter who got pissed off because he feels that the mainstream media does not report on the country's most important stories. He expects, with the rest of the country, that the journalists' job is to be muckrakers and not prostitutes to the Democrats or the Republicans," Alex says.

"I'm not familiar with the Americanism *muckraker.* What does it mean?"

"Well, at one time, in this country, it was the job of our journalists to keep the public informed—you know, they would investigate politicians taking bribes and things. In one instance, John D. Rockefeller Senior accused Ida Tarbell of being a muckraker when she wrote her book *The History of the Standard Oil Company,* wherein she documented some of the company's more devious practices. It's a term attributed to President Theodore Roosevelt. It is mostly political rhetoric used against one's opponents," Alex explains.

"The term we use in Britain would be a sleaze writer," Wally says. "Well, then, it could be a good thing, as in the reporting of the Watergate scandal?" Wally says.

"Any time truth can be discovered and reported to the people, it is a good thing. The problem in America is that the oil-soaked monopoly press does not always report the truth to the public. The opinions of the mainstream media are bought and paid for by large corporations, and everyone knows it," Alex says.

Chapter 25

Joey turns on the radio as the limo moves south along Third Avenue.

"Turn that blasted thing off. We need to get through this dossier," David says to Joey.

"I thought I would check the weather report. I heard it may rain later today," Joey says as he pushes a button to shut off the radio.

"Section 13 of our dossier reads," David says as he turns a page, "'The Van Rensselaers, with the governmental authority of New York, had issued warrants for the arrest of many of the Green Mountain Boys from Vermont. The British crown had given the authority of these lands, known as the New Hampshire grants, to the government in Albany, but this was rejected by the militia controlled by Ethan Allen. By the 1770s, the Green Mountain Boys had become the de facto government of this northeastern province of New York. The Van Rensselaers pushed Congress to have George Washington invade Vermont, but Washington was certainly too busy fighting the British forces. Vermont eventually declared itself an independent nation in January, 1777,'" David reads.

"Vermont was an independent nation? That sounds a lot like

Texas, before they became a state. I think it was considered to be its own country as well," Joey says.

"Yes, we know, Joey," David says before he starts back into the dossier. "'Colonel Johannas Van Rensselaer, Hendrick's first son, inherited the entire lower branch of Rensselaerswyck. Johannas served as commissioner of Indian affairs for thirty years. He was a member of the twenty-first provincial assembly of New York, on the side of the radicals. In 1743, he was appointed captain of a company of foot soldiers in the British army, later being promoted to colonel. He was an active supporter of American independence, though too old to physically take part in the Revolutionary War. He allowed an encampment of American soldiers to reside at Fort Crailo in June 1775 while on their way to Ticonderoga. Fort Crailo, being the headquarters of the northern army and commanded by his son-in-law, General Philip Schuyler, was never attacked by the British. Johannas died in 1783, just before the British withdrawal from New York City,'" David reads. "'Johannes' oldest son Jeremias died an early death, and his younger brother, General Robert Van Rensselaer, became head of the lower branch of the family. Robert was named after his maternal grandfather, Robert Livingston. He resided in the Manor House at Claverack.

"'Of all the members of the family who were able to bear arms during the Revolution, it was Robert who, in the military service of his country, was the most distinguished Van Rensselaer name identified with that war. He was commissioned colonel of the Eighth Regiment, Albany County Militia, on the twentieth of October, 1775, and was made brigadier-general, Second Brigade, Albany County Militia, on June 16, 1780. He fought at Ticonderoga under the orders of his brother-in-law, General Philip Schuyler, and commanded the militia which pursued and defeated Sir John Johnston when on his famous raid in the Mohawk Valley in 1780. From 1775 to 1777, he was the representative in the New York provincial congress of the Eastern Manor. He also fought in the battle of Klock's Field.'

"Section 14 of the dossier reads," David reads on, "'In 1776, William Tryson, the British governor of New York; David Mathews, the mayor of New York City; and Thomas Hickey, a bodyguard of General George Washington, were conspirators in a plot to kidnap Washington, assassinate his generals, and blow up the Continental Army's ammunition magazines. It was said that part of Hickey's plot to kill Washington was to poison him with a dish of peas. This was discovered by Phoebe Fraunces, a black slave working for Washington's kitchen staff and housekeeper. She had reported her knowledge of the assassination to her master, Samuel Fraunces.'"

"I've read that Black Sam, as he was called, was probably a white guy who rented slaves out on a short-term basis," Joey says.

"'In June 1776, Hickey was hanged in front of a crowd of over twenty thousand, in which Robert Van Rensselaer was in attendance,'" David reads.

"The Van Rensselaer family had members on the Committee of Sixty, as well as the Committee of One Hundred, who created a petition-signing drive to figure out who was a patriot and who was a loyalist," Laurance says.

"Hey, I've read that any person who would not sign the petition was considered a loyalist and was tarred and feathered," Joey says.

"Yes, I believe that is accurate," Laurance says.

"It's too bad we can't do that now. I'd like to tar and feather some of the traitors in Washington, D.C.," Joey says as he looks in the rearview mirror for a reaction.

"I don't believe the tar and feathering caused any harm. It was meant to humiliate people so they would leave town," David explains.

"That would be perfect," Joey says. "So all these Van

Rensselaers were patriots of the American Revolutionary War?" Joey asks.

"They were more than patriots—the Van Rensselaers donated money, food, clothing, and the manor house at the head of Broadway Street during the Revolutionary War. The house became St. Peter's Hospital and is still there today," David states.

"We don't see that kind of generosity anymore. I mean, what the country went through during the Revolutionary War. The Enlightenment of the eighteenth century must have driven these men to reason that they might one day have their own government," Joey says.

"The hospital—that reminds me, I need to take my pills," David says.

"What are you taking there?" Joey asks.

"Zanex, it is for anxiety."

"So they got you too. I mean the pharmaceutical companies. They've got everyone hooked on something," Joey says. "I don't know why the government doesn't just legalize drugs."

"That would be insane," David says.

"Well, why not? I mean if you just look at the financials of it. We have millions of what would be productive citizens sitting in prisons being fed, clothed, and educated by the taxpayers. And think of the time and money that would be saved in our judicial systems," Joey says.

"Don't lecture us, Joey. I think we have a group performing a study on that subject right now," David says.

"Well, I just think that drug abuse should be treated the same as alcohol abuse. You know, like at hospitals or clinics and not by the prison systems," Joey says.

Joey stops the car at a traffic light on the corner of Whitehall

Street. "Hey, look there on the corner—there is a historical marker. It says, 'The Great Fire of 1776 was started at this spot September 21, 1776, at the Fighting Cocks Tavern,'" Joey reads.

"There is an interesting bit of history that goes with that, you know," Laurence adds. "George Washington requested Congress to burn the city before he retreated with the Continental Army. His request was denied. Mysteriously, New York lost four to five hundred buildings in the Great Fire anyway. Washington denied any knowledge of how the fire started," Laurance says.

"I've got one for you: did you know we lost more troops to neglect while they were held captive aboard British prison ships than we lost in combat during the Revolutionary War?" Joey says.

"Yes, Joey, I've heard that as well," Laurance says.

Chapter 26

"We'll be landing at JFK within an hour," Alex announces to Wally.

"We might be able to finish the report while still in the air," Wally says, reading over his laptop.

"If not, we'll just bring it with us. What do you have next in the report?" Alex asks.

"David's older brother, Nelson Rockefeller; he passed away back in 1979. 'He was the forty-first vice president of the United States under Gerald Ford, and he was the forty-ninth governor of New York. He was a businessman, art collector, and philanthropist,'" Wally reads.

"I know he served in the Roosevelt, Truman, Eisenhower, and Nixon administrations in a variety of positions. In his time, the press would call liberal Republicans 'Rockefeller Republicans,'" Alex says.

"He attended the Lincoln School, an experimental school administered by Teachers College of Columbia University. Perhaps you're closer to the Rockefellers than you thought," Wally says.

"You have no idea," Alex responds.

"He earned his A.B. in economics from Dartmouth College,

where he was a member of Casque and Gauntlet, in 1930," Wally says.

"I could not fly in a plane; I could not drive in a train; if we must, let's try the bus," Wally sings a rhyme.

"What on earth are you talking about?" Alex asks.

"Dr. Seuss, my good man. You see, the writer Theodor Seuss Geisel was also a member of Casque and Gauntlet at Dartmouth College," Wally explains.

"Do you often embarrass yourself just to explain something so trivial?"

"It's not so trivial if you knew that Dr. Seuss was hired by Nelson to draw advertising for the Standard Oil Company," Wally says.

"Touché, my friend. Go on," Alex says.

"'Nelson, being the true politician in the family, ran unsuccessfully, seeking the Republican presidential nomination in 1960, 1964, and in 1968. He did not join the 1976 ticket with Ford, marking his retirement from politics,'" Wally reads.

"As a businessman, he was the president and chairman of Rockefeller Center. He is responsible for building the South Mall up in Albany, along with a friend of mine, Erastus Corning. It's called the Empire State Plaza," Alex says.

"'In 1930, Nelson married Mary Todhunter Clark. They had five children together. Their youngest, Michael, disappeared in New Guinea in 1961. He was presumed drowned while trying to swim to shore after his canoe capsized."

"Maybe he was out hunting toads?" Alex says, laughing at his own joke.

"Sir, please, enough of your shenanigans. 'Nelson's first public service was with the Westchester County Board of Health. He became fluent in Spanish after his service with Creole Petroleum. In 1940, he expressed concerns to President Franklin Roosevelt over Nazi influence in Latin America. The president appointed him to the new position of coordinator of Inter-American affairs, countering rising Nazi influence in the region. In 1945, Nelson was a member of the US delegation at the United Nations Conference on International Organization at San Francisco. Nelson was also instrumental in persuading the United Nations to establish its headquarters in New York City,'" Wally reads.

"You mentioned he worked for Truman and Eisenhower. What did he do exactly?" Alex asks.

"Yes, sir, just a moment. Truman appointed him chairman of the International Development Advisory Board. It was charged with providing foreign technical assistance in South America. I believe what they were really doing was to help those countries set up better militaries," Wally says.

"I'll buy that, as long as they weren't selling America military secrets," Alex says.

"'In 1952, Eisenhower asked Nelson to chair the President's Advisory Committee on Government Organizations. He was asked to recommend ways of improving efficiency and effectiveness of the executive branch of the federal government,'" Wally reads.

"So Nelson was given the run of the place," Alex says.

"Well, Eisenhower, with the direction of Nelson, did make changes to the Department of Defense and the Department of Agriculture; they also created the Department of Health, Education and Welfare," Wally says.

"So we have Nelson to thank any time we hear of some obscure Washington alphabet soup committee, organization, or office," Alex says.

"I guess so, Alex. 'In 1954, Nelson was appointed special assistant to the president for foreign affairs. As part of his responsibility, he was named as the president's representative on the Operations Coordinating Board. Other members were the undersecretary of state, the deputy secretary of defense, the director of the Foreign Operations Administration, the National Security Council, and the director of the CIA,'" Wally reads.

"Reminds me of when Senator Palpatine asks Anakin Skywalker to be his eyes and ears on the Jedi Council in the movie *Star Wars*. Do you think Nelson was the master or the apprentice?" Alex laughs.

"You are incorrigible, sir," Wally says. "'The OCB's purpose was to oversee and coordinate the execution of national security policy and plans, including clandestine operations,'" Wally reads.

"That would have included the likes of John Foster Dulles and Herbert Hoover Junior. Those two were strong opponents of communism, amongst others," Alex says.

"'In 1955, the State Department officials and CIA director Allen Dulles refused to cooperate with Nelson, and his initiatives were either stymied or ignored. In December, Nelson resigned as special assistant to the president,'" Wally reads.

"It sounds like he got fed up. Nelson was always the most ambitious of the brothers," Alex says.

"'In 1956, Nelson created the Special Studies Project, named himself president, and hired Henry Kissinger to direct the group. It was funded by the Rockefeller Brothers Fund. In October of 1957, the Russians launched Sputnik, and two months later, the Special Studies Project military subpanel's report recommended a massive military buildup to counter a then-perceived military superiority threat posed by the USSR,'" Wally reads.

Alex interrupts briefly and says, "In turn, Eisenhower fully endorsed its recommendations, as his 1958 State of the Union address indicated. Some of the project's domestic policy recommendations became part of President

Kennedy's New Frontier initiative. When Eisenhower gave his famous speech to America warning us of the military-industrial complex, he was no doubt referring to this Nelson Rockefeller group."

"It seems to be an unscrupulous way to make money, sir."

"They are the big boys on the block," Alex says.

"Nelson won his bid to be governor of New York by defeating the incumbent, multi-millionaire William Averell Harriman, by six hundred thousand votes in 1958."

"My uncle James is also an uncle to William Harriman, even though we are not related by blood. You see, my uncle James had married Annie J. Harriman, sister to E. H. Harriman. And, ah … I'm sorry, Wally, that's my mother in me again. Please go on."

"'Nelson was re-elected four times again in 1962, 1966, and 1970. During his tenure, Nelson was the driving force in turning the State University of New York into the largest system of public higher education in the United States. He also began expansion of the New York State park system, which included the Pure Waters Program, which was the first state bond issue to end water pollution. Nelson created the Department of Environmental Conservation, which banned DDT and other pesticides. He initiated the creation and expansion of over twenty-two thousand miles of highway in the state of New York. He reformed the New York subway system by creating the New York Metropolitan Transportation Authority in 1965, which merged the subways with the Triborough Bridge, the Tunnel Authority, the Long Island Railroad, the Staten Island Rapid Transit, and the Metro North Railroad. It was a massive public bailout of bankrupt railroads,'" Wally reports.

"In reality, Nelson shifted power away from Robert Moses, who controlled several of New York's public infrastructure authorities. Nelson first convinced the railroads to sell by allowing them to withdraw all the funds in their respective railroads; this showed they were bankrupt when they really weren't. Secondly, the MTA used the revenues collected by tunnels and bridges to support mass transportation operations, thus shifting the cost from general state funds to the motorist. By taking control, Nelson abandoned one of Moses's pet projects, the Long Island Sound bridge from Rye to Oyster Bay. Nelson would claim the cancellation of the project was due to environmental issues," Alex says.

"You are quite the expert, sir," Wally says.

"I would have had part interest in the new bridge, but not all was lost. I did get to sell the last of my railroad shares at a premium," Alex says.

"'Nelson created the New York State Urban Development Corporation, with unprecedented powers to override local zoning laws, condemn property, and create financing schemes to carry out desired developments,'" Wally says.

"So Nelson wins twice. I mean, it sounds good on the outside, new housing for the poor and ageing, but if Nelson was involved, there was a profit motive behind it, I assure you," Alex says.

"The UDC did complete eighty-eight thousand units of housing for limited income families. And if one can profit a little from helping the poor, I don't see it as a bad thing," Wally says.

"Of course not. I'm just a believer in small government," Alex says.

"'The Rockefeller administration carried out the largest state medical care program for the needy in the US under Medicaid. Nelson began the state breakfast program for children in low-income homes and established the first state loan fund for non-profit groups to start day-care centers,'" Wally reads.

"Nelson was also a hero for civil rights by outlawing job discrimination and increased the number of African

Americans and Hispanics holding state jobs. He admitted the first women to the state police forces," Alex adds.

"This part is perplexing. 'Nelson was a supporter of capital punishment and oversaw fourteen executions by electrocution as governor, but he signed a bill in 1965 to abolish the death penalty except in cases involving the murder of police officers,'" Wally reads.

"That is a sign of a wise man, not to let his personal opinions get in the way of public sentiment. I recall the Attica State Prison riots, where he made a command decision to send in the New York State Police and the National Guard. Some people blamed him for the deaths, but I, for one, supported his decision to use force against force. It set a precedent for American policy. Even today, it shows that the authorities will not negotiate with prisoners or terrorists of any kind," Alex says.

"Interesting to hear that. I never knew when that philosophy started or where it came from. The British government and all of western Europe share the same opinion when it comes to dealing with terrorists," Wally says.

"Nelson reminds me a bit of a great-uncle of mine," Alex says.

"How is that, sir?"

"You see, prior to the Civil War, most of the power in politics remained with the state legislators and the offices of the state governors, whereas a great-uncle of mine, Stephen Van Rensselaer III, was elected to the position of lieutenant governor, and no other family member of ours has ever reached the top spot in government. Similarly, no Rockefeller has ever made it to the top spot in the federal government of the United States. Nelson had gotten the closest, becoming the vice president of the United States," Alex explains.

"Even though separated by many years, the similarities in your two families are almost eerie, sir," Wally says.

Chapter 27

"WE ARE ON BOWERY Street, about ten minutes away. It's a big area over there. Where did you guys want me to park?" Joey asks.

"Take the Avenue of the Finest toward Wall Street, if you could, please. You could park right outside of the construction area. The police are supposed to have a spot blocked off for us. We should park just south of the post office on Vesey Street," Laurance explains.

"I know right where you're talking about," Joey answers. "Did you know the word *Bowery* is Dutch for farm? I had heard that the Wall Street trading started right around here, outside underneath a tree or something. Is that true?" Joey asks.

"Yes, a buttonwood tree. It was called the Buttonwood Agreement. It is where twenty-four traders agreed to do business together. Later, they moved indoors to the Tontine Coffee House," Laurance answers. "They agreed on and set prices of their own commissions and promised not to trade with anyone else."

"Sounds like insider trading to me," Joey says. "It should be illegal."

"There are laws today to prevent that," Laurance says.

"Where was the American stock exchange started?" Joey asks.

Laurance answers. "In 1842, curb vendors started trading outside at Broad Street and Exchange Place."

"That is right in front of one of the Van Rensselaers' mansions," David adds as he looks out the window and sees some of his own skyscrapers.

"What a coincidence," Joey says. "Well, who owns the NYSE and the AMEX now?" Joey asks.

"I believe the VOC owns both trading associations," David answers.

"Oh, another coincidence, I guess," Joey says.

"What are you getting at, Joey?" asks David.

"I don't know. I was just wondering who owns our country. I mean, I thought it was you, and it's certainly not me," Joey says.

"The matter does not concern you. We haven't finished the dossier yet," David says as he closes the folder and begins looking for his speech.

"We will have plenty of time on our return trip to finish it," Laurance says.

"Well, there is more information to get through," David advises as he pulls his speech out and starts to review it.

With the help and direction of the police officers, Joey parks the limo on the south side of Vesey Street. He immediately gets out and moves to open David's car door. After helping the aged David out of the car, Joey asks him to stay put as he rushes around the other side of the car to offer his aid to Laurance.

David informs Laurance that it is his turn this year to give the speech.

"It is?" Laurance says, playing dumb. "I don't recall any speech that I've written."

"Are you mad, Laurence?" David says, raising his voice. "My goodness, have you become that forgetful?"

"Well, I am ninety-six years old," Laurance says as Joey helps the two across the street and toward a waiting podium.

"You've been pulling that 'I can't remember' crap for twenty years," David says. "Fine. I'll give the speech. Let me try and recall what I said last year," David says as he finishes reading his handwritten notes.

"Come on, you guys, this way. You sound like a married couple, a couple of cackling hens," Joey says as he guides the gentlemen up upon the sidewalk and toward a huge crowd.

A crowd of firefighters and the loved ones who had suffered losses on the day America was attacked gather in front of the podium. There is a somber feeling in the air as clouds roll in over the city and as the old men make their way over amongst a police escort. Across the street from the gathering, near St. Paul's church, a group of protesters starts to gather, "9-11 Truthers," as they are called. The truthers are caught off-guard, as they had arrived early and were planning a big protest for the next day. The truthers hold their silence during the ceremony but draw ever closer to the podium. Top fire officials are placing wreaths on the fences behind the podium and turn their attention toward their guest speaker, David Rockefeller.

David, with Joey's help, takes one step up onto the platform and begins: "I'd like to thank Fire Chief Berry and his staff, as well as Mayor Bloomburg for allowing me to speak today, for it is my honor to do so," David starts. "On September 11, 2001, we New Yorkers lost over three thousand souls to a horrible tragedy. We come together on this day not to mourn or to cast hate, but to remember our fallen comrades and loved ones. Yes, today we remember, and tomorrow we must drive on. Though without the ones we miss and love, our world has been tightened together by outside forces that we will someday overcome. Today, we lay this wreath in remembrance of those terrible events and for the love we share with each other. Today, we should be proud of the way our first responders, along with our troops overseas, have conducted themselves, not only on 9-11, but every day and when any situation arrives that calls for heroism and beyond." David turns to Laurance and grasps half of the wreath. "At this time, I would like to ask for a moment of silence to remember and pray for the fallen."

"...Thank you all, and God bless." David finishes his speech and is helped down by Joey. Mayor Bloomberg takes the podium and asks for a round of applause. The men turn and begin walking down the sidewalk.

Once the ceremonies are over, the truthers, who had started to gather quietly, move toward the barricades that were set up to protect the Rockefellers from the crowds. The truthers feel betrayed by the event coordinators for having the ceremonies one day ahead of time. The police move to set up a defensive line, but it is too late. One truther toting a bullhorn slips through and approaches the Rockefellers. When the megaphone voice pierces Joey's ear, the sound is deafening. Joey goes straight into combat mode; his instincts take over. First, Joey lands a kick to the side of the knee, breaking the man's leg; then, as the bullhorn flies through the air, Joey spins 360 degrees and lands an impressive left elbow into the left ear of the same man, slamming the man to the ground. He isn't going to get up. Joey backs up closer to David and Laurence. He stands in a defensive position and is combat-ready. Another, younger man comes through the barricades. Joey's combat instincts take over once again as his advanced combat training at Fort Benning takes over. Joey steps forward and lands a straight-leg kick to the man's sternum. Before the young man can exhale his first breath, Joey lands a left upper-cut to the chin, closing his mouth, as three of his teeth are dislodged and fall onto the sidewalk.

"Joey, my God!" David screams.

"Don't worry. I've got it under control," Joey says calmly, with fists clenched.

Even the police are impressed when a third man comes through and Joey provides him with a spinning sweep-kick to the legs which lands the guy on his backside. The crowd grows silent as Joey rushes across the street and sees that the brothers are already in the back of the limo. Joey quickly closes the rear door of the limo for them.

Joey gets behind the wheel. He looks back and says, "Don't worry. I'll get us out of here."

"I knew he would make a good wheelman," Laurance says to his brother David.

"Thanks. We almost got killed out there," Joey says.

"I hope you can drive as well as you can fight," David says.

Joey, driving the limo in reverse and at speed, spins the wheel as the limo does a 180-degree turn and heads north on Vesey Street. "How is that for some stunt driving?" Joey asks.

There is no response from the brothers, as their eyes are closed. They are both exhausted.

"Hey, what's-a matter with you guys back there?" Joey shouts. "I'm up here panting like a dog, and I just saved your lives."

David opens one eye and says, "It is our nap time. Could you be a dear and wake us up in twenty minutes?"

"Well, you're welcome, you old bastards. I guess it's about lunchtime, and I'm hungry. I've got to stop somewhere and eat something," Joey says out loud.

Again, there is no response from David or Laurance.

"I guess I'll stop and grab a hotdog down here somewhere," Joey says to himself as he sees the two men sleeping comfortably with mouths wide open.

Joey looks back and adjusts his rearview mirror. Joey sighs as he appreciates what a good nap can do to soothe one's soul. Joey takes a deep breath and turns the limo left onto Broadway.

Chapter 28

As the private jet crosses the invisible boundary between Canada and the United States, Alex asks. "Tell me, Wally, do you believe in folklore or old wives' tales?"

"No, of course not, but I do love a good mystery now and again. Why do you ask?"

"You see, in my family, there is story that has been passed down for generations. It goes like this. Back in 1615, a great ancestor of mine, Kiliaen Van Rensselaer, came across a desperate sea captain looking to trade a precious golden quill. It was said to have been endowed with some magical properties," Alex begins by saying.

"Quite common for that day, sir. Superstitions, folklore, and the belief of witchcraft was the norm, I believe," Wally says as he set his laptop aside. "Please go on."

"Yes, as my mother puts it, the man was a pirate, of course, of dubious character. He claimed the owner of the quill would become fabulously rich in all manors of life. This sea captain called the quill 'The Quill of Prosperity,' but he had warned Kiliaen that the owner of the quill would always have to answer to a higher authority," Alex says.

"A quill—do you mean a pen that one would write with?" Wally asks.

"Yes, it is said to be made of a golden sleeve about four inches long and had two white tail feathers from the now-extinct dodo bird. In a letter written by Kiliaen, he was of the belief that the higher authority was that of Prince William of Orange, and of course he, being on good terms with the prince, had no fear of such superstitions. Kiliaen, being a man of means and carrying deep superstitious beliefs, did indeed trade a ship for this golden quill," Alex says.

"He traded an entire ship? Well, the whole thing sounds rather preposterous to me," Wally says.

"Yes, quite so, but in those days, many people still believed the world was flat, amongst other things. Anyway, my mother, of all people, believes that it was Stephen Van Rensselaer III who had lost, sold, given away, or had it stolen from him by a man who my mother claims was Godfrey Rockefeller—he was the grandfather of John D. Rockefeller Senior—while he was living in Albany some time ago," Alex says.

"That is an incredible story, sir. It would be best if you didn't speak of any of that nonsense. We live in the real world of the here and now. Golden quill? Please. That sounds like the J. R. R. Tolkien story, *The Lord of the Rings*. Can we please get back to business, sir?" Wally asks as he sets his computer back onto his lap.

"Yes, of course, Wally. Let's move on with your report. We were discussing Nelson, I believe," Alex says.

"Yes. 'Nelson Rockefeller was named vice president after Gerald Ford was elevated to the presidency. Ford, in fact, almost gave the job of vice president to George H. W. Bush,'" Wally reads.

"President Ford never seemed to give poor Nelson anything to do while he was vice president, as he himself put it. He donated his entire salary back to the government and even flew his own Gulfstream private jet instead of Air Force Two," Alex says.

"It is rather quite nice, sir. I mean your plane, of course," Wally says as he gives the leather chair a good squeeze.

"They finally talked him into flying the DC-9 on account of the fact that the secret service was spending too much money flying agents around the country to meet his needs," Alex says.

"'Nelson was a noted collector of both non-western and modern art. He continued his mother's work at the Museum of Modern Art as president,'" Wally reads.

"You know, I was at his mansion once at Kykuit. The man had turned his entire basement into a world-class art gallery. He had this damn helicopter to move different sculptures around his yard. He was enamored with the stuff," Alex says.

"'Nelson and Mary got divorced in 1962, and on May 4, 1963, Nelson married Margaretta "Happy" Murphy.'"

"You know, after his divorce from Mary, she kept their apartment at 810 Fifth Avenue, but Nelson moved into the top three floors at the same address with his new wife. To avoid his first wife, Nelson bought the adjoining property at 812 Fifth Avenue and had the two apartments connected. He and his new wife used the entrance at 812, and Mary used the entrance at 810," Alex says.

"'David and Nelson, through the New York and New Jersey Port Authority, had the twin towers of the World Trade Center built,'" Wally reads.

"We used to call the north tower David and the south tower Nelson, or was it the other way around? Either way, they were pure New York icons," Alex says.

"Did you mean the brothers or the buildings, sir?" Wally asks.

"Nice one, Wally. Both, I suppose," Alex says.

"'Nelson died of a heart attack on January 26, 1979, at age seventy. His ashes were interred in a private Rockefeller family cemetery, also at the Sleepy Hollow Cemetery, New York,'" Wally reads.

"Did you know he was with his mistress Megan Marchack, one of his aides, when he died? I remember his brother David and Henry Kissinger, along with two of his children, gave the eulogies. Everybody who was anybody was there at the Riverside Church—presidents, senators, and foreign dignitaries. The place was a madhouse," Alex says.

Chapter 29

Dʀɪᴠɪɴɢ ɴᴏʀᴛʜ ᴏɴ Bʀᴏᴀᴅᴡᴀʏ, the group has a straight drive to Midtown Manhattan and Rockefeller Center, but they are still a good four miles or fifty blocks away from their destination. As the New York traffic picks up, horns honk, and pedestrians crowd the busy sidewalks.

You know, that incident back there ... that crowd and the fight remind me of when I was in the war over there in Iraq, Joey thinks to himself silently. *I had some good friends there. Pandorf and I ... Pandorf, he was a good friend from Jersey, and Sergeant Cotton, him and I used to golf together before the war. He was from Georgia. Then there was Sergeant Griffith—he was a big dude about six foot six. He was from the Virgin Islands, and from all the stories he told, I know I'd like to go there someday. I'm not sure if that is even part of America. Doesn't matter, I guess. And Jackson, one of my closest friends, he was from Philly; he should have been a football star, or maybe a professional basketball player, a great athlete. Oh yeah, Sergeant Keesey—I'm not sure were he was from, but he looked like MC Hammer. And Sergeant Chabot, he was from Maine. He was the only guy in our unit that was older than myself. I'm glad I was with him when the Boston Red Sox finally won the World Series. I remember the tears rolling down his face. My roommate, his name was Kava, Prince Robert Kava, probably the most interesting guy with us, even though he was a bit on the quiet side. His mother was the high priestess in Samoa, another place I would like to visit one of these days. Oh yeah, Master Sergeant Sampson, he was a good guy. He would have been killed in his own tent if it weren't for the call of nature. And Sergeant Gonzalez. I remember the one time him and I were standing just outside of our tent when a crazed suicide driver drove his car into the front gate of the base and we hit the deck like a couple of schoolgirls as it exploded over our heads. Like most of us, we shared a lot of close calls with death while we were over there. It's funny, the army—it's the only place were you can bring total strangers together, black, white, Latino, from anywhere in America, and we all get along like brothers. Well maybe all of America is alike, and we just don't know it. The whole experience sucked, minus knowing my buddies, but at least we all made it back, praise be to God.*

Joey pulls to the curb and gets out. He waits in line at one of the many hotdog vendors in New York.

"Hey, gimme two chilidogs with onions," Joey says. "You better make it four. You never know, these guys might get hungry," Joey says.

"Nice ride. Who's back there, the Smothers brothers?" the smart-alecky vendor asks.

"No, not the Smothers brothers. What are you, a comedian?" Joey strikes back with his quintessential New York attitude. "You don't want to know who's back there."

As Joey and the vendor stand alone together, Joey asks, "What would you do if you were the president?"

"You've got the president in there?" the street vendor asks.

"No, I don't have the president in there," Joey says. "I mean if you had the power to change the world or something, what would you do?"

"I'd feed the world—you know, end starvation. Do I win a prize or something?" the vendor asks.

"No, you don't win a fucking prize, you idiot," Joey says as he walks back around the car.

"I was just trying to help," The vendor says as a few customers walk up and Joey gets in the limo on the driver's side. Joey sits in the car and starts in on his first of two hotdogs.

"Only in New York. What do I look like, the Cash Cab Limo?" Joey says to himself. "'Do I win a fucking prize?'"

Chapter 30

W<small>ALLY</small> <small>CONTINUES HIS BRIEF</small> to Alex on the history of the Rockefeller family.

"'David and his brother Winthrop A. Rockefeller were the youngest two sons of John D. Rockefeller Junior. Winthrop attended Yale University from 1931 to 1934. Winthrop was expelled for his misbehavior before earning his degree. At the age of twenty-nine, he enlisted into the Seventy-seventh Infantry Division in early 1941 and fought in World War II, advancing from a private to colonel while earning a bronze star with clusters and a Purple Heart for his actions aboard the U,S,S, *Henrico* after a kamikaze attack during the battle of Okinawa,'" Wally reads.

"No one in the military goes from private to colonel—well, unless you're connected. Either way, he sounds like a head case. Though heroic and brave, he was still a head case," Alex says, relaxing in his chair.

"Did you know him, sir?" Wally asks.

"Yes, but not much outside of reading newspaper headlines. His wife was something of a treat. She was a former model and showgirl. Her name was Barbara, but they called her Bobo. After Bobo the Clown, I guess. At their wedding in Florida, they supposedly hired a Negro spiritualist to sing songs," Alex says.

"You mean African religious rituals like spiritual possession, speaking in tongues, and communal chants?" Wally asks.

"I don't know. I wasn't there. The man had issues, I think, and his wife was no different," Alex answers.

"It says here that they got divorced in 1954. She claims he had an extensive collection of pornography. I have a quote here from her. It reads, 'I want him to suffer the way he has made me suffer, as he has humiliated me before the whole world,'" Wally reads.

"'I suffered in front of the whole world,'" Alex repeats in his best female voice. "Do you think she was a fucking drama queen, or what? As far as his porn collection, maybe he needed it with the likes of her. Maybe he should be in charge of the SEC. I hear they watch a lot of porn over there while they are supposed to be regulating the stock market."

"I don't think so, sir. 'Winthrop moved to Arkansas in 1953. In 1956, he married his second wife, Jeanette Edris Barrager Bartley McDonnell,'" Wally reads.

"My goodness, how did she get all those names?" Alex asks.

"Well, sir, it says here she was previously married to a pro American football player, a lawyer, and a stockbroker," Wally answers.

"So he jumped from the frying pan and into the fire," Alex says as he rumbles around in his chair.

"'Winthrop won the governorship of Arkansas in 1966.' So that would mean he and his brother Nelson were governors at the same time," Wally says.

"Very good, Wally, you've read your own report," Alex says. "Do you think his name and fortune had anything to do with his winning the election?" Alex asks.

"Well, although slanted toward the wealthy, you know the American way of democracy is still the envy of the all the world, sir," Wally says.

"Yes, how misconstrued we all are," Alex says.

"Winthrop served two terms as governor, in which he fought against prison scandals and illegal gambling. At the 1968 Republican National Convention, Winthrop received 18 votes for the nomination for the presidency, mostly from the Arkansas delegates, to his brother Nelson's 277. As a dramatic last act as governor of Arkansas, he commuted the sentences of every prisoner on Arkansas's death row and urged other states to do the same. Do you think that his brothers had influenced him to do this?" Wally asks.

"I doubt it. I told you, he was a head case," Alex says.

"'He was diagnosed with inoperable cancer of the pancreas and went through chemotherapy. He died in February 1973. He did die quite young compared to the rest of his brothers. His son, Win, died very young as well; he was still serving as lieutenant governor back in 2006 when he himself passed away,'" Wally reads.

"I'm sure Win Junior was the richest man in Arkansas when he died," Alex says.

"'*Forbes* magazine ranked Winthrop "Win" Paul Rockefeller at #283 of the nation's wealthiest people in 2005, with a fortune estimated at 1.2 billion dollars,'" Wally reads.

"Good gracious, I've always thought he was the poor one in the family," Alex says.

"Yes, sir, he may have been," Wally says.

"Listen to this week's *Forbes* magazine headlines. 'The top ten richest Americans of all time, according to their net worth versus the GDP of the United States economy,'" Wally reads from his laptop as he surfs the Internet.

"Let me guess—John D. Rockefeller is number one," Alex says.

"Yes, he is, but do you know who number ten on the list is?" Wally asks.

"I have no idea," Alex says.

"Mr. Stephen Van Rensselaer III. It says here his accumulated worth in today's dollars would have been ninety billion dollars. Did you hear that? Billion with a b," Wally says proudly as he looks up to witness Alex's reaction.

"I heard you the first time, Wally. He was my great-great-great-grandfather. I believe he passed away back in 1839. It makes you wonder where all the money went. Did you know that I probably have more than two hundred living relatives just in this country alone?" Alex says, leaning back in his chair, pondering his own question.

"I'm sure you have received your fair share, sir," Wally says, trying to bring Alex back to the reality of his own wealth.

"Yes, quite right, Wally, quite right," Alex says boldly.

Chapter 31

J OEY PULLS AWAY FROM the curb and turns on the radio. "I think the Yankees have a day game today in Detroit," Joey says to himself as the alarms on the brothers' watches go off simultaneously.

"Oh, dear God, is it that time already?" Laurance says as he rolls over to his left side. "Just give me five more minutes, please."

"Wake up, Laurance. No time to dilly-dally. We must get back to our dossier," David says, rubbing his eyes as if he had slept for hours. "Now, let's see where I was."

"Your dossier left off somewhere during the American Revolution," Joey says has he turns and shows them a tray with two hotdogs on it. "Hey, I got you guys a couple of chilidogs. I figured you guys might be hungry. You can eat them on our way to your office."

"How delightful. I haven't had a chilidog in years," Laurance says. "Thank you."

David reaches and grabs the cardboard tray from Joey. David sits back, unwraps one of the hotdogs, and begins to eat.

"What is the score of the ballgame?" Laurance asks.

"It's 2-2 Tigers in the fifth," Joey answers.

"Is Kirk Gibson playing?" Laurance asks. "He is my favorite baseball player."

"No, Kirk Gibson isn't playing. He hasn't played for the Tigers in twenty-five years," Joey answers.

"You must forgive my brother. He is forgetful at times," David says.

"Hey, Laurance, DiMaggio, Gehrig, and Ruth are due up next inning. You think we have a chance?" Joey asks sarcastically.

"That is not funny, Joey," David says.

"Oh, come on. I like the old feller. He is a funny one," Joey says. "What do you say we trade Derek Jeter for Pete Rose, or maybe A-Rod for Ty Cobb? Kirk Gibson, come on, get real." Joey roars with laughter.

"Enough already," David says, chewing down his last bite. "It wasn't funny the first time."

"Where did you get that suit?" Joey asks of Laurance as he looks through the rearview mirror.

"This is a tailor-made suit," Laurance answers while looking down at his sleeves.

"Yeah, from, like, the 1980s. Welcome to the new millennium already," Joey says.

"Ah, yes, here we are, section 15," David says as he finds his spot. "I'll try and stick to the highlights. There are far too many namesakes to get to. All the marriages that have intertwined the Van Rensselaers with the Gansevoorts, Van Cortlandts, Schuylers, and Livingstons are just too confusing.

"Here is an interesting spot. 'Catharine Van Rensselaer was born in 1734 to her father, General Robert. In 1755, she married Major-General Philip Schuyler. She is said to have set fire to as many wheat crops as she could in the fall of 1776 so the British could not use them. Their daughter Elizabeth would marry Alexander Hamilton. The marriage of Elizabeth and Alexander took place at the Schuyler mansion in 1780,'" David reads.

"Wow, that is right in the middle of the Revolutionary War. Could you imagine who showed up at that wedding? You aren't saying that Alexander Hamilton married into the Van Rensselaer family, are you?"

"Yes, Joey. It was with Van Rensselaer money that Hamilton was able to start the Bank of New York," Laurance says.

"Here is another. 'Major James Van Rensselaer was born in 1747. He served as aide-de-camp, with the rank of captain, to Major-General Richard Montgomery from August to December, 1775. He served through the Canadian campaign at Fort Chambly, St. John's, Montreal, and Quebec. In April 1776, he became captain in the Second Regiment of the New York line under Colonel James Clinton and from June to August of the same year was aide-de-camp, with the rank of major, to General Philip Schuyler in the northern army. James married Catharine Van Cortlandt,'" David reads.

"I have more. 'John Jeremias Van Rensselaer was born in 1769. He fought in the American Revolution as lieutenant colonel of the Fourteenth Regiment, Albany County Militia. John was the only son of Jeremias and Judith Bayard. He inherited the Greenbush lands, with the ancient mansion, under the terms of the will of his grandfather, Colonel Johannes Van Rensselaer,'" David reads.

"'Colonel Jacob Rutsen Van Rensselaer was born 1767, second son of General Robert Van Rensselaer. He was associated with Governor De Witt Clinton in the building of the Erie Canal. While waiting for orders expecting him to march to Niagara, he was assumed the leading candidate as governor of New York,'" David reads.

"'Jeremias Van Rensselaer was the third son of General Robert. He lived in Utica, New York. He was the head of the firm Van Rensselaer and Kane, which brought grain from the west and also had a large trade in coffee and spices from the West Indies. He married Sybil Adeline Kane of Albany. Their eldest daughter would go onto marry Francis Granger of the highly regarded Granger family,'" David reads.

"'James Van Rensselaer, fifth son of General Robert, moved to Indiana in 1835, where he purchased a large tract of land in Jasper County, about seventy miles south of Chicago. In February 1840, a town was laid out and was named Rensselaer. Most of the street names are of family origin. The Daughters of the American Revolution have established a General Van Rensselaer Chapter in honor of General Robert in the city of Rensselaer, Indiana,'" David reads.

"The Daughters of the American Revolution has quite an honor roll of members, I do believe," Laurance adds.

"Yes, I have a short list here. 'Many female members of the Van Rensselaer family are included on its rolls. Other members include Susan B. Anthony, Clara Barton, Grandma Moses, Ginger Rodgers, Caroline Scott Harrison, Rosalynn Carter, Laura Bush, Elizabeth Dole, Janet Reno, and Bo Derek,'" David reads. "'Cornelia Rutsen Van Rensselaer was invited to one of the first meetings by her close friend, Mary S. Lockwood of New York City, in 1890.'"

"Bo Derek? You're kidding, right?" Joey asks.

"No, not at all, Joey," David says, rereading the last part, not fully believing it himself.

"'Solomon Van Rensselaer was a US representative from New York, a lieutenant colonel of the New York Volunteers during the War of 1812, and a postmaster. He was the son of General Henry Killian Van Rensselaer, who fought in the Revolutionary War at the Battle of Saratoga,'" David reads.

"Hold on a minute. What you're saying is that most of today's New York elitists and most of our country can in one way or another trace back their names and roots to all the glory of this one family?" Joey says as he slows the limo and stops at the corner of West Twelfth Street.

"One can look at it that way, yes. Why is that, Joey?" Laurance asks.

"It just seems to be pretty important. I mean, maybe we should add them into our American history books somewhere."

"'Stephen Van Rensselaer III was the tenth *patroon* of Rensselaerswyck. He was heir to the greatest estate in New York at the time, which made him the tenth richest American of all time. He founded the Rensselaer Polytechnic Institute in 1824. He was the father of Henry Bell Van Rensselaer, who was a general in the American Civil War. His younger brother, Philip Schuyler Van Rensselaer, was the mayor of Albany from 1799 to 1812. He was the great-grandson of the mayor of New York, Stephanus Van Cortlandt, and Catherine Livingston, daughter of Philip Livingston, the signer of the Declaration of Independence. His father died when he was only five years old. His uncle was Abraham Ten Broeck and was in charge of his estate until he came of age. He went to Princeton and graduated from Harvard in 1782. One year later, he married Margarita Schuyler. Over time, he would be landlord of over three thousand tenants.'"

"He had three thousand tenants? That is more people than my entire high school had, when I was there," Joey says.

"As the head of Rensselaerswyck, he did not press the tenants for the rents and had actually lowered the rent of most to one percent."

"Well, at least he sounds like a nice guy," Joey says.

"'He served in the New York State Assembly and the New York Senate, and was elected lieutenant governor. He voted for universal male suffrage, against most of New York's upper class. In 1786, he was a major of the United States militia, and by 1801, he became a major-general. He led the fight with his cousin Solomon in the battle of Queenstown Heights. They lost the battle, but his men did kill British general Isaac Brock. During the War of 1812, Stephen built the Watervliet Arsenal in 1813, just north of Albany on the Hudson River. It is the oldest continuously active arsenal in the United States and today produces much of the artillery for the army, as well as gun tubes for ships, mortars, and tanks.'" David stops to turn the page and take a breath.

"Did you know the Watervliet was the first place in America to use the Bessemer process?" Joey asks.

"Yes, we did, Joey. 'Stephen initiated the building of the Erie Canal and was on the canal commission for twenty-three years, from 1816 until 1839. He also served as the president of the canal commission for fourteen years. In 1823, he was elected to the House of Representatives. He was the chairmen of the Committee on Agriculture. Stephen Van Rensselaer served as grand master of Masons of New York in 1825, 1826, 1827, 1828, and 1829.'" David pauses again.

"Hey, that is the same group I'm in. Wasn't that around the time that William Morgan wanted to publish an anti-Freemason book, but ended up disappearing?" Joey asks.

"Yes, in fact, it was the night of September 11, 1826, when William Morgan was first arrested. His friend, David Miller, owner of the local newspaper, went and bailed him out, but several hours later, he was rearrested for not paying back a loan and supposedly stealing some clothing. Later that same night, three men appeared at the jail, paying his bail, and had him released into their custody. Some say he was taken by carriage to Niagara Falls and thrown over. In October of 1827, a badly decomposed body was found washed up on the shores of Lake Ontario. Many assumed the body was that of Morgan," Laurance says.

"Yeah, right, and the three men who had obtained his release were believed to be Freemasons. It started the whole anti-Masonic movement at the time. Well, the Van Rensselaers could not have anything to do with it. They all lived in Albany or New Jersey at the time," Joey says.

"I guess we'll never know for sure. Do you want to hear the weird part of his story?" Laurance offers.

"Does it get any weirder?" Joey asks.

"Well, you see, Morgan was married to a woman named Lucinda Pendleton, and after his disappearance, she later became one of the plural wives of the Mormon Church founder, Joseph Smith Junior," Laurance says.

"Get the hell outta here," Joey says.

"Not only that, but William Morgan was given one of the first official baptisms for the dead by the Church of Latter Day Saints," Laurance adds.

"The Mormon Church actually baptizes dead people? I've never heard of that," Joey says.

"It's a practice that they still do to this day," Laurance says.

David begins to get inpatient with the two and reads on loudly. "Well, now you know. Now, please be quiet. 'In the election for president of the United States in 1824, it was Stephen Van Rensselaer who cast the deciding vote that put John Quincy Adams into the White House. He was regent of the University of the State of New York from 1819 to 1839. He died later that year at the age of seventy-four. After the death of Stephen Van Rensselaer III in 1839, the antirenter party was established. The first meeting was held in 1839, and by 1845, they called for political redress of grievances. The Anti-Rent Movement led to the Homestead Act. After his death, the land was split into two by his sons, Stephen IV and his brother William. Stephen IV called upon Governor Seward to send in the militia to help collect the back rents owed to him. Dr. Boughton, who was one of the leaders of the Anti-Rent Movement, dressed himself up as an Indian and named himself Big Thunder. Not able to deal with the chaos caused by the Anti-Rent Movement, the Van Rensselaers began to sell off their land. From 1845 through 1850, the Van Rensselaers had sold off most of their land in upstate New York. The vast and powerful Manor of Rensselaerswyck was no more. The Van Rensselaer Land Company was formed in 1848 to deal with this issue and was also set up to reinvest the family's vast wealth,'" David reads.

"So that was it? It took an uprising by the people to end the feudalism in America? It's too bad that the colony disappeared, but it took almost to the eve of the Civil War to do it. Right across the Hudson River from the city of Albany, the county of Rensselaer is still there to this day," Joey says as he drives the limo north on Broadway and across Twenty-ninth Street.

David continues with the dossier. "'Henry Bell Van Rensselaer was another son of Stephen III. He graduated from West Point 1831. He was elected representative of New York in 1841. At the outbreak of the Civil War, he was made a brigadier general in the Union Army. He was appointed chief of staff under General Winfield Scott. It is unconfirmed, but some say he was wounded during Pickett's charge at the battle of Gettysburg in July of 1863. He was later transported to Cincinnati, where he died from the wounds he sustained.

"'A cousin to Stephen III was Schuyler Van Rensselaer. He was the only son of John Cullen and Cornelia Van Rensselaer. He was born at 42 Clinton Place, New York City. In the summer of 1862, he enlisted as a private in the Newport Company of the Rhode Island Regiment, was promoted to sergeant, and was offered a commission on the staff of General Burnside. He only served four months and then decided to go to Harvard. He married Mariana Alley

Griswold, eldest daughter of George Griswold of New York City,'" David reads.

"Here is an insert of a list of the *patroons* of Rensselaerswyck in chronological order," David says to Laurance.

"Let me see that, if you would, please," Laurance says, reaching for the list.

"Don't forget that it took an uprising by the people, the farmers, to end the feudalistic arrangements that benefited the *patroons*," Joey says.

"Yes, the Anti-Rent Wars lasted for almost a decade," David says.

"I have two more notes left here in the first folder. The first reads, 'After the duel between Hamilton and Burr, Hamilton was taken across the Hudson River to the house of William Bayard and his wife, Mrs. Van Rensselaer Bayard, where he had died later the next day,'" David reads. "I still own those dueling pistols. I have them on display on the fiftieth floor at JP Morgan Chase on 270 Park Avenue. And the second and last note is about the Ship of Gold, the Ship of Gold being the side wheel steamer S.S. *Central America*. 'Captain William Herndon and first officer and paymaster, Charles M. Van Rensselaer, lost control of the ship on September 11, 1857, during a hurricane off the coast of the Carolinas and were lost together with the ship on the next day. The ship was heavily laden with ten tons of gold prospected during the California gold rush,'" David reads.

"That is the ship with America's lost treasure. The loss actually contributed to the bank panic of 1857," Joey says. "I think the wreck was found by a group from Ohio State University."

"Yes, it was, and it's a good thing the Van Rensselaers were insured at the time. They may have lost a fortune. Of course, the insurance claim was highly debated amongst the Wall Street insurers who had lost out. The strange thing is that the ship was found 130 years later to the day, on September 11, 1987. A team led by a man named Tommy Thompson discovered the wreck and recovered the gold. Almost immediately after the announcement of the discovery, thirty-nine insurance companies filed suits, claiming that because they had paid damages to the Van Rensselaers in 1857 for the lost gold, that they had the right to it. In 1996, courts awarded ninety-two percent of the gold to the discoverers. The total value of the gold was estimated between 100 and 150 million dollars," Laurance says.

"I recall one of the gold ingots, named Eureka, weighed eighty pounds and was worth eight million dollars. I guess the guy who bought it wanted to remain anonymous," Joey says as he looks back at the two billionaires as if one of them may have been the purchaser. David and Laurance both look out the windows, trying to put on their most innocent-looking faces as if to say it wasn't them.

"Yeah, I know that look. Hey, maybe it was your buddy Alex who is the mystery man who bought the huge chunk of gold," Joey says.

The *Patroons* of Rensselaerswyck

Kiliaen Van Rensselaer   1631-1640

Johan Van Rensselaer   1640-1652

Jan Baptist Van Rensselaer   1652-1658

Jeremias Van Rensselaer   1658-1674

Kiliaen Van Rensselaer   1674-1687

Kiliaen Van Rensselaer   1687-1719

Jeremias Van Rensselaer   1719-1745

Stephen Van Rensselaer   1745-1747

Stephen Van Rensselaer II   1747-1769

Abraham Ten Broeck 1769-1784 (de facto)

Stephen Van Rensselaer III   1784-1839

"That finishes our first folder on the Van Rensselaer family background," David announces.

"Wait, wait, wait, is that it? What about the war of 1812 or their politics or their businesses? You've gotten us right up to the Civil War. What about World War I or World War II, or today, even? You don't know anything about this guy Alex. Where is the family today? Did they pull a Houdini and disappear or something?" Joey asks.

"We know plenty about Mr. Van Rensselaer. After all, he is a friend of ours," David says, checking his watch.

"He is a friend of yours! Then why would you do a background check on him?"

"That is a standard business practice of ours," Laurance answers.

"Then you must have done one on me too. You're bastards," Joey says, trying to make his way through the New York City traffic.

"Of course, it's S.O.P.," David says.

"What does S.O.P. stand for?" Joey asks.

"It stands for standard operating procedure," David answers.

"I've got an acronym for you—S.O.B. It stands for sons of bitches," Joey says. "Have you guys ever read the Constitution? I have the right to some privacy, you know. I'm sure it's in there somewhere."

"It is just a formality, Joey," David says. "Well, let's take a look at this folder number two, shall we?" David says.

Chapter 32

"WE ARE ON APPROACH to New York's John F. Kennedy Airport. Please fasten your seatbelt, Wally. We have gained clearance to land," Alex announces.

Wally hurries to close his computer and collects the men's luggage by his side. The Gulfstream 650 slows to a moderate speed after racing over the North Atlantic. The nose gently rises as the wheels reach downward, searching for the tarmac. The plane takes one gentle hop and slows its way down the runway. Alex looks at Wally with a big smile. Alex knowingly takes the plane to the private hanger where the plane has been kept for over a year.

"I've always loved the landings. It's exhilarating," Alex says as he looks intensely out the front window.

The plane rolls to a complete stop directly next to an extending platform inside of the hanger.

"There is no need to refuel the plane while we are here. I'll just leave it here in the hanger for now." Alex undoes his seatbelt and walks out of the front cabin. "I don't plan on any other flights for a least a week or so."

Wally and Alex secure their bags and walk out and onto the enclosed platform.

"I've got ten minutes to two, sir. I called ahead, and your pilot Paul is waiting for us in the whirlybird. Are you hungry at all, sir?" Wally asks.

"I'm famished. We should have had the plane loaded with food. Write that down for next time, Wally," Alex says.

"You made it a point, while in London, not to try eating any British cuisine, sir. You Americans love your cheeseburgers," Wally says as he must gallop to try and keep up with the long strides of Alex.

"I forgot about your tastes, Wally. I feel bad. A big cheeseburger sounds great right about now. We'll stop and get something to go. We'll go through the food court. It has just about everything," Alex says as the two walk their way through the terminal. "Let me help you with those," Alex offers, taking the smallest of the four bags that Wally has been wrestling with.

"Thank you, sir," Wally says as he heads his own way to get his lunch.

Wally and Alex purchase separate lunches and head though the airport for the helicopter landing pad.

Alex's helicopter is not far off as Wally and Alex open a side exit door of the airport and walk out and onto the tarmac. A huge gust of wind blows from the already spinning blades of the helicopter. Wally and Alex climb aboard, fasten their seatbelts, and lift the radio headsets onto their heads.

"Good afternoon, sir. Where can I take you today, Mr. Van Rensselaer?" Captain Paul asks as he turns and looks over his left shoulder and offers a friendly wave.

"You are a sight for sore eyes. We're headed to the Holland Society. You can take us to the East Thirty-fourth Street helipad," Alex says.

"Yes, sir, not a problem," Captain Paul says as he agrees with choice of the landing spot.

With a slow liftoff, the bird spins 180 degrees and heads directly over Van Wyck Highway and towards downtown Manhattan.

"Sir, in the Rockefeller report, we have yet to go over the files on Laurance or David."

"It can wait, Wally. Try and enjoy the view. Relax," Alex says as he opens the wrapper of his cheeseburger and bites in. "You might want to eat now. We won't have much time later."

"Yes, sir." Wally turns and looks down and has some anxiety while looking over the fast-moving landscape. As the helicopter gains in height, Wally looks through the front glass bubble and can see the downtown skyline of Manhattan and wonders if the skyline is more impressive during the daytime or at night. Either way, he thinks it is truly awesome every time he crosses the pond and sees New York City.

"It's truly the only way to view the city, sir," Wally says.

"I love it. The view of New York City never gets boring, especially flying at fifteen hundred feet," Alex says as he wipes his chin with a napkin.

"Do I need to call ahead and have a limousine meet us at the landing zone?" Wally asks.

"No, no. The Holland Society is on Forty-fourth Street. We'll just take a cab over; it's not too far," Alex answers.

As the whirlybird approaches the East River, it slows down to avoid other birds and waits to move forward. Wally mentions, "The Chrysler building looks great."

"Yes, they had cleaned it up a few years ago. As regent to the Union College, we actually own the land on which it sits," Alex says with some pride.

"I take it they never built automobiles there?" Wally asks.

"No, of course not. Everyone knows cars are built in Detroit. Walter P. Chrysler leased the land from the college and built the world's tallest building on the site. About a year later, the Empire State Building was completed, and it remained the tallest building for over forty years. It's right over there," Alex says, pointing at the tall peak on the New York skyline. "Like with many of United States skyscrapers and bridges, there were hundreds of Mohawk Indian ironworkers that worked at the top. They lack the fear of heights, I would guess," Alex says.

Paul flies the helicopter across the East River and down to the helipad, making a pinpoint landing. As the winds swirl about, Wally and Alex step off of the helicopter, and Alex thanks the pilot and waves goodbye.

Wally and Alex walk to the north side parking lot, where a waiting taxicab is parked, and they get in.

"Twenty West Forty-fourth Street, please," Alex says as both men climb into the back seat of the cab.

The driver turns and announces with a French accent, "The Huguenot Society, sir, right away. Are those all the bags you are bringing? the driver asks.

"Yes, these are all our bags, and no, we're headed for the Holland Society, actually," Alex responds.

"Oh, yes, sir. They actually share the same address, sir," the driver says.

The cab pulls up just outside of the Holland Society's front door at 2:20 pm. Alex reaches into his wallet and pays the man with a twenty and a ten-dollar bill. "Keep the change," Alex says.

"Well, we made it with five minutes to spare," Wally says proudly.

"Yes, of course. That is why I hire professionals like you, Wally. Whatever you do, do not bring up the bomb to my mother. She will have David's balls for breakfast if she finds out," Alex says as the two men greet James the doorman just outside of the Holland Society.

"How are you today, sir?" James the doorman asks.

"I couldn't be better, James, and yourself?" Alex asks.

"I'm okay, I guess," James answers.

"Could you watch our bags for a moment? We won't be staying long," Alex says.

"Yes, of course, but it is your mother's birthday, sir ... They'll be right here when you come out, sir," James says, correcting himself.

"Thank you, James. This way, Wally," Alex says as they walk through the front door.

"Good day, sir."

"Good afternoon, James," Wally replies.

The men make their way through the front door and approach the open elevator door. After striding in, Alex presses the fifth button. Wally stays in the corridor near the elevator as Alex mingles his way through a ballroom filled with guests of his mother. Alex sees his mother in the middle of the room, chatting with some friends, as he makes his way over to her.

"Happy eighty-seventh, Mother. You look great. How are you feeling, my dear?" Alex says as he gives a slight bow to his mother's friends and takes her hand. "And ladies, you look wonderful as always."

"Why, thank you, Alex," the group of women seems to say all at the same time.

"Well, I could be better. As for you, you look terrible," Mrs. Van Rensselaer says to her son, Alex. "Your pilot Jimmy called and said you were in trouble. Is everything all right?"

"Yes, we had a small problem with the replacement pilot, but everything is fine now."

"It was that bastard David, wasn't it? We can't let people fuck with us. You let them screw with you once, and they'll never stop. I'll have him wearing cement shoes by morning."

"Easy, Mother. Everything is all right," Alex says.

"I've got news for you, mister: you better stop all your gallivanting around. It's time for you to settle in with a nice woman. I have some ladies here you might like to meet. Let me introduce you," Mrs. Van Rensselaer says.

"If you are done embarrassing me, Mother, I need to speak with you. And as for fixing me up, it is a bit too late for me now. I'm sixty-eight years old. I'm no spring chicken, you know," Alex says with a smile.

"Well, after your divorce, you just plain stopped looking. No wife, no children. Alex, you could at least try and look decent," Mrs. Van Rensselaer says, fixing his tie.

"Could you excuse us for a moment, ladies?" Alex says to the group as he pats down his suit jacket and turns, walking away with his mother as he holds her arm.

"Yes, of course. We'll see you again later, Cornelia," one of the ladies says.

"I have news on a different front for you. I know that you are going over to see David Rockefeller this afternoon, along with those Chinese or Japanese diplomats. Just ignore what happened on your flight. Try to act casual. I'll take care of him later," Cornelia says.

"They are both Chinese and Japanese, Mother," Alex says as the two walk back out into the main corridor. Wally seems to be enjoying himself, as he is standing and looking at the various paintings on the walls.

"Well, either way, I have to inform you ... is he okay?" Cornelia whispers and asks about Wally's presence.

Wally turns and approaches the two. "Mrs. Van Rensselaer, it's my honor to see you again." And with a slight bow, "Are you enjoying your birthday, Mama?"

"Yes, it has been delightful. Thank you for asking, young man," Cornelia offers with a big smile.

"Your art collection is exquisite, my dear," Wally says to Cornelia.

"Oh, thank you. It's taken a lifetime to collect, and I'm still not completely happy with it, but that is the joy of it, I suppose."

"Yes, Mama, Wally has been my private secretary for almost ten years now. He knows everything about my business," Alex says to his mother.

"Well, maybe so, but I have something for your ears only," Cornelia says. "It's been nice seeing you again, Wally."

"Would you excuse us for a quick moment, Wally?" Alex asks as he escorts his mother away from the crowd of people gathering in the hallway.

"Yes, of course, sir, May I remind you, sir, our schedule is a bit tight?" Wally says hesitantly as he returns his attention back to the art hanging in the corridor. "I'll be right here if you need me, sir."

Mrs. Van Rensselaer is not happy with their privacy and leads Alex on a slow walk down the corridor and toward a salon near the back of the building.

"Alex, friends of mine in the Black Dragon Society have informed me of the fact that the Chinese have flown several dozen of their top assassins over here to New York City, some of whom are staying in Chinatown, and the Japanese are staying over at the Ritz-Carlton near Central Park," Cornelia says.

"You don't think they are here to kill Mr. Rockefeller, do you?" Alex asks.

"No, of course not, Alex, I'm not sure why they are here exactly, but the scuttlebutt is they will have the Rockefeller Center surrounded tonight. Hopefully, they are just a security detachment here to protect the delegates. I've heard that one of the diplomats, a Mr. Yoshihiko Noda, will be present. You know his boss, Mr. Naoto Kan, has become president of Japan, and the people were upset about one of our bases remaining open in Okinawa, but you never know," Cornelia says.

"What are they, ninjas or something? We don't even own the land anymore, Mother," Alex says.

"All I know for sure is, the meeting has nothing to do with that land contract that everyone keeps talking about. I've learned that the negotiations are a false front; they must want something else," Cornelia says. "You do know why you were invited to see them today, Alex?"

"Yes, of course David is going to make an offer to repurchase the property at Rockefeller Center from the Green and the Red Societies."

"You must think of it like a poker game, Alex. We know that the Rockefellers want their buildings back and the Green and the Red Societies don't want to sell. You know of the clause, don't you, Alex?" Cornelia asks.

"Well, I do need to speak to you about Father's safe, Mother. Dad had the contract and the details in his safe," Alex says.

"Hogwash. You don't need to see the contract; I know all about it. There is a clause in the contract that states only the regents of Columbia University can approve the sale of the land. It makes no difference if we own the property or not. Personally, I don't care if the Rockefellers or the Asians own the property. They have asked you to be present to approve the deal, and that is it, as far as I know. The way

I see it is that David will offer to buy the property at an extremely high price and the Asians will refuse unless they receive something else in return. It is that 'something else' that I'm not sure about. They may ask David to close or move the base in Okinawa," Cornelia says.

"I'm not sure where you get your information, Mother ..."

"You know the ladies do more gossiping than you can shake a stick at. Please, Alex, just listen. It's like a big poker game. You will be more like the referee, Alex."

"You mean the dealer, Mother," Alex says.

"Yes, that is it. No matter what happens, just know that it will be the Asians that will be bluffing, because there is no need to bring such people here for a simple property deal. After your meeting with the members of the Asian societies, you will be meeting David later on, no?" Cornelia asks.

"Yes, Mother. You women, I swear. You are the leader of a bunch of busybodies. What does your heart tell you, Mother?" Alex asks.

"It tells me the situation could be extremely dangerous. You be careful tonight. And another thing: do you remember the story I used to tell you as a child?" Cornelia asks.

"Which story would that be, Mother?" Alex asks as he clasps his hands together behind his back and starts a nervous pace back down the corridor.

"You know, the one about our long-lost golden quill. I have received close word from a friend that David keeps it in his upper chest pocket. This may be our best chance to get it back," Cornelia says.

"The Quill of Prosperity? Please, Mother, I think you have said enough already. Even if there were such a family heirloom, we have lived without it for four generations. And who is to say that we did not sell it to the Rockefellers fair and square in the first place? And besides, why don't you just walk right up ask him for it? A little charm might go a long way, you know. It might be just another fairytale that your grandfather had created."

"It's no myth, Alex. You know of the Book of Ages, right?"

"Yes, of course, Mother. I have it locked away in the basement of the library at the University. It is in a safe place."

"Well, you can accept that as real. Why not the quill, then? The time in the second Book of Ages draws nearer."

"Well, it sounds like your granddad really has you convinced about the quill, God rest his soul. And yes, the first Book of Ages ends on the winter solstice, December 21, 2012, and the second begins the next day on the twenty-second. I know all about it," Alex says.

"I'm not sure if I'll live long enough to see it, but let me tell you this: from time to time, the holder of the older book, the first Book of Ages, allows certain members of secret societies to view it—only when it profits him to do so," Cornelia says, holding onto Alex's right arm.

"And who are they? The Skull and Bones? The Freemasons? Or maybe it's the Jesuits, Mother? It all sounds ludicrous," Alex says as he stops in the center of the corridor and turns to his mother. "Have you or any of your network of spies ever seen it?"

"I'm still working on that. Will you stay and present my birthday cake to me, my dear Alex?" Cornelia asks as the two make their way back from their short walk.

"I would love to, Mother, but Wally and I need to get to the Ritz-Carleton right away. Tell the others I said hello," Alex says as mother and son walk together back toward the fifth-floor elevator.

"Of course I will. You be safe. Keep an eye on that Wally of yours," Cornelia says as she looks down the corridor at him.

"Yes, Mother. I love you, and I will call you first thing in the morning. Please enjoy your birthday," Alex says.

"Are you ready, sir?" Wally asks.

"Yes, go ahead and wave us down another cab. I'll be down in a minute," Alex says.

"Yes, sir," Wally says as he retreats into the elevator.

"I don't trust him, Alex. It's that British accent," Cornelia says as Alex kisses her goodbye.

Chapter 33

JUST BEFORE DAVID BEGINS to read from the second folder, Joey shouts out.

"Hey, that guy just stole that lady's purse. We have to stop and do something," Joey says in a slight panic.

"Let it go, Joey. That is why we pay taxes. Let the police handle it," David says, as he is ready to begin.

"But we have a chance to help, I can do something."

Just then, the man with the purse runs out into the middle of the street.

"Should I stop?" Joey yells.

"Hit 'em!" Laurance screams. "Use the car to stop him."

Joey slows just a little before the man's legs crunch over the front of the car and his body is flung toward the windshield. The man slowly flops off the side of the car as Joey gives the wheel a quick right and then a left. Laurance powers down the right side rear window.

"Crime never pays, loser," Laurance shouts out the window.

"Holy shit! I just ran a guy over," Joey shouts.

"He'll be okay," David says.

"So you just want me to leave him there?" Joey asks.

"Yes. Keep driving, Joey—that is an order," David says.

"What about the cops?" Joey asks.

"What about them?" Laurance asks.

"I mean I can get in big trouble for a hit and run," Joey says.

"They'll do their job. You do yours," Laurance says. The guy is a scumbag, Joey. You're doing the right thing. If we stop now, we'll be here for hours."

"You guys have been living in New York too long. I think the city is starting to affect your judgment," Joey says.

"Fuck 'em," David says loudly.

Joey starts to laugh at David's reaction. Laurance joins in the laughter, and now David joins in the laughter. All three are laughing hysterically.

"Yeah, fuck him. Who does he think he is, anyway?" Joey screams. "You guys are some sick bastards, you know that? We're all going to hell for this one."

David turns to look out the rear window. "He's getting up. He'll have a limp, but he looks to be okay."

Chapter 34

ALEX MOVES THROUGH THE front doors of the Holland Society and out onto the front sidewalk, where Wally is waiting.

"Did everything go all right, sir?" Wally asks.

"Yes, of course. My mother hasn't changed much over the years. I'm sorry about her behavior; she can't bring herself to trust anybody outside of her circle of friends," Alex says.

"That is quite all right, Alex. There is no need to apologize," Wally says.

James the doorman successfully waves down the men a cab and opens the cab door for them.

"Thank you, James," Alex says.

"No problem at all, Mr. Van Rensselaer. I'm just doing my job," James the doorman says as he tips his hat.

"Say, could you have these three bags sent over to the Waldorf-Astoria at 301 Park Avenue? You can just have them be given to the doorman there, and I'll pick them up from the front desk on my way up," Alex says.

"Yes, I'll make sure Mr. Belvedere gets them, sir. He is a

friend of mine. You know how us doorman stick together, sir," James says.

"Yes, of course," Alex says as he and Wally climb into the rear of the cab.

"Fifty South Central Park, please. Take a right onto the Avenue of the Americas, if you would," Alex commands the taxi driver.

"We are only about ten minutes away, sir. That is not enough time to review our report," Wally advises.

"It will have to wait. Could you find anything on the Red or Green Societies on that computer of yours, Wally?" Alex asks.

"I can try. Let's see if I can get a connection first," Wally says as he is opening up his laptop.

"I've found the Red Hat Society, The Red Nation Society, and the Red Society. Nothing, sir. I'll try the Green Society. Again, I have found nothing, sir," Wally says.

"Try Asian Secret Societies," Alex says.

"Yes, sir. Wow, would you look at that? I found an article titled 'Asian Secret Society Challenges Illuminist,'" Wally reads.

"That's the one, Wally. Let's see what you've got," Alex says.

"Lets see. 'A spokesman who claims to be a member of a secret Asian society says that the group is determined to stop the implementation of plans for a very large-scale mass genocide by the secret world elites from around the planet. The spokesman says the Asian society is in particular targeting the American elite. He claims the society is composed of over one million gangsters and thousands of assassins. The Asian society believes the global elite have plans to depopulate the world and have attacked Asians by introducing the SARS virus into the Asian culture. The society claims to have ancient roots, and the last time they were active above ground was when they backed Chiang Kai-shek against the communist party of Mao Zedong.' The article claims they still use the oracle bone script of the Shang Dynasty, which represents the oldest forms of Chinese writing, in their initiation rites and even predates the Ming Dynasty. You don't think this is legitimate, do you, Alex?" Wally asks, looking up from the computer.

"I don't know for sure, but anything is possible, I guess," Alex answers.

"Does Mr. Rockefeller know that you are meeting with these people?"

"I'm sure he knows, but I haven't mentioned it to him. This whole thing doesn't add up. David must know that I've been in contact with the Green and the Red. He wants to speak to me about this land deal. I'm positive he knows they are here, but in what numbers?" Alex says.

"Your mother shared some information with you, sir? Do you wish to discuss it?" Wally asks.

"She mentioned a story about an old family heirloom," Alex says trying to change the subject.

"What is it—a book, sir?" Wally asks nonchalantly.

"No. The story is too fantastic to be believable," Alex says.

"Is it interesting, Alex?" Wally asks.

"Well, if you like fairytales. Remember the quill I mentioned earlier? Well, my mother says that back in 1615, a great-uncle of ours, Kiliaen, had traded a yet-unnamed ship for the quill to a pirate named Captain Enrique Brower," Alex says, continuing the story.

"Yes, sir, you had mentioned it earlier. An entire ship for a magic quill—he must have lost his marbles," Wally says.

"Well, apparently, the quill is described to have two parts.

The handle is said to be of pure gold about four inches long and has the two dodo feathers pushed through it. Of course you know the Dodo was last seen on the island of Madagascar. One of the feathers is four inches long and the other eight inches long. As the story goes, Captain Brower claimed he acquired the quill through trading with the Persian shah, Abbas I. The quill, as it was told to Kiliaen, was said to have been owned by Hermes Trismestigustus," Alex says.

"Not the writer of the *Corpus Hermetica?* That seems highly unlikely," Wally says.

"Yes, and even more unlikely was the fact that the ship that my great uncle traded, upon its completion in the 1640s, was named *The Flying Dutchman,*" Alex says.

"I've heard them all now. Your mother believes this story to be true, doesn't she?"

"Of course she does. The funny thing is, she thinks that David Rockefeller keeps the quill in his upper breast pocket."

"Why on earth would your grand-uncle trade a ship for a quill, even if it was magical? Any wise trader would have asked for proof," Wally says.

"Wally, you've heard of the Charter of Freedoms and Exemptions, haven't you?" Alex asks.

"Of course. That is the document written by the Dutch West India Company in an effort to settle its colonies of New Amsterdam in North America," Wally says.

"It also established the *patroon*ships here in America," Alex adds. "My mother claims our great-uncle Kiliaen Van Rensselaer used the quill to write that document and more."

"Unfortunately, that ended badly for your family, with the Anti-Rent Wars in the 1840s, sir," Wally says.

"Well, it was inevitable, with the Enlightenment and all. The Anti-Rent Wars lead to the abolitionist movement and eventually ended the slavery in the South. My mother says the quill came to America and, as she claims, was used in the signing of the Declaration of Independence, the New York State Constitution, the Jay Treaty, or the Treaty of London of 1794, as you Britons would know it, the Dongan Charter, the US Constitution, and many other documents," Alex says.

"Wow, that is a magic quill. And your mother says David now has this so-called quill today?" Wally asks.

"She did."

The cab pulls up to the front door of the Ritz-Carlton and gently stops curbside. The doorman of the hotel opens the door and says, "Any bags I can help you with, sirs?"

"No, just our bodies today, Michaels," Alex says, acknowledging the doorman.

"Oh, it's you, Mr. Van Rensselaer. Anything I can get you, sir?" Michaels says.

"Yes, directions to conference room 1A, if you would?" Alex asks.

"Straight down the hall. It will be on your left, sir," Michaels says.

"Thank you, Michaels," Alex says as he and Wally gather themselves on the sidewalk.

Alex knocks on the door labeled 1A and enters. Alex and Wally walk into the room, where they are greeted by three men.

"I'm Benjamin Fulford. I'm an interpreter for Mr. Yoshihiko Noda, the minister of finance for Japan, on your left," Ben says as all four men bow and Alex shakes hands with Mr. Noda.

"And this is Mr. Xie Xuren, the minister of finance of the People's Republic of China," Ben says.

The men take their seats around a majestic mahogany table. Wally says, "I was of the understanding we were to meet the leaders of the Green and the Red Societies in the matter of the Rockefeller Center property."

"Wally, these are the leaders of the Green and Red Societies," Alex says, correcting his secretary with a look that is discrediting.

"It's nice to meet you, Mr. Fulford. I can't quite place your accent, though," Alex says as he pulls in his chair.

"I'm originally from Ottawa, Canada, but I've been living abroad for about ten years now, mostly in Japan. I'm a former editor of *Investment Magazine.* I have recently been initiated into Mr. Noda's association. I've been asked to mediate and interpret on behalf of these gentlemen and the groups they represent," Ben says as he takes his chair in the center of the two groups.

"We are glad to be here in assistance with your property dealings with Mr. Rockefeller, but I must say, I'm not quite sure how I could be of any help to you," Alex says.

"The gentlemen are of the understanding that Columbia University was the original holder of the property in question and that you represent the regents," Ben says.

"Yes, that is true, but the Green and the Red currently own the property, and the university has no issue with their ownership," Alex says.

Mr. Noda, Mr. Xuren, and Mr. Fulford speak in Japanese for some time.

"Mr. Van Rensselaer, we are here today to discuss Mr. Rockefeller's request. We are of the understanding that it is Mr. Rockefeller's inclination to offer a substantial amount of money to repurchase the entire property," Ben says.

"Yes, that may be true, but I'm in no way representing Mr. Rockefeller in this deal, one way or another. I am here simply to approve of the final transaction," Alex says.

"Yes, these men here know that you have final approval of any deals involved with the land. I believe they wish to convey to you that they are not interested in selling any of their property at this time," Ben says.

"Well, there again, I am not part of Mr. Rockefeller's real estate team, and I have no idea of what his intentions are," Alex says.

The men speak together again in Japanese.

"The gentleman asks if you are to meet Mr. Rockefeller later today," Ben says.

"Well, yes, I am, in a very short time from now," Alex says.

"The gentlemen are asking if you would look favorably on them and if you could invite them as well to this meeting," Ben says.

"Well, yes, of course. I seem to be the monkey in the middle here. Let the gentlemen know I think it would be best if Mr. Rockefeller met directly with Mr. Noda and Mr. Xuren. Allow me to go ahead and meet with David first, and I'll call you to set up a time and place," Alex says.

"The gentlemen would also like to convey their wish to you. That is, it would be beneficial to them if you could decline the deal on behalf of the university so the men could save face. It would be most embarrassing to them if it looked like they refused any generous offers. They do have shareholders to answer to. The gentlemen feel that it could make them look bad if they were the ones to refuse the deal," Ben says.

"Yes, I understand their predicament. I'll keep the idea in mind, but you have to see it from my point of view. My family has been doing business with the Rockefellers for years. I just can't jeopardize any future relations with Mr. Rockefeller, and it could prove extremely detrimental to my interest," Alex says.

"We are sorry to put you in such a position, and we fully understand your point of view. In fact, these gentlemen have correctly predicted the situation," Ben says. "We will not be at the Ritz-Carlton for long. We will be moving over to the Sony Building in Rockefeller Center later this afternoon. You can reach me directly on my cell phone," Ben says, handing Alex a small business card with his number on it. "The men are looking forward to seeing some of their interest up close and personal, but they have suffered from a long flight, and they do have accommodations in that building for us. It would be generous of you if you would call before eight o'clock eastern standard time," Ben says.

"Yes, of course. I'll try my best," Alex says as he and Wally stand up. "I hope your stay in New York is a pleasant one. I'll be in contact with you as soon as I can," Alex says as all the men stand and bow toward each other.

Wally and Alex turn toward the door of the conference room and walk out into the hallway.

"I don't think that went very well," Wally says.

"We'll talk in the car, Wally," Alex says as he opens the door to the conference room.

The men move through the building quickly and out onto the front driveway.

"Mr. Michaels, a cab, please," Alex says.

The doorman quickly hails a cab. Wally and Alex open the doors together and climb in.

"Rockefeller Center, please," Alex says.

Chapter 35

"Before I was rudely interrupted, I was ..." David starts to say.

"Rudely interrupted? We just ran a guy over, for Christ's sake," Joey says.

"Ah yes, section 16. It is labeled 'Agents and Associates'. It seems to be in alphabetical order," David says. "'Benedict Arnold was an associate of the Van Rensselaers. They fought and captured Fort Ticonderoga together in 1775. Arnold also fought in the Battle of Saratoga in 1777 while he was under General Schuyler, until General Gates' arrival later that year,'" David reads.

"Screw that guy. I don't want to hear about no damn American traitors," Joey says.

"You're correct; he did try and surrender the fort at West Point to the British," Laurance argues.

"Yeah, yeah, I know. It's bad enough that I have to hear about Barack Obama and how bad our Congress is every day. Both the Democrats and Republicans, they are all traitors. Look, Benedict Arnold looks like a hero compared to our Congress of today. They started two illegal wars, all based on lies—now, that is what I call treason. I'm not saying Arnold was a good guy. I'm just saying you have a million Iraqis dead and God knows how many Afghanis. If I were the president, I'd end both wars. I would have the United States drop out of NATO and return all troops from Germany and Japan. Hell, I would also close all bases outside the United States and redeploy some of our troops to our southern border here in the United States," Joey says.

"I think that would hurt our economy and ruin any friendships we share with our allies," David says.

"That is bullshit," Joey says. "None of our allies backed the wars, not the people anyway—not the British people, the Canadians, the French, nobody. Bringing the troops home would have two economic positives. First, it eliminates the high cost of overseas installments. And second, all the economic strength of our troops stationed anywhere is highly valuable. In Hawaii, the army, marines, navy, and air force are responsible for over one-third of the local economy. That's all I'm saying," Joey says.

"Next up is Aaron Burr Senior. He was an associate of the Van Rensselaers. 'He was one of the founders of the College of New Jersey, later named Princeton. He attended Yale College with Johannas Van Rensselaer and obtained a B.A. in 1735. With the patronage of the Van Rensselaer family, he supervised the construction of Nassau Hall in 1756. He was elected president of the college at the age of thirty-two, the youngest person ever to serve as their president,'" David reads.

"'Aaron Burr Junior attended the College of New Jersey, later to be Princeton, while his father Aaron Burr Senior was serving as the president. Aaron Junior served with the Van Rensselaers during the fighting in Saratoga. Burr served under Benedict Arnold, George Washington, and General Israel Putnam during the Revolutionary War. After the war, he had to go to Albany to pass the bar exam, which was administered by one of the Van Rensselaers. In 1799, Burr started the Bank of Manhattan Company with the Van Rensselaers' backing, which in later years evolved into the Chase Manhattan Bank and later J. P. Morgan Chase,'" David reads.

"That is our J. P. Morgan Chase Bank," Laurance says. "He lived in New York City most of his life. We own the pistols that were used in his duel with Hamilton," Laurance says.

"You told us already. He's the guy that married that prostitute. I think she was some kind of succubus or something," Joey says. "I read that she had killed her first husband."

"Yes, her name was Eliza Jumel. She had an interesting life. After the battle of Waterloo, she offered Napoleon safe passage to New York, but he refused. Burr married her when he was seventy-seven years old. She is buried at the Trinity Church here in New York," Laurance says. "It is believed that she was the richest female in America at the time of her death."

"There must be some good money in the world's oldest profession," Joey says.

"I have a quote here from Mr. Burr: 'In the past, even I was afraid of my own greatness; therefore, I could not stand in front of mirrors,'" David reads with a smile.

"My God, egos don't come that big," Joey says. "Maybe he and that broad were meant for each other."

"'George Clinton, first governor of New York in 1777, was believed to be an agent of the Van Rensselaers. He was the fourth vice president serving under Thomas Jefferson as well. He was one of America's founding fathers and was close friends with George Washington, riding with him to the first inauguration, and gave Washington a dinner party to celebrate it afterward, in which three members of the Van Rensselaer family were in attendance,'" David reads.

"'Alexander Hamilton, as we already know, married into the Van Rensselaer family during the Revolutionary War. He started the Bank of New York with the backing of the Van Rensselaers. He married Elizabeth Schuyler, whose mom was Catherine Van Rensselaer. His duel with Aaron Burr was on July 11, 1804. He also was buried at the Trinity Churchyard Cemetery. Fifty-three years later, his wife Elizabeth would be buried next to him,'" David reads.

"'General Horatio Gates stayed at the Van Rensselaers' Fort Crailo home before he took over the command of General Schuyler on August 4, 1777,'" David reads.

"I heard he is buried at the Trinity Church in New York, but the location of his grave is unknown," Laurance says.

"We were just near there. Do you want to go back and look around?" Joey asks. "Maybe we can find the poor guy."

"That is not amusing, Joey," David says.

"'John Jay started his career in politics as the secretary to the New York committee of correspondence after being discovered by members of the Van Rensselaer faction,'" David reads.

"Great. What did this committee do to help the world?" Joey asks.

"It was a public committee set up by the conservative faction to protect property rights," Laurance answers.

"By conservative faction, you mean the rich landowners like the Van Rensselaers, who probably feared true democracy and the mob rule that comes with it," Joey says.

"'In 1764, John Jay graduated from Kings College. He practiced law with Robert Livingston. He was president of the Continental Congress from 1778 to 1779. He was chief justice of the United States from 1789 to 1795. Jay was also the governor of New York from 1795 to 1801. That is the same year that Stephen III became lieutenant governor,'" David reads.

"In 1799, John Jay signed into law the first anti-slavery

law in the state of New York, amongst a great many other things he did as governor," Laurance adds.

"As a Federalist, it sounds like his whole political career was backed by the Van Rensselaer family," Joey says.

"All the Van Rensselaers were Federalist, and they did back Jay and a number of other candidates as well," David says.

"'Robert Livingston 'the younger' went to Kings College and started his political career when the Van Rensselaers appointed him the recorder of New York City,'" David reads.

"The Freemason lodge's library where I'm a member is named after Robert Livingston. It was started 1782," Joey says.

"Yes, Joey, and in 1784, Robert Livingston was appointed grand master and served in that position for the next sixteen years," Laurence adds.

"'Many members of the Van Rensselaer family were present when Robert Livingston presided over the swearing-in of George Washington. The ceremony was the only time a president of the United States took the oath of office in New York City. The Bible that was used to administer the oath of office to President Washington is owned by St. John's Lodge No. 1. It is still used today when the grand master is sworn in and, by request, when a president of the United States is sworn in. He was born at Clermont Manor and built for himself Belvedere Manor. Both were burned down by the British Army in 1777. He was a member of the Committee of Five that drafted the Declaration of Independence. He was friends with John Jay and Alexander Hamilton, but later would change sides when he joined with George Clinton and Aaron Burr. He ran for governor of New York, but lost to John Jay in 1789. During his time as minister to France, he met Robert Fulton, with whom he developed the first steamboat, the *Clermont*. The *Clermont's* home port was

Clermont Manor. On her first voyage, she left New York City, stopped at Clermont Manor, and preceded to Albany to visit the Van Rensselaer estate, as they too were investors in the steamship. Both Livingston and Fulton became members of the Erie Canal Commission in1811 upon the approval of Stephen Van Rensselaer III,'" David reads.

"Well, weren't they all related, like cousins or something?" Joey asks.

"Yes, the Van Rensselaers were first or second cousins to most of the Livingstons, including Phillip Livingston, who graduated from Yale College in 1737. Philip was a member of the Committee of Sixty, Assembly of the Province of New York, Albany Congress, and Continental Congress. He also signed the Declaration of Independence in 1776," Laurance says.

"Hey, do you remember the story of the Collyer brothers?" Joey asks. "They were these eccentric brothers that lived together in a clusterfuck of a house over in Harlem. I guess they were hoarders of the worst kind. After their bodies were discovered, the city had come in and removed more than fifty tons of garbage from their house. I guess they lived like paupers, but as it ended up, they were really millionaires. Anyway, I heard that they were descended from the Livingston family."

"That was a very interesting story, Joey, and probably true. Our next subject is Gouverneur Morris. 'After leaving the US senate, Van Rensselaer had hired him to serve as chairman of the Erie Canal Commission. He also graduated from Kings College 1768. He was on the three-member commission that in 1811 redrew the street maps of New York City,'" David reads.

"'Robert Morris was known as the Black Prince for his ownership of many privateering ships. The Van Rensselaers had invested with him and were co-owners of many of the ships. On March 12, 1791, Robert Morris, along with the Van Rensselaers, contracted with Massachusetts to purchase what is now all of western New York, west of the Genesee River, for $333,333.33. Morris sold the Phelps and Gorham Purchases (in western New York) to the Van Rensselaer family, who were the said owners of the Holland Land Company in 1792 and 1793,'" David says.

"I've heard the Holland Land Company was a front for some rich bankers back in Holland. At the time, it was illegal for foreigners to own land in America, so the Van Rensselaers had set up the company to disguise the fact the real owners were from Europe," Joey says.

"That could be true, I suppose. Robert's son Thomas Morris met with the Seneca Indian chief Red Jacket, who was against selling the property, but Thomas freely distributed liquor and trinkets to the Indian women during their meetings. Red Jacket and Thomas eventually signed the Treaty of Big Tree, which granted the group all the land in the area."

"Were Gouverneur and Robert Morris related?" Joey asks.

"No, they were not," Laurance answers.

"I have an article here on Joseph Smith Junior. It says its origin is unknown," David continues. "'In the early spring of 1816, while the Smith family was migrating west from Vermont on their way to the Erie Canal, they moved south along an old Indian trail toward the Greenbush estate. In the early morning of April 19, they met a group of Indians that were friendly to the Rensselaerswyck estate. The young Joseph, being formally trained by his family in magic and sorcery, wowed the Indians with several tricks of deception. One of the Indians traveled quickly by horse to the manor, in which he described the amazing feats performed by the young child. Joseph, at the age of ten or eleven, wore a white top hat made of rabbit skins and used a cane to help him walk, due to a crippling bone infection. In the early afternoon, on the steps of the manor, the young Joseph was called in front of the *patroon* to show off his magical abilities. After a short presentation, the young man promised the *patroon* he could find buried treasure on the property if he were allowed to look. The *patroon,* being much amused by the young lad, had conveyed a staunch disregard for such theater. The *patroon* said to his mother, Lacy Mack Smith, "I'd like no better than to find a treasure here on my property, but I can assure you will not. Perhaps you will find your treasure at the other end of the canal. I think it would be best if you were on your way. A canal barge is leaving within two hours; it would be prudent if you and your family found yourselves on it. And as for the boy, perhaps you should start him in on some proper religion."

"'Mrs. Lacy Smith, with her poor hearing replied, "Start a religion? Why, that is a great idea. Thank you for your time, sir. Good day."'"

"That is an awfully far-fetched story," Joey says.

"Well, it is dated 1816. Who knows?" David says.

"There is no way," Joey says. "How can this Van Rensselaer family be involved in so much American history? I told you they should be called the boss of bosses, or maybe the *patroon* of *patroons.*"

"Okay, now on to section 17. Columbia College was formerly Kings College," David announces.

"Why is this important?" Joey asks.

"That is where Alex works, Joey. It may be favorable to review a little of its history," Laurance says.

"'Kings College was renamed Columbia College in 1784, after the British abandoned Manhattan. The college alumni, which were primarily loyalist, had left for Canada. After the war, the remaining board of governors of King's College petitioned Van Rensselaer and the New York legislature for a new charter. On May 1, 1784, Kings College became Columbia College. A board of regents was set up to oversee the administration, and it was the Van Rensselaers who placed Brockholst Livingston as its treasurer. The Van Rensselaers have been on the board of regents since that date in 1784 and up to the present. At the request of the regents, George Washington gave the first commencement speech at Columbia in the year 1790,'" David reads.

"No way, in 1790? Washington was still the president of our country at that time," Joey says. "So this family commanded that much respect, to just call the president of the United States and have him come on down and give a speech. That is incredible. It makes you wonder why one of their pictures isn't on the twenty-dollar bill, or why one of them didn't become president themselves," Joey says. "I know all these guys were responsible for our constitution and founded our country, but they screwed up in the way we elect our presidents. We should change our national election of the POTUS from the Electoral College to a direct election by the people. The people should demand it, and we should get rid of those electronic voting machines. It's just another way for the elite to steal and control our elections and keep the common man down," Joey says.

"You would use a paper ballot that could be double–checked, Joey?" Laurance asks.

"Of course. That is the only way. Our country should show leadership as a democratic society and stop being the laughingstock of the free world. Look at the 2000 and the 2004 elections. Our country's election was an embarrassment seen by the world," Joey says.

Chapter 36

THE CAB PULLS AWAY from the Ritz-Carlton. Wally quickly opens his laptop and brings it to life.

"Mr. Van Rensselaer, I must say this is beginning to look like some sort of setup. I mean, why would the Asians wish to go to the Sony Building so soon? They claim they are tired from their flight, but they are already at a hotel; why don't they just go up to their rooms right there?" Wally says.

"I agree, it doesn't add up. They could simply refuse Mr. Rockefeller's offer and go home. Why bother coming at all?" Alex says.

"I can drive around all day if you'd like me to," The cab driver says.

"I'm sorry. Could you take us to Rockefeller Center, please?" Alex asks as he ponders what lies ahead.

"Sure, no problem. That's only nine or ten blocks," the cab driver says.

"We are missing something, sir. Was there anything else your mother mentioned?" Wally asks.

"If you must know, she brought up your Book of Ages," Alex says.

"I've only heard stories about it," Wally says.

"I'm not familiar with it. Could you elaborate?" Alex asks.

"Now you're asking me to tell fairytales. Anyway, as the rumor goes, there is an ancient book written by the gods and owned by the devil himself. It is supposed to be twenty-six thousand years old. It's believed to be written in the Sumerian language. The master of this world reads from it daily and follows its directions. He uses it to control the world. It is said to be the complete history of the world starting from day one and ends on the date December 21, 2012," Wally says.

"The same date of the Mayan calendar?" Alex asks as he tries to act surprised.

"Yes, of course. Rumors say it is kept in the dungeon of a castle in Holland. I've also heard the P2 Masonic Lodge in Italy may have it. I've met some men at my lodge in London that claim they have actually seen it. They told me it was in the Black Castle or Dark Castle. I'm not sure where it is at, and I've never been to Holland myself. They tell me it is in the possession of a Mr. Rothschild," Wally says.

"You mean Nathan Rothschild, the London banker?" Alex asks.

"Yes. I don't think he is British per se, but related nonetheless. The book's purpose was to guide mankind through his quest in life. The strange thing is, the world doesn't seem complete, does it? I mean, why end the world now? Whatever mankind's ambitions are or whatever man's true destiny is, it seems to be incomplete. In fact, I've been told that there may be a second book. The first book, as I've been told, speaks of a second Book of Ages directly. The old Book of Ages says that the new Book of Ages is in the hands of the last *patroon* and that it starts on December 22, 2012," Wally says.

"Did it ever cross your mind that if a second book did exist, there would be powerful forces looking for it?" Alex asks.

"If I believed in such fairytales, one could come to the conclusion that the Prince of Darkness himself, certain world powers, and possibly the Church in Rome would spend every waking moment in pursuit of such a book, if it existed," Wally says.

"One could also deduce that all the powers of good would be working to keep such a manuscript hidden away from evil," Alex says.

"Sir, you called it a manuscript—why?" Wally asks as the drive through New York to meet Mr. Rockefeller takes the men through Midtown Manhattan, the heart of New York City and home to some of the tallest buildings in the world.

"I haven't been fully honest with you, Wally. I've seen the first Book of Ages. In fact, I've seen it and read from it at one time. It is written in old Sumerian. I haven't set eyes on it for years, probably thirty or forty years now," Alex says.

"My God, is it true? I mean, does it really exist? There has been kings and queens, armadas, and entire crusades looking for it since time has begun. In God's name, man, where is it?" Wally asks.

"It is hidden. It is hidden very well," Alex says. "Turn here if you could, please," Alex shouts at the driver.

"Radio City Music Hall is right here, if you like," the cabbie says, as traffic has completely stopped after they make the turn onto West Fiftieth Street.

"This will be fine. We'll get out here," Alex says while searching though his pockets for some money.

"I've got it, sir. You always have me carry around some petty cash," Wally says as the men exit the cab, still a block away from their destination at the GE Building, which lies at the heart of Rockefeller Center.

"If you do know where it is located, sir, it would be the

archeological find of the decade, of the century, of the history of the world for that matter," Wally says.

"We must get a move on, Wally," Alex says, hurrying down the sidewalk.

"Is it at the St. James Lodge, sir?" Wally asks.

"Now is not the time to discuss it, Wally," Alex says. "Try and concentrate on the meeting with Mr. Rockefeller. Can you remember, months ago, who asked to meet with us first? Was it David or the Asian societies?" Alex asks.

"I don't remember, sir, but I can check our day planner and see when I entered the events, once we stop and sit down somewhere. Is that fact important, sir?" Wally says.

"Of course it is important. It would at least let us know who this meeting is more important to, and that could give us the reason why the intended meeting is a fake," Alex says.

"I would assume it was Mr. Rockefeller's idea, just because he is the one interested in purchasing the property back. The Asians sounded as if they wanted nothing to do with the deal," Wally says as he hurries down the busy sidewalk.

"Never assume, Wally. We'll check it out inside."

Wally and Alex arrive at the GE Building and walk inside. They head directly to the information desk after checking in with security.

"I'm sorry, but Mr. Rockefeller has not checked into the building yet," the young woman at the information desk says. "Is he expecting you?" she asks.

"Yes, of course he is," Alex says, checking his watch.

"If you wait one minute, I can check with his private secretary. Your name, sir?" she asks.

"My name is Alex Van Rensselaer, my dear," Alex says.

"I'll be right with you, sir," she says.

"A Mr. Alex Van Rensselaer for David Rockefeller ... Yes, yes, I see, thank you," she says over her headset. "Mr. Rockefeller is en route, sir. I can prompt you upon his arrival. Just take this phone with you, and I'll ring when Mr. Rockefeller is available. Marguerite, his secretary, says it won't be long," she says.

"Thank you, my dear. We'll wait here in the lobby," Alex says, reaching and taking the private phone. He slips it into his pocket.

"Okay, Wally, we have been given some time to think. Let's check that day planner of ours," Alex says.

Chapter 37

J OEY TURNS THE LIMO right onto Fiftieth Street.

"If you turn left here, Joey, it will take us down to our private parking garage below the center," David says.

"Yes, sir," Joey says as he turns on the parking lights and turns the limo down into a series of circular ramps and into an extra-wide parking spot near a set of elevator doors.

"The Van Rensselaers did manage to get one of their men elected president back in 1837," Laurance says.

"Ah, yes, our eighth president, Martin Van Buren," David says. "He was elected in 1837 and took office in 1838."

"Do you know where the term *okay* comes from, Joey?" Laurance asks.

"Of course not. It's just a saying," Joey answers.

"During his bid for reelection in 1840, the term *OK* came to be popular; it stood for Old Kinderhook. Van Buren grew up speaking Dutch as his first language," Laurance says.

"I believe Kinderhook is on the Rensselaerswyck grounds," David says.

"Was he the first president from New York?" Joey asks as he puts the car in park and shuts the engine off.

"Yes, he was, and before he became the president, he had a long political career in Albany, New York," Laurance says.

"His ancestors came from Holland back in 1631. Along with many of the Van Rensselaers, he was a member of the Albany Regency, a group of politicians who for more than a generation dominated much of the politics of New York and the nation," David says.

"Besides being elected US senator from New York, he managed the presidential campaign for Andrew Jackson," Laurance says.

"Don't forget that Van Buren was elected governor of New York in 1828 and served as secretary of state in the Andrew Jackson cabinet," David says.

"And in 1831, he was appointed minister to the Court of St. James's," Laurance says.

"The Jackson-Van Buren ticket won the election by a landslide in 1832," David says.

"I didn't know you were a couple of Van Buren slappies," Joey says. "You need to get out more and away from those history books. You guys still don't know jack. Wouldn't you be better off studying the Asians that you're about to deal with?" Joey says as he gets out of the limo and moves toward the rear of the car.

"I have complete knowledge of the Asians, and I have Alex's personal dossier right here," David says, pointing to his skull as Joey opens his door.

David Rockefeller's cell phone rings. It is his private secretary calling from Rockefeller Center.

"Yes, yes, we're in the garage now, will be right up," David says and hangs up. Joey helps the older gentleman out of the car and onto his feet.

"Who didn't eat their hotdog? I could have sworn I only order four of them," Joey says.

"Just leave it there. We are going this way, young man," David says as he shuts the car door.

"What about Laurance?" Joey asks.

"He won't be coming with us," David says.

"We can't just leave him in the car," Joey says.

"He'll be fine," David says as the elevator doors open and the men enter.

"Press the lobby button, please, Joey," David says.

Chapter 38

"You were right, sir. Both meetings were scheduled on the same day, but it was the Asian societies who had first contacted us for the meeting at the Ritz-Carlton," Wally says.

"I thought as much. My mother was right—the Asians are up to something. Whatever happens, watch your back, Wally," Alex says.

"Do you think we have time to go over some more of the Rockefeller report, sir?" Wally asks as he opens the file.

"Sure, let's go for it. Whenever you're ready, Wally," Alex says.

The elevator doors open. David and Joey walk out and into the massive lobby floor. At once, all four men make eye contact. Wally closes his laptop as both he and Alex stand up. David looks horrified to see the men standing in the lobby.

"Mr. Rockefeller, how are you doing?" Alex says from a distance.

"Oh, you know better than that, Alex. Just call me David. This is my assistant, Joey Patroni," David says without any look of guilt.

"Joey, this is Mr. Alex Van Rensselaer," David says as the men shake hands. "You didn't have any problems crossing the Atlantic, I see."

"No, not at all. Should we have?" Alex asks.

"No, of course not. Let's just say I wasn't expecting you until tomorrow," David says.

"I'm Wally Niles, Alex's secretary," Wally says, introducing himself and shaking both David and Joey's hands.

"It seems we caught you in the middle of something. Would it be all right if we took this upstairs?" David asks.

"Yes, of course," Alex says as he turns and gives the phone back to the receptionist.

As the men walk back toward the elevator and get in, David says, "I hope you haven't been waiting too long for us. Push fifty-six, please."

"To be honest with you, we were just starting to go over your dossier, David," Alex says.

"Of course you were. It's the standard business practice that your grandfather started a long time ago. Would you care to entertain an old man? You wouldn't mind if I listen in on my own dossier, do you?" David asks as the elevator rushes them skyward. "I understand you've met with my Asian friends today?" David asks knowingly.

"They didn't seem too happy to be here in New York," Alex says.

"We'll get to that later. First, let's hear the report," David says.

The doors of the elevator open up into David's private office. On the walls hang many paintings: a Van Gogh here, a Monet there, and a few Rembrandts spread around.

"Please take a seat. Make yourselves comfortable. You too,

Joey. That couch there will be fine," David says as he takes a seat behind his desk. "I would offer you a drink, Alex, but as you know, I don't keep any around."

"That is all right. I have no need at the moment. Wally, go ahead and open the report."

"Would you like me to address Laurence's dossier, even though he is ..." Wally asks.

"Though he is what?" Joey asks.

"Don't tell me you have the boy believing in it too?" Alex asks David.

"Have me believing, in what?" Joey asks anxiously as he waits for an answer.

"I keep telling you, it's a matter of one's conscience," David says to Alex.

Wally begins the report. "Laurance Spelman Rockefeller was born May 26, 1910, deceased July 11, 2004."

"What did you say? Deceased July 11, 2004? No way. I've been talking to him all day. You guys are putting me on, right? Are you saying it wasn't real? That he wasn't real? I don't believe it. I'm a good Catholic. Are you guys playing tricks on me?" Joey says as he takes a long walk around the room. "I should have known. Back at Ground Zero, he didn't give the speech, and he climbed into the car so quickly—he'd be too old to ... he didn't eat the hot dog, his suit from the 80s ... I should have figured it out. I was talking to a ghost the whole time." Joey stares dumbfounded at David. "I believe in God, not ghosts."

"Like I said, it is a matter of conscience," David says.

"Go on, Wally," Alex says.

"'Laurance was a venture capitalist, financier, philanthropist, an important conservationist, and a third-generation member of the prominent Rockefeller family. He was born in New York City and graduated Princeton in 1932. He went to Harvard Law School for two years and concluded that he did not want to be a lawyer. Laurance married Mary French in 1934 and had three daughters and a son, Larry Junior. In 1937, he inherited his grandfather's seat on the New York Stock Exchange. He served as trustee of the Rockefeller Brothers Fund for forty-two years and was a trustee of the Rockefeller Family Fund for ten years,'" Wally reads.

"What's the difference? Their both tax shelters, another way the rich don't pay their fair share of taxes," Joey says sarcastically.

"'Laurance's Venrock Associates investment interest ranged across aerospace, electronics, high temperature physics, composite materials, optics, lasers, data processing, thermionics, instrumentation, and nuclear power and provided important funding for Intel and Apple Computer, amongst many start-up firms, including major health care companies. Laurance had a major interest in aviation. He became friends with Captain Rickenbacker after the First World War. Laurance learned to fly and found Rickenbacker's stories of a coming boom in commercial air travel to be convincing. Laurance became the largest shareholder in Eastern Airlines, after World War Two, as it became the most profitable commercial airline in the United States. He also funded the military contractor McDonnell Aircraft Corporation. Through his resort management company, Rockresorts Inc., Laurance opened environmentally friendly hotels at Caneel Bay in the Virgin Islands, Puerto Rico, the British Virgin Islands, and Hawaii. Another interest of Laurence's was the Lindisfarne Association, the think tank and retreat of William Irwin Thompson,'" Wally reads.

"I never heard of him," Joey says.

"He is a kind of teacher, dealing with social philosophy and culture," David says.

"I heard he was some kind of mystic, teaching some kind

of planetary consciousness or something to that effect. He was a crackpot, trust me," Alex says.

"So you believe in ghosts, at least in your own brother's ghost, and Laurance was some sort of whack job," Joe says.

"'Laurance had an interest in Buddhism and Asian cultural affairs, which included spiritual research. Lady Bird Johnson labeled him 'America's leading conservationist,' and he was a leader in the protection of wildlife. Laurance served on dozens of federal, state, and local commissions advising every president since Dwight D. Eisenhower on issues involving ecology, recreation, and wilderness preservation. He funded the expansion of Grand Teton National Park and was instrumental in enlarging parks in Wyoming and California. In 1992, Laurance and his wife Mary donated their Vermont summer home and farm to the National Park Service, which is dedicated to the history of conservation. His JY Ranch, which covers 1106 acres of Grand Teton National Park, was donated to the park and was accepted by Vice President Dick Cheney on behalf of the federal government. In 1993, after becoming interested in UFOs, he established the UFO disclosure initiative to the Clinton White House, asking for all UFO information held by the government, including the CIA and the air force,'" Wally reads.

"How did that work out for him?" Joey asks David.

"He didn't get very far. I think he was interested mainly in the Roswell incident. It shows that money and power can't buy you everything. I told him he was crazy at the time, but he didn't listen to me," David says.

"I think you're both crazy," Joey says as he sits back down on the couch. "And now you got me going crazy."

Chapter 39

"It's time we talk about our friends, the Green and the Red," Alex says to David.

"Not yet, Alex. We're not done," David says.

David stands up and begins his dossier on Alex from memory. "Mr. Alex Van Rensselaer was born December 5, 1941, a pre-war baby by a day or two. Alex was known to be a world traveler and playboy in his youth. He is known as a brilliant raconteur and possesses a great personal and social charm. He is man of the truest nobility of character and equally esteemed and admired for his elevation of mind and generosity of heart," David says.

"You are the spitting image of that king who abdicated the crown for the American woman. You know, the king just before Queen ElizabethII. What was his name?" Joey asks.

"He's right. You could be Edward VIII's twin brother. He was known as the Duke of Windsor. He was king for only 325 days, but was never crowned. The Duke of Windsor is actually Queen Elizabeth's uncle," Wally says.

David continues, "It has been said that if he had continued practicing his law profession, Alex would have had won a leading place among the lawyers of New York."

"That is my mother talking," Alex interrupts.

"Alex graduated top of his class at the Columbia Law School in 1962. A few years later, married one of his first cousins, in which there were many to choose from. His choice was Cornelia Rutsen Van Rensselaer of Waverly Place, whom he married in 1969. If the lordship of the manor had continued, Alex would have been the tenth lord of the manor, or the fourteenth *patroon,* as the Dutch prefer. Alex is a prominent member of many social and patriotic clubs, including the Holland Society, the Orange Club, and the River Club. Like his father and grandfather before him, he is the current president of the Federal Albany Savings Bank, the largest institution in the city of Albany. He is also president of the Savings Bank Association of New York State, president of the Albany Terminal Warehouse Company, vice president of the New York State National Bank, and the vice president of the Union Trust Company of Albany. Alex sits on the executive committee of the New York State Board of Regents and is the active president. I've recently heard you had an audience with Queen Elizabeth herself as early as yesterday. It must have been of some importance. Care to share with us, Alex?" David asks.

"No, I wouldn't," Alex answers.

"The Van Rensselaer family has been in the business of selling armaments to the federal government since the war of 1812 and probably before. It is said his wealth is in the millions, but yet his total net assets are unknown," David says, returning to the chair behind his desk.

"Bravo, David, you've done your homework," Alex says as he begins a slow pace as if he were in a courtroom. "Now it is my turn. David Rockefeller Senior is the current patriarch of the prominent Rockefeller family. He is the youngest and last surviving third-generation grandchild of oil tycoon John D. Rockefeller Senior, founder of the Standard Oil Company. David was born in New York City at 10 West Fifty-fourth Street, in a nine-story mansion owned by his father, John D. Rockefeller Junior. At the time, it was the largest private residence in the city. He spent much of his childhood at the vast family estate of Kykuit. His summer vacations were spent at Eyrie, a rambling 100-room mansion in Seal Harbor, Maine, that had a large retinue of servants, French tutors, and German governesses. David was educated at the experimental Lincoln School, where I remind him that the institution was set up by my grandfather for the children of the rich and spoiled," Alex says.

"Careful, Alex. Some respect is in order; after all, I am some twenty years your senior," David says with a smiling grin as he enjoys the attention.

"You are twenty-four years my senior, to be exact. In 1936, he graduated cum laude from Harvard University, doing his senior thesis on Fabian socialism. After he did a postgraduate year in economics at Harvard, he spent a year at the London School of Economics, where he met a young John F. Kennedy. I've heard rumors you actually dated his sister Kathleen for a while," Alex says.

"Careful, Alex, this is a business meeting, not one of your social calls," David warns.

"In 1940, he received his Ph.D. from the family-created University of Chicago. Though it is hard, I will refrain from stating the obvious," Alex says.

"You are an ass." David laughs heartily.

"His dissertation was entitled 'Unused Resources and Economic Waste.' David became secretary to the mayor of New York, Fiorello La Guardia, working for a dollar a year. I know that you were just one of sixty interns working there, so how did you manage to work out of the huge office of the deputy mayor?" Alex asks.

"It was vacant at the time. So I just took it," David answers.

"Oh, right, it would be conducive for a Rockefeller to just fill in if the office of president, pope, or perhaps king of

England would become vacant," Alex says, raising an eyebrow toward his victim. Alex prowls the room as if he were in front of the Supreme Court of the United States, showing his wherewithal and rhetorical abilities.

"I wouldn't want to go against you in any debate—or courtroom, for that matter, Alex. Perhaps your mother was onto something," David says, jabbing back.

"In 1943, David enlisted in the war effort and entered Officer Candidate School. He served in North Africa and France for military intelligence, of course, whereas David speaks French fluently and was promoted to captain in 1945. Isn't this where you learned the invaluable lesson of networking, David?" Alex asks.

"Yes, among other things, such as the standard operating procedures of investigating your business rival's family history," David says.

"We are not rivals today, but I see where you're going with that, and it will prove to be inconsequential," Alex says.

"You are good, Alex. If you ever need a job, you've got my number," David says, paying Alex a compliment.

"After the war, you returned to the family office, Room 5600, at Rockefeller Center, in which I now stand and speak. David became a major investor, with his brother Nelson, in over fifty start-up companies through the venture capital firm Venrock Associates. In the brothers' meetings held right here, David served as secretary to the group and has preserved all of his notes for posterity. I repeat, secretary to his brothers," Wally says.

"No need to repeat it—we heard you the first time," David says.

"In 1947, David was invited onto the board of the Carnegie Endowment for International Peace, with other spies like Alger Hiss and John Foster Dulles," Alex says.

"Let me remind you of something. Your father's boy Dwight D. Eisenhower was also on that board," David says.

"Yes, as was the president of IBM, Thomas J. Watson. David was appointed director of the dubious Council on Foreign Relations, the youngest director ever," Alex says.

"I object to the counsel's opinion, on the grounds that said counsel may be insane. And besides, the CFR was created to help war-torn Europe with American financial aid. We did formulate the Marshall Plan after the war, you know," David says.

"Although members of the Council on Foreign Relations have included members of presidential administrations from Harry S. Truman through to our current administration of Barack H. Obama, his detractors would state that he is the secret ruler of the world. What say you?" Alex asks David.

"I love that one, Alex. In my defense I offer that I am the secret ruler of only part of the world. Join with me, Alex, and we could rule the galaxy together." David laughs, recalling the *Star Wars* trilogy.

"David became the family's first and only banker in 1946, when he joined Chase National Bank, now known as J.P. Morgan Chase. Wasn't it your uncle Winthrop Aldrich who hired you?" Alex asks.

"Yes, he put me at the commodities desk trading coffee, sugar, and metals. I worked my way up and became president in 1960. I was chairman and chief executive of the bank from 1969 until 1980, when I was made CEO," David says in his defense.

"Not so hard when you are the largest individual shareholder the bank has ever seen. In 1960, it was your decision to build the headquarters of the bank at One Chase Manhattan Plaza on Liberty Street, was it not?" Alex says.

"It was. That project revived our city's downtown financial

district and, at sixty stories, was at the time the largest bank building in the world," David says.

"Yes, and with five stories underground, the largest bank vault then in existence. It is funny how your bank sits directly across from the Federal Reserve Bank of New York," Alex says.

"It's not funny—it is strategic," David offers.

"Is it also strategic that J.P. Morgan Chase, better known as The Rockefeller Bank's, biggest competitor is Citigroup, better known by its nickname the Oil Bank, by its association with the Standard Oil Empire?"

"Well, you got me there. Don't forget, together we helped set up the World Bank and the IMF," David reminds Alex.

"Oh, I haven't forgotten. Forgive me if I skip your associations with the likes of Henry Kissinger, Allen Dulles, and the whole crowd at the CIA. Wasn't it you, David, who set up room 3603, Rockefeller Center, to be the OSS command post liaison relating closely with British MI6, whose principal operating center was also in the center? Nor will I mention your lifelong friendship with CIA asset William Bundy, who instrumented the Iran coup of 1953, bringing the shah to power," Alex says.

"I thought you were going to skip that part," David says.

"Perhaps I should skip the facts that surround your extensive world travels in your private jet. That would include meeting a range of world leaders, including Fidel Castro, Nikita Khrushchev, Mikhail Gorbachev, and Saddam Hussein. Your personal friends include members of the Rothschild and Henry Ford families. Such relationships could be misconstrued, of course," Alex says as he paces back and forth in front of David's desk.

"That is equally not important. You can also skip the philanthropy, conservationism, and world class art collection I have obtained," David says.

"Yes, let's not get into your affiliation with the Bilderberg group or your famous Rolodex that contains over 150,000 entries of the most powerful people in the world," Alex says.

"Well, it's in the next room, if you'd like to see it," David says.

"No, it's okay. Just let me finish by saying I am sorry to here of your wife Margaret's death. I haven't seen you since before that unfortunate incident," Alex offers.

"Thank you, Alex. I hear your mother is doing fine. She was quite a looker back in her day," David says.

"And may I ask about your children and grandchildren?" Alex asks.

"Oh they're doing fine, just fine ..." David answers.

"Excuse me, I don't mean to be a bother, but we are here because the Asian societies have agreed to a meeting with Mr. Rockefeller, and I think it would be appropriate to consider our options, or lack of options in Mr. Van Rensselaer's case, on what to do," Wally says.

"It was just getting good, wasn't it, Wally?" David says.

"Okay, then, let's get this meeting started. David, I just left a meeting with the Asians, and I believe they are in no way going to agree to any terms. They plainly don't want to sell you back the property at any price. They contacted me as a way of saving face in this deal. They wish the terms of the deal not to be published," Alex starts off by saying.

"I may have to double my offer. I wouldn't consider any more than that," David says.

Chapter 40

David begins by saying, "Let me start with what I know of the Green and the Red Societies. My family has had a long relationship with them. Our dealings started out with them when they were an ultra-nationalist, right-wing group of Japan—that, of course, would be the Red, even though the groups may be hundreds of years older. Our goal was to support efforts to drive the Russian Empire out of East Asia and included a secret society in China, which would be the Green, of course. At the beginning, we pushed to eliminate the criminal elements of the two groups, because their memberships included cabinet ministers, high-ranking military officials, and professional secret agents. However, as time passed, we found it necessary to use the criminal activities to be a convenient 'means to an end' for many of their operations. We established and operated an espionage training school, from which we dispatched agents to gather intelligence on Russian activities in Russia, Manchuria, Korea, and China. We also pressured Japanese politicians to adopt a strong foreign policy after the war. We lent financial support to revolutionaries such as Sun Yat-sen and Emilio Aguinaldo. During the Russo-Japanese War and the annexation of Korea, the societies made use of their network for espionage, sabotage, and assassination. They organized guerrillas against the Russians from Chinese warlords and bandit chieftains in the region, the most important being Marshal Chang Tso-lin. The Chinese, in conjunction with the Japanese, spread disinformation and propaganda, waging a very successful psychological warfare campaign against the communists. Initially, we directed our efforts only against the Russians, but expanded our activities around the world in such places as Ethiopia, Turkey, Morocco, and South America."

"Have you ever directed any of the society's activities here in the United States?" Alex asks.

"Yes, during World War Two we sensationalized their activities with novels and short stories, connecting them with all sorts of nefarious criminal acts, so that the United States government could use this as an excuse to set up the internment camps during the war," David says.

"But aren't they friends of yours?" Joey asks.

"Well, yes and no. After the war, many of their members became prominent citizens with our financial help. In fact, those same families are in control today. In the 1970s, it was clear to us that the rest of the world was not treating the Asians fairly. So that is when we started the Trilateral Commission. We held the founding session of its executive committee in Tokyo in October of 1973. You see, the Asians felt they were being left out of world affairs," David says.

"David, how did the societies come to own part of Rockefeller Center?" Joey asks.

"Well, they were well aware of what was going on here in New York, with the United Nations and all, and they had demonstrated an interest to me about allowing them closer access to the U.N. The five buildings here at Rockefeller Center were the closest I could get them at the time, so we sold them—with your father's permission, of course, Alex—the same buildings they occupy now," David says.

"Is that the Mitsubishi Real Estate Group?" Wally asks.

"Yes, it is, but the deal was more than just a goodwill

gesture. It freed up a considerable amount of money for our family to invest in more lucrative investments," David says.

"Would it surprise you that the leading members of the groups are here now in New York?" Alex says.

"No, that tells me they are probably pissed off about something. I'm sure they want to meet with us," David says.

"They do, David. They're over at the Sony Building under the impression we are to meet together to negotiate your repurchase of their five buildings here at the center," Alex says.

"How did they want to set this meeting up?" David asks.

"They didn't say. They want for me to call them when your party is ready. Sometime tonight, I'm afraid," Alex says.

"I am my party. I don't need to confer with anyone else concerning this matter. Tell me, Alex: you've long known my intensions of reacquiring this property. Did the Asians contact you about it before I did?" David asks.

"Yes, as a matter of fact, they did," Alex answers.

"I should have guessed. Careful we must be. These guys are warriors when it comes to business. I'm afraid they may not be here for any kind of real estate deal," David says.

"I agree, David. Why do you think they are here?" Alex asks.

"They probably want to start a war with some third world country we've never heard of," David says.

"Do they need your approval, Mr. Rockefeller?" Wally asks.

"No, of course they don't. You go ahead and call them, and let's see where they want to meet with us. If they want us to meet them over in the Sony Building, tell them we would prefer a neutral site. Let's try and make it somewhere that we are familiar with. Let them know we can be there in less than an hour, Alex," David says.

Alex pulls his cell phone from his jacket and dials Mr. Ben Fulford.

Chapter 41

THE HAND-HELD CELLULAR BEN Fulford is holding rings. It is Alex Van Rensselaer.

"Good evening, Benjamin. It is Alex Van Rensselaer. I'm over at the GE Building with Mr. Rockefeller now. David and I wish to invite you and your group over to the fifty-sixth floor. We are willing to negotiate the deal tonight, just like you asked," Alex says.

"That is great, Alex. I've talked it over with Mr. Noda and Mr. Xuren, and they would feel most comfortable negotiating the deal over here at the Sony Building," Ben says.

"How would you feel if I offered a neutral site—let's say Columbia University?" Alex asks.

"Wait just a moment," Ben says as he confers with the leaders of the Green and the Red Societies. "That will be fine, Alex. Where exactly on campus would you like to meet?" Ben asks nervously.

"We can meet you at the front steps leading to the Low Memorial Library. It is a very public place, and the library will still be open for another two hours. The building is on West 116th Street between Amsterdam Avenue and Broadway," Alex says.

"Yes, we are good with that. Just give us an hour or so to meet you there," Ben says.

"Okay, great. Let's say seven o'clock, then," Alex says as he hangs up the phone and looks down at his watch. "Columbia University is perfect, David. It has an extensive underground tunnel system that was built more than a century ago. Though some of the tunnels are open to the students so they can walk from building to building, most are closed, I know it very well. As regent, I have a code key that allows me total access," Alex says.

"I thought you might," David says.

"I have to let you know something, David," Alex says. "I've got a good notion that the Green and the Red have brought with them a team of specialist bodyguards, and perhaps assassins," Alex says.

"Your mother informed you, I suppose. How many does she think?" David asks.

"I've heard twenty-five men, maybe thirty altogether," Alex says.

"That makes sense. They usually work in five-man teams. I have a security team of my own," David says as he glances over in Joey's direction.

"Don't look at me. I'm just one man," Joey says.

"Joey take this. It might come in handy," David says as he pulls a revolver from his desk drawer and hands it to him. "Wally, you no doubt have some military training. There is another revolver over there in the cabinet drawer, if you would, please," David says as he points across the room.

"Yes, of course, I spent three years in Her Majesty's service," Wally says nervously, making his way to the cabinet.

"I don't keep the guns loaded, of course. There are some bullets in there as well," David says as Joey walks over next to Wally. Both men load the chambers of their guns and place the small-caliber weapons in the rear of their pants and in the crooks of their backs.

"Really, David, do you think that will be necessary?" Alex asks.

"Let's hope not," David answers.

"I feel like a gangster from the 1950s," Joey says.

"Yes, very James Bondish," Wally adds.

Alex, Wally, David, and Joey move toward the elevator and get in.

"We really should get there as soon as possible," Alex says.

"I have an SUV parked down in the garage that should get us there safely. It is bulletproof. I have friends in the NYPD. I'll give them a call. We'll park it out front of the Low Memorial Library building, and I'll have the police keep an eye on it while we are inside," David says.

"I think you are being a bit overdramatic," Alex says.

"Better safe than sorry, I always say," Joey says.

"I'll have them place a few men around the campus as well. Here are the keys, Joey. You're driving," David says as he reaches into his pocket and hands Joey the keys.

"I'm in charge of security for Mr. Rockefeller, and I agree—we should take every precaution," Joey says.

The elevator doors open onto the LL3 level, and all four men walk out.

"It's right over here. Follow me," David says.

Joey pushes the unlock button on the GMC Denali keychain. The lights flash, and the horn toots on the SUV briefly as the doors unlock. Wally gets in the passenger side front seat as Alex climbs in directly behind him. Joey opens the rear door for David directly behind the driver.

"Driving you guys around is a heavy burden I don't like to bear. You know, I've got my own dreams of being rich. I'd like someone to chauffer me around once," Joey says.

"Is that right? What is your big idea that's going to make you rich?" Alex asks.

"Well, I got a million of them. Here's one; tell me what you think. Okay, so you guys know I have twin daughters, right?" Joey says as he backs the SUV from its parking spot.

"So you think your daughters may be your golden ticket?" Alex asks.

"No, just listen. I have this idea for a reality television show. It goes like this. It's a finishing school for girls. My girls they are only fourteen and are being raised by my ex, and she is not doing a very good job, so I think they will need to go to a finishing school for girls. I think it would make a great reality show. I was thinking of calling it *Zsa Zsa Gabor's Finishing School.* She would be the star and be like a headmaster or a drill sergeant. She would be like a Nazi or something. She could use a cane or stick to straighten the girls out. It would have eight to ten girls, where at the end of the series, Zsa Zsa would get them prepared for a ball or to meet the president or members of royalty. I think she is some kind of aristocrat or something herself," Joey says.

The back seat erupts with laughter.

"That is a ridiculous idea. That would never fare well in Britain," Wally says.

"I think it's a good idea. I just need someone like Donald J. Trump to present it," Joey says as he drives the SUV forward.

The laughter gets louder as Joey takes the SUV up the circular ramp.

"Good luck with that, Joey. You're a regular raconteur," Alex says.

"I've got another one for you. I always dreamed of being a country music singer. I have written a few songs," Joey says.

"You're an Italian from Brooklyn, right?" David asks.

"Yes, so, what about it?" Joey answers with his heavy New York accent.

"I can't see a short Italian from Brooklyn singing country songs," David laughs.

"What's wrong with that? Just listen," Joey says, clearing his throat. "Now, just think more like Jimmy Buffet than Clint Black, and no laughing. It's almost Hawaiian-sounding–like, with light strumming of a guitar," Joey says.

> "I woke up one morning,
> and I said, 'Aloha, Mom,
> the time has come
> for me to go to the big, big city.
>
> 'I've got my kayak stacked;
> it's parked out back.
>
> I've got the warm summer breeze,
> and dreams that please to keep me at ease.
>
> 'It'll take me three long days,
> but I need a job that pays.
>
> 'I'll use my kayak some,
> and I'll drift in the sun.
>
> 'Until I make it there,
> Momma, don't be scared,'"

Joey sings.

"And this is where the female voice comes in," Joey says.

> "Oh my son, do not forget your banjo, baby,
> and take your ukulele.
> You'll find a pretty wahina lady,
> and you can use your guitar as an oar."

Joey stops singing because of the laughter from the back seat.

"What are you laughing at, Wally? At least my name isn't Wally," Joey says.

Joey continues singing:

> "I'll be back in time,
> to enjoy the sweet sunshine.

Ah, fuck you guys. I'd like to see you do better," Joey says.

"It'll be in the top fifty in no time," Alex laughs.

"Only not on the big island—more like a very small island no one ever heard of," Wally laughs.

Joey stops and looks both ways before pulling out onto the darkening streets of New York. Making a right on Forty-ninth Street, exiting the south side of the garage, the SUV slows to a halt directly behind one of New York's finest.

"I'd like to get there before our Asian friends, if at all possible," Alex says.

"What in the fuck do these cops think they're doing blocking the road?" Joey shouts.

"Easy, Joey, they are our escorts. Alex, how fast would you like to get there?" David asks as he presses his cell phone to his left ear.

"Well, I've heard the rumor that we might encounter some extra company associated with the Asian societies. I would like to look around a bit before they arrive, if we could," Alex says as he reaches for his seatbelt.

"Captain Wilson, we are ready for your escort. We are headed to the Low Memorial Library on the campus of Columbia University," David speaks to his cell phone.

On Captain Wilson's command, an army of police officers jump into action, he being in authority over some thirty police cruisers and over fifty officers on foot. They move as if in combat mode. Quickly, the city's police react as if in extreme emergency conditions. As sirens blare, all roads are blocked from entering Broadway, and all the cars on the road are immediately stopped and pulled over.

Captain Wilson has commanded some of his plainclothes officers to take up books in their hands and scour the Columbia University campus for Asian agents disguised as students. The only problem is that Columbia University has a total population of fifteen hundred Asian students enrolled there, a small fact that gives an advantage to the secret societies.

"Follow the little red siren in front of us, Joey," David says.

Joey punches the gas pedal to the floor to keep up with the police cruiser. Making a right onto Broadway, the SUV leans upon the two left wheels, wanting to roll.

"Hold on, baby. She's a heavy son of a bitch. This is the first time a Patroni has gotten to chase a cop car, if you know what I mean. This is the fastest truck I have ever been in, God bless Detroit. I think I can pass him," Joey says, laughing.

"Take it easy. This isn't NASCAR. Just get us there, please. I did have it custom-built at the General Motors Truck and Bus Validation Center," David says as Wally and Alex begin to turn white.

"Trust me, it is validated," Joey screams as he races the GMC Denali through red light after red light.

Chapter 42

Joey suddenly slams on the brakes, and the SUV comes to a complete halt in the middle of Broadway and West Seventy-second Street.

"What on earth are you doing? Get going, you idiot," David yells at Joey for stopping the truck.

"I just had a thought. You know, I've always ranked wisdom higher than money. Why is it that we don't use our knowledge of history to help direct mankind's future, anyway? It should be used like a crystal ball to see and change the future. Not to see the future, but to affect the future. You know, to make it better. You guys right here, Mr. Van Rensselaer and David Rockefeller, you can use your money and power to make the future a better place for mankind, but you refuse to do it. Why?" Joey says, looking over his shoulder.

"You don't believe in destiny Joey—you know, where the future may be predetermined?" David asks.

"No, of course not. I mean, look, you had all these prophets like Daniel, Isaiah, Nostradamus, and John from the book of Revelations. None of them predicted airplanes, television, electricity, the Internet, or even automobiles," Joey says. "If they couldn't foresee electricity coming, then all books on prophecies are garbage," Joey says. "What we need to be doing is investigating our true past, and not the revisionist history as it is written in some of our books.

"Look at all corruption we have in Washington and New York. Our founding fathers are rolling in their graves. Let me tell you, God will smite us in the end. Whatever happened to free will?" Joey asks. "I've got it. I will be the one to change things, right here and right now. I'll show you some free will," Joey says as he spins the steering wheel counter-clockwise and floors the gas pedal, launching the SUV west down West Seventy-second Street and through a police roadblock.

"Where in hell are you going?" Wally shouts.

"If the people knew of the crooked way the Federal Reserve came into power, we would have a second revolution tomorrow. We should eliminate the Federal Reserve Bank, the Central Intelligence Agency, and another dozen of the alphabet agencies. The power of the government should be given back to the people. I think most of the politicians are there to protect the interest of the rich anyway," Joey says as he keeps the accelerator pressed to the floor.

The SUV swerves to the right and onto New York's Westside Highway, heading north. Joey hits the power locks on all four doors as the truck heads down the highway.

"I'm taking control of our destiny. I'm going to drive us off the George Washington Bridge," Joey says.

"What in God's name has gotten into you? Have you lost your mind?" Alex asks.

"I'm making the same sacrifice that our forefathers made. I'm not talking about all the rich landowners like George Washington or the *patroons,* but for the little guys, the everyday people like the ones that served our country under Washington. Do you know how many patriots died at Valley Forge, not from being attacked by the British, but from the cold and lack of food and support from others? Or when, after we won the war, the army officers rebelled afterward in Newburgh because they didn't get paid? Nothing has changed in this world. The poor sacrifice for the rich landowners every day, year after year. Since you guys can't find it in your hearts to change, it's time we all meet our maker," Joey says as the SUV passes the West Seventy-eighth Street exit, reaching eighty-five miles per hour.

"My God, man, come to your senses. They trained you in the army to do the right thing. Think of your future," Wally says.

"Future? I have no future! I've suffered with PTSDs and a bad back for years because of my time spent in the army. And the army has hardly done shit for me or any of my sick soldier friends," Joey says.

"That just proves that the time you have spent overseas has made you crazy," David says as he holds on.

"No. I have been crazy since I was a kid. It's people in power like you that make us all crazy. I remember as a kid, we were forced to watch *Willy Wonka and the Chocolate Factory.* The whole movie is a psychological operation meant to scare the hell out of kids and keep them in line. I mean, what kind of kids' movie shows the head of a live chicken being cut off right in the middle of it?" Joey asks. "It's still happening today. Even our president, he was never on the side of the people who elected him. All of our elected officials are in the pockets of the rich."

"I remember that scene. It happened when Willy Wonka took the group into the tunnel," Wally says.

"The only future Americans have is indebtedness to the banksters. The Federal Reserve and our politicians have made sure the future of mankind will be enslaved forever. The only true source of war is politics. I'm still not buying that fact the first American Revolution was fought for the right reasons. The founding fathers had some good ideas, but they set things up for just the rich, landowning, white folks of our country. I mean, fuck the landless peasant class. I read a quote from that John Jay the other day; he said something to the effect of, 'The people who own the country should run it.' Do you think that is right? You treat the working class as if you want to return to serfdom and the dark ages. We all live in this country. Whatever happened to 'We the people,' 'by the people and for the people?' The White House and Congress are just subsidiaries of the rich and powerful. We need to reinstate the Glass-Steagall Act to protect the people's savings from the vultures on Wall Street. You know, the Van Rensselaers may have been the old masters of New York, and you Rockefellers may be the current masters of New York, but it will be us common people that will be the future masters of New York, and we will take back this great country of ours that we built. Its greatness came from the hard labors and sacrifice of the people, and not from your money and the thieves on Wall Street," Joey says as his eyes glaze over, showing no fear whatsoever.

"Please slow down, Joey. You don't want to do this. Have you gone mad, Joey? What, may I ask, have you ever sacrificed?" David asks as the SUV passes along the west bank of the Hudson River, reaching ninety miles per hour, and as the George Washington Bridge comes into full view.

"The biggest thing I learned in the military was how to sacrifice for others. All of us veterans sacrificed for each other daily. We put our lives on the line for our country, and I personally sacrificed for my family. Let me tell you a story. Right after basic training, I received custody of my twin daughters. The army flew them out to my first duty station, where I raised them on my own as a single parent," Joey says.

"You don't have them now?" David asks.

"No, I don't. I lost custody of them when I got deployed to Iraq. I'm still mad about it because as it turns out, I'm not fighting for my country, but for some mega-giant corporate oil companies. When I got back, I did not even receive a thank you note, nothing. Look, I know life isn't all bunnies and rainbows, but it could be—hell, it should be," Joey says.

"We know it must have been tough not having any contact with your daughters while you were deployed, but killing us is just plain crazy," David says as he holds on for dear life.

"How did you know that?" Joey asks. "I've never brought that up."

"Well, I read it in your report, Joey, so it must be true. Just remember, what doesn't kill you makes you stronger. You need to be stronger for your children's sake," David says as the SUV speedometer reaches the hundred-mile-per-hour mark.

"Think of what your daughters' future would be like without you. Who is going to help them through school and the tough times in life? You are a strong man, and certainly stronger than this," Wally says.

That hits Joey pretty deep. Joey lets off the gas and quickly slows the vehicle down. Tears roll down his cheeks.

"I'm not looking for any pity ... Just a good-paying job would be nice. I just want to make enough to buy my daughters the braces they need," Joey says as he lets out a soft whimper. "I have a confession to make. Back in Iraq, I killed an innocent Chaldean family. It was my job to guard our Humvee while a team kicked in the front door of a house. We suspected they were hiding weapons in there. A guy appeared in the upstairs window caring an AK-47. I didn't have time to think—I just fired my AT4 at him on instinct. The rocket glanced off the man's chest and exploded in the back room of the house, killing one of our own men and an entire innocent family," Joey says as he cries out loud, remembering the experience vividly. "God will not forgive me. I have no chance of going to heaven now. I'm a sinner. I'm a baby-killer."

"Don't lose your faith, Joey. Perhaps God has bigger plans for you," Alex says. "God never gives anyone more than they can handle," Alex says.

"Sometimes our duties and responsibilities are tied to the social class in which we were born. Is it that bad, being a member of the working class?" David asks.

"Of course it is. You know, people are still willing to work to make a living, and I'm surprised at that. To help the working class, we need to raise tariffs to protect American jobs. I'll tell you why it doesn't happen. It's because it's not in the best interest of the rich globalist like you. When I say interest, I mean money. It's people like you that push for deals like NAFTA and CAFTA that gave all our jobs away. We've been working like dogs for years. The real labor movement has been brutally suppressed in the United States. Did you know the average amount of annual vacation days in Finland is forty-four days? In Italy, it is forty-two days a year, and here in America, it is twelve days a year. Before I joined the army, I never received a vacation day for any job I've ever worked at. It is insane," Joey says.

"Do you think the people are better off in Europe?" Alex asks.

"Yes, I do. Getting a higher education here puts people back about a hundred grand and in debt for years. In Europe and the rest of the world, higher education is either free or highly subsidized. The people are tired of getting Jim Joyced all the time," Joey says.

"Who is Jim Joyce?" Wally asks as he grips the overhead door handles.

"He was that idiot first base umpire who blew the perfect game for the Detroit Tigers' Armando Galarraga. The umpire put himself above the game. I understand a bad call here or there, but it should never have happened when history is on the line. It was unforgivable and the worst call in the history of baseball. The man obviously had his head up his ass. It was as if he gave the middle finger to the fans, the players, the coaches, and all of sports in general. After that call, I've decided to boycott all sports. I won't even watch on television anymore, until I get a personal apology from that jerk himself. It is the same feeling everybody has toward our government," Joey says as he wipes away a tear.

"Look at all this traffic. Now we'll be stuck here for another half hour. Take the next exit at West 158th Street," David says.

"If you feel that passionate about it, you could always run for office, Joey," David says.

"Run for office and be beholden to someone of the likes of you? It takes a lot of money to win a small-time position. The only opinion a politician has is the one that corporate interests tell them to have. That lacks any form of a conscience or belief system," Joey says.

"How would you change things, Joey?" David asks.

"First, the people should petition the Congress to adopt a new amendment to the Constitution," Joey says.

"Asking for what?" David asks.

"It should be declared that no federal employee could have or ever have had a dual citizenship. I mean from the office of the president down to the newest mail clerk hiring, with no grandfather clauses," Joey says.

"Well what would that do?" David asks.

"It would keep out anyone that does not have the interest of the American people first. Our country should be the country that our forefathers built and the rest of our generations have helped make great," Joey answers.

"That sounds like a pretty big task," David says.

"Well, that's not all I would do. I think we should end the tax on labor. Our tax code treats labor as assets in a ledger, as if we were cattle or sheep," Joey says as he begins to move through traffic.

"I don't quite understand what you mean," David asks.

"I already think it is unconstitutional to tax labor, but I see it like this. There should be a tax on profits, not labor, because it is unfair in an exchange of goods and services. If you ask me to build you a wooden deck for your house, and you are willing to pay me three hundred dollars for my labor, and I say that will take three hours of my time to complete, then my labor is equal to one hundred dollars an hour," Joey says.

"I still don't understand. You just made three hundred dollars that can and will be taxed," David says.

"It's like this. You just received three hundred dollars in labor, and I received three hundred dollars in cash. That is considered a fair and equal exchange of goods and services. So does the government tax you for your deck? No, of course not, so why should I pay thirty percent for my labor? It's bad for business, especially for the working class," Joey explains. "You see, profit is an unfair exchange of goods and services, and so it should be taxed."

"If we work at it together, I'm sure we could make our country a better place," David says.

"True change needs to start with people like you, with money. You should stop interfering in Washington. The government is meant for everybody, not just the rich. We should force our government to stop the Keynesian economic theory. One would think that the government of the United States would have the world's largest savings account, but it doesn't. It is the world's number one debtor nation. And besides, the Bible says usury is a sin. It is a system to keep the people bound and chained. Usury is slavery; the people just now are starting to see it," Joey says as they move along.

"I can't agree with that. There is no slavery in America,"

David says. "And America is still the greatest country to ever exist."

"Bullshit. We, the people, are economic slaves to the system, and so are our children and our grandchildren," Joey says. "Our country can do better. We used to be the envy of the world, and we can be again."

"How is it that usury is slavery?" David asks.

"It's like this. If I borrow a hundred dollars from a bank, I might owe them a hundred and five. The only way for me to create the extra five dollars is to work for it. So I just spent some of my time working for free. So it is simple. Interest equals free labor, and free labor equals slavery. With the government running up high debts to be paid from the taxes of the working class, it is the working class that is working to pay the interest on the national debt," Joey says.

Joey rushes down the West 158th exit ramp and slows the SUV down in order to make the hairpin turn onto West 158th Street.

"Do you feel better now that you got that off your chest?" David asks.

"Yes, thanks for listening. I get like that once in a while," Joey says.

"We're almost there. I'll take Edward Morgan Place back to Broadway and ..." Joey says.

"Look out for that horse and carriage!" Alex shouts.

"What in the hell does this Amish guy think he's doing in New York City?" Joey asks.

"He's not Amish. He's one of the carriage drivers on his way to Central Park," David says.

"Oh, yeah, right. I'll go around him. Speaking of the Amish, there is a group of people who know how to live right. I mean, look, they all get together a build a house or barn in a couple of weeks, and bam, they're done. Not us idiots—we take out thirty-year mortgages and work half our lives paying interest on a damn house. It's ignorance at its best, but the people don't have a choice," Joey says.

"America is not so bad. I think the people in Britain have it even worse," Alex says.

"It's not so bad if you're rich. We could always do better. We are Americans, damn it. We need to stop 'K Street' governance and bring governance back to the people. Why can't we run a simulation on the Internet where the people write their own laws and are invited to vote on them, including the spending? Right now, we have a do-nothing Congress. The members of Congress are all about stealing as much from the trough for themselves as possible," Joey says.

"You must love the new Obamacare plan?" David asks.

"Mandating health insurance is the same as back in the seventies when the states passed laws mandating auto insurance. The insurance companies lobbied hard for it and became rich from it. America should never force any citizen to buy goods and services of any kind, including military defense," Joey says.

"What in the world are you saying?" David says.

"Listen, I've been to Iraq and all kinds of places in the world, and people and generally all the same. They are good loving, good natured, and live by the creed 'Do unto others as they would do onto you,'" Joey answers.

"Joey, there are evil people out there that can and will do evil things to you," David says.

"Yes, and you're one of them. That is why I carry a gun, and that is why we have police forces. There is no need for standing armies anywhere in the world."

"I disagree, and I think you are a loon," David says.

"You are one of those paranoid freaks that think with the R-complex part of your brain," Joey says.

"What do you mean by that?" David asks.

"Well, that is the oldest part of the brain, the part that thinks in terms of survival—you know, to run or to stop and fight. All of our psychopathic world leaders think the same way. Men who think without compassion are the evil ones," Joey says.

"So you think America should just give all of our military secrets away to the enemy?" David asks.

"No, that is not what I said. What I'm saying is there is no need for secrets, period. We are all humans. I think everyone, rich and poor, should be for the advancement of the human race," Joey says.

"Well, we can't advance until we end our differences," David says.

"I agree one hundred percent. Now you're with me. If we were to let the world know of all our weapons capabilities, war production would stop by tomorrow," Joey says.

"I don't quite follow, Joey," David says.

"The world would be scared shitless, including our own population and our allies," Joey says.

"So you don't think the government works right now? You do have the right to vote, you know," David says.

"Here, I'll give you an example. While George W. Bush was in office, he had the chance to outlaw subliminal messages broadcast on the television and the Internet, and he voted it down. What in the fuck was he thinking? You think secret mind tricks to keep the public in the dark and have them buying shit they don't need is okay? I guess it is okay to have men think with their dicks instead of their brains or have women think it is okay to destroy the family way of life," Joey says.

"Can I ask who you voted for in the last election?" David asks.

"You mean for president? I've only voted twice for president. The first was Ross Perot, and the second, I was going to vote for Ron Paul, but he wasn't on the ballot, so I voted for the Libertarian ticket straight across the board," Joey answers.

"A revolution cannot be the only answer," David says.

"You can quote me for saying this: 'There never ever has been any change to the improvement of the human condition without blood being spilt,'" Joey says.

"You wouldn't be advocating violence, now, Joey?" David says.

"I'll give you another example. In 1848, a revolution spread over Europe, and in Italy, the people started their protest of Austrian rule by stopping playing the lottery, and the people stopped smoking tobacco products, and where did that get them? Nowhere," Joey says.

"Is that true?" David asks.

"Of course it's true. The people stopped buying lottery tickets, and the reactionaries attacked and killed the people for being unruly," Joey says.

"What's a reactionary?" Wally asks.

"You never heard of the Congress of Vienna?" Joey asks. "Well, right after the French Revolution, members of European royalty—kings, princes, archdukes, and the like—went to a meeting set up by their host, Austrian emperor Francis I. It was ten days of concerts, balls, feasts, fireworks, and hunting parties. They were the representatives of all the states that had fought against Napoleon. The reason they got to together was to restore any legitimate monarch to their throne who would preserve the status quo. The leader of the congress was Prince Klemens Von Metternich; it was his idea to use the principle of legitimacy. In general, they agreed if there were to be any uprising of any kind in any country by the people, they would help each other and crush any and all revolutions by the people. It feels like that agreement is still in effect today. I think the guy was the true anti-Christ," Joey says.

"How can you think of such nonsense, Joey? The people of America are nowhere near starting a second revolution," David says.

"I don't think you know the temperament of the people. It's a lot closer than you think. It's guys like you who hire the likes of Henry Kissinger," Joey says. "It's all about control. Did you know that in Kissinger's doctoral thesis, he wrote about Prince Metternich, like the guy was his hero or something?" Joey says.

"We don't have an interest in controlling the people. We just want to preserve our interest," David says.

"You are out of touch. If it takes a second revolution, then so be it. It may come to that," Joey says.

"Joey, you would make a great politician," Alex says.

"Yes, a real Churchill," Wally cracks.

Chapter 43

Joey pulls the black SUV over to the curb and stops directly in front of the Low Memorial Library. Just then, a white Honda Pilot pulls nose-to-nose with their SUV. It is the Asian society, along with their interpreter, Ben Fulford. There are police and students everywhere as daytime turns to dusk. The semi-warm fall day has turned cool and breezy.

"My friends from the orient are surprised by your lack of trust in them. Is this much police protection necessary?" Ben asks as he steps up onto the sidewalk.

"It wouldn't be necessary if we didn't have such an influx of your Ming Dynasty guards in the New York area this week," David says as the men stop on the stairway leading to the library.

"We will call off our warriors, if you call off your wars," Ben interprets after listening to Noda.

"And what wars would he be referring to?" David asks as he turns and proceeds up the stairs.

Ben starts without interpreting Xuren's words. "Your wars of aggression in the Middle East and the financial wars you've started in the Far East. We know that America's economy and the whole of the West's economy are based on war and military spending. We demand that it come to an end. That is why we are here," Ben says.

"I was under the impression that we were here to negotiate the property in Midtown, the five buildings that remain in their portfolio," David says, reaching the top of the stairs just outside the library.

Ben turns to Xuren and Noda and speaks in Japanese. Both men agree on what to say next.

"You can have the buildings for nothing and all of our assets here in the United States if you agree to our terms," Ben says as all the men gather at the top of the stairs outside of the library.

"That is a generous offer from those who speak without knowledge and authority," David says as he motions to Joey to open the doors to the library.

Joey opens the door as Wally, Ben, Alex, Xuren, Noda, and David walk through in that order.

"Mr. Rockefeller, that sounds like a great offer. It is a win-win situation for everybody. I mean, peace on earth for all, and you get to increase your personal holdings. You could never spend all that money anyway. You have to accept it. Don't let us all down."

Alex moves forward. Knowing the library well, he escorts the men toward the center of the rotunda and motions to one of the librarians. Captain Wilson of the NYPD sees Mr. Rockefeller and moves close to his side. David then whispers something in his ear. Captain Wilson nods his head in the affirmative and walks out front of the library, barking commands into his hand held-radio. After conferring with the librarian, Mr. Van Rensselaer escorts the men to a private room just off the right side of the main gallery. Mr. Xuren and Mr. Noda talk amongst themselves. David and Joey are the only ones to sit down at the table, while the other men gather around a large table but refuse to sit.

"My friends here feel insulted. They insist on knowing what was said to the officer outside," Ben says.

"If they must know, I just ordered the police to round up all the males of Asian persuasion on this campus and have them locked up under the suspicion of espionage," David says as his storm troopers outside no doubt get to work.

"This does not show that you are willing to negotiate in good faith," Ben says as he speaks in Japanese and fills in the Asians.

"They should have thought of that before bringing their ninjas over here and sticking their noses into my business," David says as the intensity in the room increases.

"Easy, fellows. What's all this talk of war and money? The world is big enough for both of your concerns. We can all just walk away and live in peace," Alex says, offering to calm things down.

"I'm afraid their part of the world is not big enough for the both of us. We have many ongoing concerns in Japan and China. I'm afraid our concerns interfere with Mr. Noda and Mr. Xuren's way in which they would like to run their countries, at least financially," David says.

"I'm staying out of this one," Joey says as Ben and the Asians speak in Japanese.

Ben turns and says, "My friends agree that it has been you and your family that have ruined our economy and have been ruining it since the end of World War Two. The gentlemen believe that the first act of war is always on a financial level. They feel that Mr. Rockefeller here has launched an all-out attack against their homelands and wish not to escalate the war. They only wish for peace," Ben says.

David stands up and says, "How can it be that I have attacked that part of the world's economy, when it is I who owns it?"

Ben interprets David's words to the Asians. They, in turn, speak amongst themselves for a long while.

"We only wish for peace, but we wish to remind Mr. Rockefeller that it is we who possess long-range missiles that can attack the home continent of the United States. We know of your earthquake machine known as HAARP, and we are not afraid, because we have secretly built big enough underground facilities to support our entire nation, not just the rich and prosperous. Your nation will not survive, but ours will. We also have submarines trailing every one of your aircraft carriers. If you choose to go to war with us, your entire navy will be sunk on the first day of the war," Ben says, interpreting for the Asians. David's face has grown furious, but before he can speak, Wally's cell phone rings, breaking some of the tension.

"Wally Niles here. How may I help you?" Wally says calmly in the way only a Brit could during a time of tension. He listens carefully to an unfamiliar voice on the other end. "Your Majesty, how can I be of help to you?" Wally says nervously as the room goes silent. All of their attention turns to Wally and the unexpected phone call. Ben quickly interprets what is happening to the Asian diplomats.

"You have served your queen and country well, and for over ten years, you've been in pursuit of the book for us. Now the time has come to bring it back with you to your queen, your country, and the Temple Lodge. Now, please listen carefully to these instructions," Queen Elizabeth says as she hands the phone over to one of her associates.

A male voice starts out saying, "Good to hear from you again, Niles."

"Who is this?" Wally replies.

"It is the grand master of the Temple Lodge here in London, Nathan Rothschild. You've done a great job so far, my friend. You have honored your queen, your government, and your brethren. You must listen to me explicitly. Do you remember your time at the Tavistock Institute?" Nathan says.

"Why, yes, of course. Why?" Wally says.

"So you should remember your Shakespeare as well. Let me ask you, then. What's in a name? That which we call a rose?" Nathan asks.

"By any other name would smell as sweet," Wally answers as an altered personality instantly takes over his thoughts and which was triggered by the Shakespeare saying.

"As you can see, the men in front of you are about to start World War Three. Now, you don't want that to happen, do you? There is only one way to stop this war. Remove the revolver you have and point it at Mr. Alex Van Rensselaer's head," Nathan says, now directing Wally.

"I can't do it. It's not right. He is not involved with starting this war. This is espionage, and he's a friend of mine. I'm not a spy," Wally says as he grasps the revolver and lowers it to his side.

"It is the only way to stop this disaster from happening. The crown will reward you. Just do as I say, and you won't have to shoot anybody," Nathan says after he has triggered Wally's split personality syndrome.

"What is it that you want me to do?" Wally asks, unable to control himself.

"Point your weapon at Alex," Nathan says while Wally extends his right arm.

"I'm pointing it right at him. Now what do you want me to do?" Wally asks as David returns to his seat and gives Joey a nod, as if he knows what to do. Joey's mind reverts to his army training, and he readies his revolver as his adrenaline increases. Joey rests the weapon on his lap, under the table, and has it pointing directly at Wally.

"Now, just hand Alex your cell phone, please," Nathan says as he passes his phone to his boss and Wally reaches out with his left hand, giving Alex the phone.

"It is for you, sir," Wally says in his dry British tone, trying to show that he means no harm.

"Yes, this is Alex Van Rensselaer. You have gone mad. I demand an explanation," Alex says, not knowing who he is talking to or what to expect.

"As you can see, I have the American and Asian societies at each other's throats, and a gun aimed at your head," a man with a Dutch accent says.

"Who is this? Who am I speaking to?" Alex demands.

"That is not important. Just know that I'm Nathan Rothschild's boss, as you Americans would call it," the voice says.

"What do you want with me?" Alex asks.

"I want the book, Alex, the book," the voice says.

"I have no idea what you're talking about," Alex says.

"Will you deny me until the end, Alex? I have known for many years that you alone are the last *patroon,* if you will, and I know you are in possession of what we both know to be mine. Listen to me carefully, or I will continue to ruin the world's economy and have these fine men start World War Three. The future of the world rests on your shoulders," the voice says.

"The book belongs to no one. It belongs to the people," Alex says, finally admitting that he knows of the second Book of Ages.

"I need you to walk Mr. Niles down to the basement where you keep it and deliver to him the book. When Mr. Niles has the book in his possession, I will give you further instructions," the voice says.

"Is it true, Alex? The second book, it's not a myth?" Wally asks.

"What do you want me to do with Mr. Rockefeller and these other gentlemen?" Alex asks of the strange voice as he looks over at the gun Wally is holding.

"I have it taken care of. Leave their fate to me," the voice says and hangs up the phone.

"The book, I must have it. Take me to it. It is my master's book. It belongs to him," Wally says as if he is possessed by some outside forces.

"I'm only doing this to prevent a war, Alex. I mean nothing else by it, sir," Wally says, fighting the demons inside him.

"I understand, Wally. You're a good man," Alex says, trying to appease him. Captain Wilson and two armed officers enter the room in full riot gear with their pistols drawn.

"Perhaps you were right, Joey. You should have killed all of us back there on the highway. The world might have been a better place," Alex says as he puts his hands up in response to the police.

Captain Wilson looks at Alex and Wally and says, "Don't you two have somewhere else to be?" He turns and points his gun at David Rockefeller.

"Yes, of course. We are on our way," Alex says, seeing the new threat that is now imposed on the men.

David's anger is at its peak. "You son of a bitch, don't you know who signs your paycheck? I'll have your badge before morning."

"What badge? We are not even policemen. We work for a higher power," Captain Wilson explains.

Captain Wilson and his guard of men have penetrated the NYPD years before. They are on the payroll of the Temple Lodge and have carried out its assassination orders in the United States for years.

"You can't trust anybody in this city. It's a den of vipers," Joey says, redirecting his weapon toward the fake police officers.

Alex directs Wally to pull on a book that is on the shelf nearest to him. "Could you be so kind and give the 'Icke' classic a pull, Wally?" Alex asks, pointing to a row of books on the shelf.

"I only see one, *The Biggest Secret,*" Wally says as he gives it a yank and the bookshelf begins to spin.

"I thought that book was somewhat fitting," Alex says as a descending staircase appears from behind the shelf.

"I'm right after you, sir," Wally says, directing Alex down the stairs with a wave of his gun. The two slip down the stairs and into the darkness. The leaders of the Green and the Red become scared at the fact that they may be facing execution and start yelling at Ben in Japanese.

"God just wants us to love one another. It's man's job to rid the world of sin, to rid our own hearts from it and from the hearts of our neighbors ..." Joey begins to preach.

Ben suddenly, being a big man and full of fear, jumps from his chair and goes for the gun in Captain Wilson's hand, knocking him over in the process. Captain Wilson's gun fires and blows a lethal hole in David Rockefeller's chest. Joey opens up on the other two policemen, killing them instantly. As Ben and Captain Wilson struggle over his gun, Joey races around the table and delivers a coup-de-grace to the captain's head.

"My God, we have to get out of here," Ben says as he shuffles to his feet.

"We are all going to be arrested. We'll be disgraced in our home countries if this gets out," Noda says in English.

"Not to mention life in prison, if you go out there with all of New York's finest waiting for us. I've got a plan, Ben, you take these books and Mr. Rockefeller, and he's got some spectacles here in his pocket you can wear. The glasses will make you look more like a professor," Joey says while he goes through Rockefeller's front chest pocket. Joey first finds and pulls out the funny-looking feathered quill.

"Look at this. It looks like an old quill. I think is made out of gold, and look at these funny-looking feathers. I'll make sure it makes its way to one of David's museums," Joey says as he puts it in his rear pocket with the feathers sticking out. "Here they are," Joey says, raising the glasses into the air and hearing the men converse in Japanese. "What are they talking about?" Joey asks Ben.

"It's not good. They think it would be best if they ... They have decided to take their own lives. Today has been a humiliating failure for them. They were here hoping for peace. If they leave here now, they will surely go to prison and be disgraced in the eyes of their countrymen. Even if proven innocent in a court of law, they will be disgraced. This cannot be an option for these two proud men," Ben explains as he takes the glasses from Joey.

The two men start bowing and praying respectfully in their different religious heritages.

"I like my plan better. Ben, pick these books up. You look like a professor with those on. When you leave the room, just keep on walking, like you are preparing for a history exam or something. Here are the keys to the SUV. When you get inside, lock the doors and get down. I'll try and meet you out front. If I'm not there in an hour, leave," Joey says.

"Where are you going, Joey?"

"I'm putting my faith in God, and I'm going down the staircase to try and save Alex," Joey says.

"Hurry up, then. I'll spin the bookshelf shut for you," Ben says as Joey bolts down the stairs and into the dark.

Chapter 44

Ben spins the bookshelf shut and heads toward the heavy oak door that, not long before, the men entered the room from. Seeing the Asians pick up the dead officers' guns, he opens the door quickly and shuts it again, leaning against it tightly. *Bang, bang.* Two shots ring out, being muffled slightly behind the heavy door. Ben closes his eyes as he knows what has just occurred. *The oldest tradition, code of the samurai,* he thinks to himself. Ben takes a deep breath and begins a low whistle as he tries to calm himself as he walks toward the entrance to the building. Ben quickly opens the top book of his shallow stack and begins to read as two policemen quickly approach him coming through the front entrance. Ben gives a quick nod as the second policeman holds the exit door for him. Ben then moves slowly down the long staircase in front of the building. The same stairs that the men had walked up earlier seem to be a marathon of a walk this time. *Down to the waiting SUV and to safety,* he thinks. Ben, seeing the swarm of police activity in the street and around the SUV and being overloaded with adrenaline, gets scared. Instead of playing his part as a schoolteacher, Ben makes a break for it and jumps over the stairway wall and into the bushes. Ben's mind begins to race.

Why did I do that? Now I'm stuck in these bushes with nowhere to go. It's dark. It's cold. Should I run for it? Where does that tunnel that the others went down lead? I'm a dead man if I get caught. Breathe, breathe, Ben thinks to himself.

The two officers that entered the library were under orders to search the entire building. Not before too long, they turn the knob and walked upon a ghastly scene. Six bodies total.

"What on God's green earth?" one officer shouts.

"Man down, man down," the other officer shouts into his hand-held radio.

The scene of three dead uniformed officers and two dead Asians is incredible, not to mention Mr. David Rockefeller slumped over in his chair. All the chairs are pushed back away from the table as the bodies lie like dominos that had fallen on top of one another from left to right in a clockwise motion. Mr. Noda is layered on top of Mr. Xuren; in turn, he is layered on top of the first downed officer, who lies on top of the second, who lies on top of the so-called Captain Wilson.

"That professor we walked past—I'd swear he was coming from this direction," the first of the officers says.

"Okay, I'll get out a bulletin. You stay here and don't touch anything. My God, look at all the blood," the second officer says.

Ben Fulford stays in the bushes as he overhears a perfect description of himself over a nearby policeman's radio. *They are onto me. I am a dead man,* Ben thinks. *Every cop in the city is now looking for me.*

Chapter 45

W<small>ALLY</small> H<small>URRIES</small> A<small>LEX</small> D<small>OWN</small> the dark and dank hundred–year-old tunnel beneath the buildings of Columbia University. Alex's mind races with the thoughts of the many dead ends in the tunnel system and how he might escape from his old friend. Some of the tunnels are open and are used by the current students and staff of the college, mostly as shortcuts from building to building, while others in the system haven't been used in decades. *What to do, what to do?* Alex tries to think.

"Where is it? We know it's down here somewhere," Wally shouts, fighting the demons within.

"I can't give it to you. It belongs to the people," Alex says as the men have now traveled over a hundred yards into the dimly lit tunnel system.

"The book belongs to my master. Only he can decide what to do with it. I must return it to him, for I'm in the graciousness of the Light Bearer himself," Wally says as his face contorts with a menacing gaze.

"You are sadly mistaken, for you worship a false god, with promises of false treasure. Your master is a liar and deceiver," Alex says, as he is now convinced he is no longer speaking to his friend Wally.

Wally tries and opens a door at the end of one of the tunnels. As he cracks the door open slightly, he sees that it leads into huge courtyard in the center of campus.

"You are the deceiver. We've gone the wrong way. Now, where is it?" Wally shouts at Alex while pointing his gun at his face. "I will shoot you. Now tell me where it is."

"It is in a vault beneath the rotunda back under the Low Memorial Library," Alex says.

"I should have known not to trust a Dutchman. Get a move on. Let's go," Wally says as the men turn and head back down the tunnel toward the underbowels of the library.

Joey hears the footsteps of the men far off in the distance. Joey remembers his time spent in the barracks with his army buddies. They would launch ambushes on each other in the middle of the night, just for fun. The key to a successful surprise attack was the removal of his shoes, as the stomping of heavy army boots always gave away their positions in the darkened hallways. *That's it,* Joey thinks. *An ambush.* He has to think fast, as he can hear the men getting closer and closer. The tunnel is semi-lit with lights that are centered above the semi-circled arches, and where the lights are a good forty feet distant from one another, the tunnel is intermitting with light and darkness. *Position,* Joey thinks to himself, *position would be the key.* Joey hurries to remove his shoes as a second brilliant idea strikes him. In one of the many side tunnels, Joey lies down on his stomach in the semi-prone position, with his gun pointing in the opposite direction from where the men are coming from. He will lie and wait for the men to pass, hoping to get a clear shot as the men move into the light.

Wally and Alex are now moving at a quick jog back toward the Low Memorial Library, when they come upon a pair of shoes sitting directly under one of the tunnel lights.

"What in the heck? Where did those come from?" Wally says. "There is someone else down here with us." Before the men can move, a shot rings out. Joey had taken dead aim and hit Wally center chest.

Never has an easier shot been taken, Joey thinks. *Not on the practice range, not in combat, not even in the play fights with my buddies in the barracks.*

Wally gasps for air and begins to pull the trigger on his weapon. The first shot pierces Alex right through the thigh. The second flies down the hall harmlessly, but the third ricochets off the wall and into Joey's lower back near his spine. Joey's eyes quickly dilate as he gets to his feet and moves from the darkness and into the light in the center of the tunnel.

"Alex, are you all right?" Joey shouts as he dives to his knees and to Alex's side.

Joey takes a quick glance at Wally and sees that he is not breathing as he takes off his jacket and hastily wraps it as tourniquet high around Alex's thigh.

"You've been hit in a bad spot. You won't be able to walk. I've gotta get you to an ambulance. You're bleeding pretty badly," Joey explains.

With a weak breath, Alex says, "I know these tunnels very well. There is a short cut through the library basement, if you could just get us there."

"Yes, sure, which way, Padre?" Joey asks while picking Alex up and maneuvering him onto his own shoulders.

"You've been hit as well," Alex says as the men make their way down the darkened tunnel passageway.

"Turn right at the next light," Alex says, giving directions.

"I haven't done the fireman carry since basic training," Joey says as he makes the turn and begins to feel the pain in his back.

"It is the last door on your left. You'll have to set me down to open it," Alex says.

Joey struggles down the long hallway leading to the unknown door. He slowly sets Alex on his feet and helps to balance him against the outer wall.

"Take this key, Joey," Alex says as he removes a chain from around his neck. "It's the key to your future and this door."

Joey grabs the chain and key from Alex and opens the century-old oak door. The door creaks open as if it were an old dungeon.

"We do have electricity down here. There is a light switch on the inside," Alex says, directing Joey.

Joey enters the room and hits the switch. The room is a dead end. Joey suddenly realizes Alex's fate.

"I'll never be able to get you out of here in time," Joey says to Alex as he steps back into the darkness of the tunnel.

"I didn't plan on making it, Joey. This is my destiny, as it has been written in the Book of Ages," Alex says.

"What are you talking about?" Joey asks as he wraps his arms around Alex and helps him into the brightly-lit room.

"Set me down right here, Joey. That's it. This is fine," Alex says as his breath slows. "Sit with me for a moment," Alex says as he and Joey rest on the floor together.

"Many years ago, when I was allowed to read from the old Book of Ages, it had spoken to the fact that it would be me who would pass the new Book of Ages on to the last *patroon,* and that I would die doing it. The book states that *patroon's* name would be Joey. I always believed I would have a son, of course, and that I would have named him Joey. But as the years went by, there were some of us who thought the book was wrong. It is strange in the fact that man has the ability to change his destiny, and sometimes, when we achieve this, the old Book of Ages would change with it, as if by magic. You see, man's destiny is not written in stone. It is as if it were an open book, yet to be written. I realize now I must pass the book onto you, which has been my destiny from the beginning," Alex says, breathing heavily.

"What book are you talking about?" Joey asks.

"Man has been enslaved by the devil and his minions since the beginning. You see, it is the devil who is the holder of the old Book of Ages, which allows him to see and control man's future. The problem for him is, the book has an end date. It will expire on the winter solstice in 2012. After that date, the devil will be lost and confused, unable to see the future and control man's destiny," Alex says.

"That is the same date that the Mayans predicted. What does that have to do with me?"

"On the same winter solstice, there is a second Book of Ages that will begin. That book contains your destiny, Joey. Read from it and do the right thing," Alex says as he sees the feathers sticking out of Joey's pocket. "I see you have found the quill of prosperity. Where was it all this time?"

"I found it on Mr. Rockefeller while searching for his glasses. It was in his upper chest pocket," Joey replies as he holds it up to the light and they both take a good look at it.

"Ha, ha, ha, my mother was right all this time. Would you be a dear and please return it to her? It belongs to her. It would make her extremely happy," Alex says as his breathing slows.

"Sure, I will, no problem, Alex."

"Use the key I gave you earlier to open the door behind the shelf. Beyond the door, you will find a long hallway. Follow it until it ends, then use the key to open the vault. Share the book with the world, Joey. The book belongs to all of mankind. It will be your destiny to help free all of mankind from the work of the devil," Alex says.

"How would I be able to do all that? I'm just one man. One man can't change the world," Joey asks.

"The key to man's salvation while on this earth has always been our faith and belief in Jesus, our savior. He will teach you how to supply free food and free energy to all, Joey," Alex says.

"What do you mean, free energy?" Joey asks.

"Read the book. Search out Nikola Tesla's early experiments. Trust in Jesus. You will find the answers," Alex says as his eyes slowly close and he breathes his last breath.

Joey starts to panic and begins sweating profusely. "Holy shit, I don't believe any of this. I can't just leave him here," Joey says to himself as his adrenaline rises.

Alex's cell phone begins to ring. *My God, should I answer that?* Joey thinks to himself. Without finding any reason not to, Joey slips his hand into Alex Van Rensselaer's jacket. "Hello."

"Joey Patroni, please. This is Mrs. Van Rensselaer," Cornelia says over her cell phone.

"This is Joey Patroni," Joey says, amazed at hearing a female voice at the other end of the phone.

"My name is Cornelia. I am Alex's mother. I already know of my son's fate. Don't you be too bothered by what has happened, Joey. We have all been aware of today's events for quite some time now," Cornelia says.

"But your son ... He is ..." Joey begins to say.

"He was a wonderful son and performed his duties to the world well. Well in the fact that he found you, Joey. We are waiting for you, Joey. Leave the gun. Follow the tunnel. Say a prayer for Alex. Friends of ours are already on their way to retrieve my boy," Cornelia says.

Joey finds the hidden doorway just where Alex had told him. He puts the old key into the rusty slot and opens the door. Joey takes one last look at the room where Alex's body lies and slams the door shut. Now in complete darkness, he feels for the outer wall with his hands. The wall is there. Hard. Damp. Cold. He starts a steady jog down the long tunnel, keeping one hand on the wall. *This tunnel only leads one way,* Joey thinks to himself as he follows the tunnel. He starts to remember the long nights he had spent in Iraq on patrol, wearing his night vision goggles; they could have certainly helped him guide his way right now. Joey runs a hundred yards, and then two hundred yards, and then three hundred yards with the bullet still lodged in his back. *I'm lost in the darkness,* Joey thinks to himself. *Just keep going,* his inner voice says, pushing him further. Joey starts to think. *The stonemasons, the secret societies, the secret government, the quill, and the Book of Ages, what does it all mean?* Joey slows his pace to a steady walk as he realizes he is not in as good shape as he was in his old army days. He begins to have flashbacks of his time spent in the war, remembering the scariest of all events that lead the army doctors to diagnose him with post traumatic stress syndrome. It was that one night when the company headquarters came under attack and it was his duty to guard the arms room, alone. A room full of all sorts of weapons: AT4s, M16s, M14s, and many others. Joey stops and rests against the wall. With his mind racing, Joey tries not to remember how scared he was while the mortars and rockets rained down on him like a once-in-a-year hailstorm, and what he had done to get through it. Joey suddenly remembers. He prayed. He remembers praying that night for hours. He remembers the barrage of incoming missiles and bombs that lasted for some three hours, hitting his building and starting fires in the brush that surrounded it. Mostly, he remembers thanking God for getting him through it and how it was God's good grace that allowed him to live and see his children again after the war. And it was God's good grace that has come to him now. "That is what I will do. Have I forgotten the grace of God, our holy scripture, and the word of his only-begotten son, Jesus Christ?" Joey says out loud as if he could speak out to the lord himself. Joey begins to run again, as his thoughts have rejuvenated his energy. The tunnel has only one light, which offers a good view of the only ninety-degree turn that is coming up ahead. The tunnel turns and heads south, and Joey follows its path. His muscles ache. His mind goes numb. His running turns into a slow jog and finally slows to a walk. Trapped in complete darkness and bleeding, he remembers the words to the Lord's Prayer. "Our father who art in heaven, hallowed be thy name. Thy kingdom come. Thy will be done on earth as it is in heaven. Give us this day our daily bread, and forgive us our trespasses, as we forgive those who trespass against us, and lead us not into temptation, but deliver us from evil," Joey says out loud, with eyes closed, as he gently rests his head on the wall of the tunnel and tears roll down his cheeks. With his ear now pressed to the wall, he hears the noise, starting as a slow rumble and growing into a large trembling. Is it small arms fire? Mortars? Rockets? *Snap out of it!* he thinks. He is in New York City. *Subways,* he thinks. Just then, a light shines through a crack from up above. Joey moves toward the light as the rumbling grows louder. He is no longer on campus. *I'm directly under Broadway Street,* he thinks. Joey catches a glimpse of the city bus that rolls by directly overhead, blocking the light for just a moment. He knows where he is. The tunnel definitely leads south, and the end can't be much further. As Joey refocuses his eyes into the tunnel, he notices a small enclave opposite the light that shines down through. There is a small statuette that sits inside, no more than a foot tall, of the Virgin Mary holding the baby Jesus. The statuette is set back into the wall of the tunnel; no doubt it has been there for at least a hundred years. Maybe perhaps before the Revolutionary War. Joey gets on his knees and prays for forgiveness. After all, he had shot what he believed to be three policemen. Joey thinks to himself, *Maybe the church elders had put it there before the construction of the church began. That's it—the church! There is a church on the other side of Broadway, across from the university campus.* Joey thanks Mary and the baby Jesus for the moment of solitude as he gets up and moves down the tunnel and towards the church. *What was the name of the church?* Joey thinks. *It's right on the tip of my tongue. The church my grandparents took me to when I was a child.*

Chapter 46

Bᴇɴᴊᴀᴍɪɴ Fᴜʟꜰᴏʀᴅ ʜᴀꜱ ʀᴜɴ out of patience. In haste, he has decided that he can't stay in the bushes all night and that it was probably a stupid idea to begin with. He waits for the last of the policemen to clear the library's stairway entrance. He slowly moves closer to the edge of the cement work. While the police at the bottom have their backs turned, he rests his butt cheeks on the top ledge and quickly whips his legs over the cement railing. His feet land squarely on the ground, and he acts as if he's been leaning there for hours. Ben adjusts the spectacles and realizes no one has noticed his escape from he bushes. Ben pretends to read over his opened book intensely as he keeps his eyes up and on the police near the SUV. He moves down the stairs and toward the street, where the safety of the SUV lies. Ben thinks to himself that it has been at least a good hour since Joey made his way down the tunnel stairs. Ben finally makes it to the sidewalk and reaches in his pocket for the keys to the truck. The unwanted jingling noise of the keys draws the officer's attention nearby.

"Hey, mister. Hey, you there!" one officer yells.

"Hey, that is the guy we seen leaving the library earlier. Stop right there, you," the second officer says, drawing his gun. "Don't move. Hands behind your head."

"I, I, I can explain," Ben says, mumbling his words.

"Explain what? I haven't asked you anything yet," the first officer says. "Is this your vehicle?"

"No, why—why no, it's not," Ben says, trying to think of something intelligent to say. "I work here. Here at the university."

"I don't care who you are or where you work. Everyone on this campus is a suspect until we figure out what happened. Take him over to the church across the street with all the others. We'll let them figure out who he is. Bring a cruiser around," the first officer says as the second officer puts the cuffs on him.

One of New York's police cruisers pull up. An officer opens the rear door and puts Ben inside. "Take him over with the others. We have a command and control center set up at the old church," the officer says, pointing north toward the old church to the driver.

The cruiser with lights flashing heads north on West 116th Street and into the church parking lot, where a mass of people are being processed, some of whom are being arrested by the police. Ben is ordered to stand in line with the others and waits his turn. He slowly makes his way to the front, wondering what on earth happened to Joey. Ben spots the mayor of New York himself taking charge of the situation. The scene is total chaos as Ben is quickly lost in the crowd of police officers and the many Asians being arrested around him.

Chapter 47

J OEY IS EXHAUSTED AS he finally reaches the end of the tunnel. There in front of him stand two locked doors. What stands behind the doors does not matter anymore; Joey just wants the nightmare to end. Joey feels an aura about himself as if God himself is with him by his side. Joey takes the key from around his neck and inserts it into the first door. He finds a switch on the wall as the room fills with light. Joey finds himself in a room full of books, scrolls, and manuscripts. There is one book that stands out among all the rest. In the center of the room lies a huge three–foot-by-four-foot book resting on a podium. Joey looks around the room in amazement as he wonders at all the treasures that lie inside. Aristotle, Plato, Baltasar Gracian, Old Testaments and New, and there is no doubt what the book in the center of the room is. It is the Book of Ages, lying unopened. Suddenly, Joey remembers the call from Mrs. Van Rensselaer. He must find his way out. There'll be time to come back later. Joey quickly turns off the light and locks the door behind him. He finds the keyhole to the next door. It must lead to the old church. He turns the key and opens the door. He is one floor beneath the chapel inside the church of St. John the Divine. *This is the church my grandmother used to bring me to as a child,* Joey thinks. Joey slowly makes his way up the circular stairs that lie in front of him. *This is St. John the Divine* on *Amsterdam Avenue. This is where my grandfather got his first job as a stonemason in his early days. The tunnel must have been a good half-mile long,* Joey thinks. Joey remembers that his grandfather told him they had to dig seventy feet underground before they hit bedrock. Joey thinks to himself, *My grandfather helped erect this church, and he may have even helped build the tunnel, and perhaps knew of the statuette of the Virgin Mary and the baby Jesus. Now, come on. Where is your New York sensibility? All that would be impossible!* Joey thinks as he climbs the lighted staircase that leads him out of the darkness.

Joey gets to the door at the top of the stairs. It is unlocked. He gives the handle a turn and swings it open. Joey finds himself behind the main altar of the church. He quickly makes his way around and finds a congregation in full prayer. As he walks closer to the people, he begins to recognize some of the faces. Joey's mom is the first to lift her head. She walks toward Joey and smiles.

"Mom … and Dad, what on earth are you doing here?" Joey says as the rest of the congregation begins to lift their heads from prayer. He starts to recognize everyone there. "Holy Jesus, Aunt Josephine and Aunt Rose …" Joey says as he gives his mother a kiss and his father a hug.

"Joey Patroni, I presume," an unfamiliar voice rings out. It is an old and fragile Mrs. Cornelia Van Rensselaer. "I took it upon myself to gather your closest family and friends so that we could share the good news with them. We understand that in the coming days and years, your time will be full. So it has always been my belief that any kind of charity should begin at home and with family and friends," Cornelia says.

"But I haven't got much to give to anyone, if anything at all," Joey says, wondering what it is he needs to do.

"We are not here to receive your charity, but to give some to you—our love, and our friendship. That is all we really ever have to give to someone," Cornelia says.

"Your son Alex, god rest his soul, mentioned a book; he called it the Book of Ages. I found it, but I did not bring it with me. I'm sure it would take at least two people just to pick it up. I did find this funny-looking feathered golden quill, though. Alex asked me to return it to you," Joey says.

"Oh dear, the story my grandfather used to tell me as child. It was true all this time. Can you imagine that?" Cornelia says as she looks over her heirloom. "Isn't it wonderful? You hang onto it, my boy. You will be needing it more than I," Cornelia says as she hands it back to Joey. "The book that Alex spoke of has been in our family's possession for many years. As you must know by now, it is twenty-six thousand years old, but amazingly looks brand new. No one knows for sure, but many of us believe it was written by the hand of God himself. Some of my acquaintances have suggested that we destroy the book, but wiser heads prevailed. We keep it here, locked away, at Columbia University—in fact, it is located down the very stairs you came up," Cornelia says.

"Yes, I've seen it, and I have locked it back up," Joey says as he shows Cornelia the key around his neck.

"That is great. Don't you worry about it for now. The book is safer more now than it has ever been," Cornelia says.

"There were many travesties today, including Mr. Rockefeller's death. And come to find out the Chinese and Japanese ambassadors that were here just wanted peace in the world. I'm sure some evil people will be after the book again. They threatened to start World War Three if they don't get it," Joey says.

"Some of those of which you speak are just pawns of the devil, while others have sacrificed their goodness to protect the knowledge of the book. You must put your trust in God and find your faith with him. Trust in him; he will show you the way. You must go and rest now. Come Monday, you will make your way down here to the university and start your new job as regent of Columbia University," Cornelia says.

"You are going to make me regent? I haven't even finished my history classes yet," Joey says.

"I'll take care of everything. We will get you transferred here as a student first. You can take all the classes you need. I will be introducing you to a special professor of history, someone that I have hand-selected myself," Cornelia says.

"That all sounds great," Joey says as he shows his wound to the group.

"We will get you to the hospital right away. As far as your new professor goes, she will help you to read and understand the Book of Ages," Cornelia says.

"My instructor will be a female?" Joey asks.

"Well, of course. You won't be the only one to read from the book for the next twenty-six thousand years. It will be shared amongst many. There will be others that follow you as well. I have insured your mutual happiness; after all, my son Alex and I had our wills written together, leaving you everything we have. Plus, your new professor is really cute. She is a nice Italian girl. She is really going to like you. I myself can hardly keep my eyes off of you. If I were only forty ..." Cornelia says, being cut off.

"Stop it. I already have two daughters. Are you saying I may have more children?" Joey asks.

"Well, I don't know about any children, but maybe a wife. And don't forget Jesus's golden rule, Joey," Cornelia says.

"Yes of course—treat others the way you wish to be treated. I can do that, Mrs. Van Rensselaer," Joey says. "The golden rule—that reminds me. Ben—I have to help him," Joey says as he limps his way toward the front of the church. "I'll be right back."

Joey pushes open the huge doors of the church. He sees

all the commotion outside as police and news cameras are gathered in the front parking lot. Joey notices the Constantia wire that straddles the top of the fence in the church parking lot as the place looks like a prison. Joey disgusted with what he sees says. "Is this New York City or downtown Bagdad?"

Joey moves through the crowd, looking, looking.

"Joey!" Ben's voice cries out as a police officer uncuffs him and sits him down on a curb.

"What are doing with this man? He works at the university with me," Joey says.

"And who are you?" an officer asks in a gruff voice.

"Well I'm, I'm ..." Joey starts to say.

"He is the regent of Columbia University," Mrs. Van Rensselaer says with authority as she leads a procession of Joey's closest family and friends out into the parking lot.

The activity catches the attention of the mayor, who is in the middle of damage control with the death of Mr. Rockefeller. He has two unknown Asians on their way to the morgue, and the three dead men dressed as police officers that are turning out to be John Does.

"What is going on over here?" the mayor asks.

"This man was seen leaving the scene of the crime inside the Low Memorial Library. And I think this man might be his accomplice," an officer says.

"Mrs. Van Rensselaer! My goodness what are you doing out this time of the morning?" the mayor asks as he bows his head to Cornelia.

"Don't you dare suck up to me, Mikie, you overpaid gofer," Cornelia says to the mayor. "I made a mistake supporting your last election. Next year, your head will be on a platter."

"Yes, Mama, but ..." the mayor begins to say.

"You've been screwing up all year. And I'm sure you're out here screwing up something else," Cornelia says.

"Cornelia, please. I'm trying the best that I can. Are these men friends of yours?" the mayor says, quivering.

"This is our linguistics teacher, Mr. Fulford. He specializes in Asian languages," Cornelia says.

"And I am the new regent of the university," Joey says as the mayor looks to Cornelia for conformation.

"Of course they're friends of mine, you idiot," Cornelia says to the mayor as the officers let Joey and Ben free.

"Please accept my apology, Mrs. Van Rensselaer," the mayor says.

Joey and Ben gather themselves and move into the circle of friends on the front steps of the great Romanesque and Byzantine cathedral. After Cornelia whispers something into the ear of the mayor, the mayor backs the crowd out and away from their group.

Cornelia enters the circle of friends and says, "We bested the devil this time, but it will take all of us to overcome him in the end."

"Tell me, how did you know it would be me who would receive the Book of Ages?" Joey asks.

"That is a fair question regarding the circumstances. There are actually two books that are called the Book of Ages: first, there is the old Book of Ages, which comes to an end soon, and the new Book of Ages, which starts where the old book leaves off. In the first book, it states that the receiver of the new Book of Ages would be a stonemason, a soldier, a priest, a student, and a teacher, and that he would be the last of the *patroons*. It also states your first name, Joey. All of the old *patroon*ships have died out long ago. But you—you Joey—you are the last in the male line of the Patroni family," Cornelia says. "It is you who was sent here by God to do his work. It will be you, Joey, who will free the people. It is you who have bested the devil on this night. It is you who will share the book with all the people on earth," Mrs. Van Rensselaer says.

"What, am I the second coming, the Messiah, or something?" Joey asks softly.

"No, no, my dear boy. You will begin with page one, chapter one in the Book of Ages down in our library and learn about the second coming, and there is so much more later on," Cornelia says.

"Joey, it's time to come home. You will need some time to rest," Joey's mom offers with a smile.

Chapter 48

One week later at Joey Patroni's home in Brooklyn

J<small>OEY SITS RESTING ON</small> his couch, watching television and flipping channels with the remote as he recovers from the emergency back surgery to remove the bullet fragment that was lodged in his back.

"We have breaking news in the tragic deaths of Mr. Noda of Japan and Mr. Xuren of China. Apparently, the men got lost and separated from their interpreter in New York and, with neither being able to speak English, were victims of a simple robbery and were gunned down on the city's Upper West Side last weekend. No suspects have been arrested," a newswoman reports from a local New York station.

"Can you believe that? They have decided to cover up the real story. I can't believe it," Joey says as he gets up with the help of a cane.

"In another sad story, the family patriarch of the Rockefeller family, David, who had died unexpectedly of heart complications Saturday night, will be interred at the Sleepy Hollow Cemetery tomorrow, where many of the world leaders will be in attendance. We have with us here now a leader in the U.N. delegation from Amsterdam, Mr. Van Kestern. Tell me, Mr. Van Kestern, how is the news of Mr.

David Rockefeller's death being accepted over at the United Nations?" the reporter asks.

"Well, it is always a difficult time when a man of Mr. Rockefeller's stature is lost. As you know, he was a man of brilliance and foresight. The world lost a great leader, and we hope that all his works will continue. He was a peace-loving man, and the world will miss him dearly," Mr. Van Kestern says.

"Here live at the United Nations, I'm Trisha Bonderman. Now back to you, Gina," Trisha says.

"New York has certainly lost a great man this week. Our prayers go out to the family. And in other news tonight, the New York Board of Regents has named Joey Patroni, a student at the university, as an at-large regent in the Columbia University district. It is a position that serves without salary and covers the administration of local libraries, museums, and schools, public and private," Gina, the anchorwoman, says.

"Without salary! You have got to be kidding me. She must be making that up," Joey says in his heavy Brooklyn accent. "That's the story of my life. She didn't even mention Alex. My God, the Van Rensselaers started this city, this state, this country, the world which we live in!" Joey shouts to himself. "I can't just let them become another forgotten name in this city. That is so typical of New York City."

Just then, Joey's front doorbell rings. He limps his way over, cane in hand. Joey peeks through the window blinds and sees a long, black Lincoln Continental limousine parked out front. *Who on earth?* Joey thinks to himself as he opens the front door.

A young man dressed in a chauffeur's outfit says, "I'm here to see a Mr. Patroni."

The young Italian man seems to be harmless as Joey says, "I'm Mr. Patroni. Come on in." Joey swings the door open as the young man walks in.

"Good afternoon, sir. I'm here to take you to ... Hey, you are the guy I've seen on television all week. I knew I would be driving someone famous. That's right—you are the new regent at Columbia College. You know, I just started there last semester. I've been going over your schedule for this week. Monday, you have a meeting at one of the banks you own, and Tuesday, we are due at the art gallery. On Wednesday, you are meeting with the police."

"Whoah, whoah, slow down there, high speed. What did you say that the police wanted with me?" Joey asks nervously.

"I just read it over in my day planner, but the mayor has invited you to a policeman's ball. And on Thursday, we have a council at the United Nations, and ..."

"Wait one minute. What did you say your name was?" Joey asks.

"Oh, my name is Tony Maseroni. I'm from the Brooklyn Maseronis. My great-grandfather moved here from Italy back in the 1920s ..."

"How old are you, kid?" Joey asks.

"I just turned twenty-one. I know I look young, but I've been around. I just back from Afghanistan, and ..."

"Hold on, let me grab my coat. You can tell me all about it in the car."

CPSIA information can be obtained
at www.ICGtesting.com
Printed in the USA
FFOW04n1019071216
30133FF